Praise for the Books

"Very real. And very good."

—Lee Child

"There's nothing soft about Campbell's writing. If you enjoy your crime fiction hard-boiled, the Jim Grant series is a must read."

—Bruce Robert Coffin, author of the Detective Byron series

"A cop with a sharp eye, keen mind, and a lion's heart."

—Reed Farrel Coleman

"Campbell writes smart, rollercoaster tales with unstoppable forward momentum and thrilling authenticity."

—Nick Petrie

"Grim and gritty and packed with action."

—*Kirkus Review*

"The pages fly like the bullets, fistfights and one-liners that make this one of my favourite books of the year. Top stuff!"

—Matt Hilton

"An excellent story well told. A mixture of *The Choirboys* meets Harry Bosch."

—Michael Jecks

"Sets up immediately and maintains a breakneck pace throughout. Its smart structure and unrelenting suspense will please Lee Child fans."

—*Library Journal Review*

"This is police procedural close-up and personal. A strong debut with enough gritty realism to make your eyes water, and a few savage laughs along the way."

—Reginald Hill

CATAWBA POINT

OTHER TITLES BY COLIN CAMPBELL

(*) Coming Soon

COLIN CAMPBELL

CATAWBA POINT

A Jim Grant Thriller

Down & Out Books
3959 Van Dyke Road, Suite 265
Lutz, FL 33558
DownAndOutBooks.com

The characters and events in this book are fictitious. Any similarity to real persons, living or dead, is coincidental and not intended by the author.

Cover design by Zach McCain

ISBN: 1-64396-105-5
ISBN-13: 978-1-64396-105-7

*For readers groups and bloggers everywhere.
But mainly for readers, without whom
there'd be no writers.*

FLIGHT CANCELLED

ONE

"A knitting circle conference? You're kidding, right?"

"Place is swarming with little old ladies."

"And they've taken all the hotels?"

Jim Grant let out a sigh and slumped in his seat at the Airport Services Counter. The assistant held out his hands and shrugged. It was 10:45 p.m., and Charlotte Douglas International was busier than any airport Grant had ever been in. Chaos reigned, and not just because the knitting circle had their needles out. People rushed past, dragging cabin luggage or suitcases. Voices were raised. Tempers flared. Everybody was trying to get somewhere else, and nobody seemed happy with where they were.

Grant closed his eyes and rubbed his temples. It had been a long day. He should be halfway across the Atlantic by now, not stuck at an airport in Charlotte, North Carolina. He flexed his neck. Bones cracked. He opened his eyes and glanced at the airport loop road through the floor-to-ceiling windows. Shuttle buses and local cabs collected stranded passengers and whisked them off into the night.

The day had started so well. Until the sign flashed up on the departure board at La Guardia. Then it went downhill faster than shit rolling into cop valley. Grant lived at the bottom, and the shit just kept coming.

* * *

Grant didn't check the La Guardia status update until an hour before his flight. The last time he'd looked, it stated the departure gate would be announced later. It was later now. He dumped his leftovers in the food court waste bin and shrugged into the bright yellow windcheater with Old Town Trolley Tours on the breast. He slung the small canvas rucksack he was using as cabin luggage over one shoulder, still adjusting to the fact they'd finally called him back to give evidence over the Snake Pass incident. Three years and half a lifetime ago.

The nearest departure board hung from the ceiling near the concession shops. A crowd was beginning to gather beneath it. The crowd didn't look happy. Grant wondered if this was how BF Cranston felt when he'd been recalled from holiday for Crown Court. Knowing the blitzkrieg cop from Bradford, he reckoned Timmo's reaction would have been a lot more colorful. Grant joined the back of the queue and craned his neck to find the flight number.

"Oh, fuck me."

Nearly as colorful as BF Cranston but under his breath. The flight status column was changing across the board. Flashing red letters informed the crowd that their flights were delayed. All the way down the list. All except Grant's flight to Manchester via Philadelphia.

"Fucking shitty death."

A little louder this time. He checked he'd got the right flight number.

"Fuck."

The status blinked red and urgent.

FLIGHT CANCELLED

Nothing else. No explanation. No instructions about what to do next. The tropical storm sweeping up the eastern seaboard was wreaking havoc with the flight schedules. The natives were restless. The only thing to do was enquire at the US Airways desk. That's when the next pile of shit rolled down on him.

The queue zigzagged around the temporary lane barriers turning the concourse alcove into a parking lot for wheelie cases and shopping bags. The enquiry counter almost disappeared behind the crush of humanity, with three harassed-looking US Airways staff trying hard to explain the delay and reroute the passengers. They weren't trying hard enough.

"This is a goddamn disgrace."

The overweight woman at the head of the queue looked like she needed two seats and hadn't even been offered one. The assistant kept her face calm and played a ditty on the keyboard. The computer screen didn't give the right answer, so she tapped some more. The other two staff did the same. Grant settled in for a long wait. The woman was given a voucher and some hushed advice, then the next person in the queue stepped forward.

Grant checked his watch.

The queue crawled forward.

Ninety minutes later he was two places from the front, and the queue was as long behind him as when he arrived. One of the staff had been replaced, and one had gone for a toilet break. That meant there were only two left. The pace slowed. Grant reached first place. The man at the counter in front of him had a complicated query. His travel plans were discussed at length with lots of keyboard action and staring at the monitor. Grant checked his watch again. He knew it was the wrong thing to do. It only made the time go slower and sent the wrong message to the airport staff.

The passenger at the next counter took her voucher and instructions and left the desk. Grant stepped forward and handed his boarding pass over. The woman behind the computer spoke as if Grant was the first passenger she'd dealt with. Grant was impressed. Being able to keep calm under pressure was a rare talent. He wondered if she'd been in the forces. She looked up from the monitor.

"There aren't any more flights on your route."

His admiration evaporated in an instant.

"What?"

Her fingers danced over the keyboard. Her eyes scanned the display.

"Let me check alternatives."

Dancing fingers. Concentrated eyes. The fingers stopped, and she nodded.

"Okay. I've got a flight leaving in an hour to Charlotte. Connection to Manchester at ten-fifteen."

She printed out fresh boarding passes for both flights. Grant thanked her, then had another thought.

"Suitcase?"

She looked at him.

"You got checked-in luggage?"

He nodded.

"One."

The woman pointed at the monitor.

"New itinerary has gone to your canceled flight. Your checked luggage should be transferred across."

Grant nodded again. The woman smiled and looked like she meant it.

"Sorry for the delay. Have a nice flight."

"Thanks."

Grant went back along the concourse to the food court. There was still a crowd beneath the departure board. He checked the boarding pass and looked up for the new flight details. New York LaGuardia to Charlotte, N.C. The status column flashed red and urgent.

FLIGHT DELAYED

Right back where he started. It felt like running up a down escalator. He supposed it wasn't as bad as having his flight canceled. He held on to that thought for another two hours, then even that fizzled out.

Grant stood up when the seatbelt sign blinked off and took his rucksack from the overhead compartment. The plane was full. Everybody straightened their clothes and retrieved their carry-on luggage. Nobody could move until the door was opened. There was only room for one person at a time. It was another hurry-up-and-wait situation. Grant waited. The stewardess opened the door.

The press of bodies surged forward. Grant was swept along as everyone dashed to make connections they'd already missed. He didn't rush. He didn't panic. He was a big believer in only worrying about what you could control; everything else was in the hands of the gods. The gods directed him to another US Airways information desk. The queue was shorter than last time. The outcome was the same.

"No more flights on your route."

It couldn't hurt to double-check though.

"To Manchester?"

The assistant wasn't wearing her stress as well as the LaGuardia staff.

"To England."

Deft fingers worked the keyboard.

"Let me check for alternatives."

Grant's patience was wearing thin.

"Alternatives to England?"

The woman looked over the top of her glasses.

"Alternatives to the flight you just missed."

Grant took a deep breath and let it out slowly. *Things you can't control*. He softened his eyes and apologized. The woman's expression softened too. Grant nodded and gave a sad little smile.

"Fire away."

The woman went back to the keyboard. Fast fingers and brief pauses. She scrolled through various screens and checked every possibility. After a few minutes, she found the only one that fit and looked at Grant.

"Next flight we can fit you on is three days. Same time."

"Three days?"

The woman was already printing out the boarding pass and reached into the drawer for a hotel voucher. She smiled at Grant to soften the blow.

"Think of it like *Three Days of the Condor*. You've got seventy-two hours to see the sights."

Grant took the papers.

"Redford was running for his life."

The woman tapped the voucher.

"Shouldn't be as hard on you then. Call the Freephone hotline. Airline has preferential rates on all database hotels."

Grant looked at the complicated instructions.

"Preferential? You mean I've got to pay?"

The woman shrugged.

"Weather-related. We only pay if it's a mechanical fault. Sorry."

Grant slung the rucksack over his shoulder.

"Aren't you going to tell me to have a nice flight?"

The woman was already clearing the screen for the next passenger.

"Come back in three days. Then I'll tell you to have a nice flight."

Grant stepped back onto the concourse and wondered where the Freephone was, then spotted a sign hanging above the walkway. Airport Services Counter. There wasn't a queue. Everybody was rushing past it to the loop road and shuttle buses. He glanced at the hotel voucher, then at the man behind the counter. He needed a little help here. The man smiled as Grant approached, then he walked right into the knitting circle blockade.

* * *

"They gave you the hotline number, huh?"

Grant relaxed in the chair. He was still absorbing the fact that he'd been laid low by a bunch of little old ladies. He waved the voucher.

"Preferential rates."

The assistant took the voucher.

"Database hotels filled up hours ago. Like I said. They're in swarm. The few rooms that were left got snapped up when the first delays came in."

Grant crossed his legs and rested one arm across the back of the chair.

"Well, I can't sit here for three days."

"Three days? Damn."

Grant watched the world going mad around him.

"That wasn't the first word came to mind."

The assistant nodded.

"I'm sure it wasn't."

He glanced over his shoulder to make sure his supervisor wasn't listening, then picked up the phone.

"Let me try a place I know."

Grant uncrossed his legs and leaned forward.

"Database?"

The assistant shook his head as he dialed.

"Off the books. It's still okay though. Used to be a Days Inn. Just not jumped the hoops yet for official recognition."

He held up a hand as the phone was answered.

"Hi. It's Jerry."

Grant listened as Jerry found him a room and gave a thumbs up. He passed Grant's description for the hotel shuttle on the loop road collection point. Grant shook Jerry's hand and thanked him. The assistant noticed Grant's rucksack.

"Luggage?"

Grant twirled a hand in the air.

"Somewhere."

The assistant went to a cupboard behind the counter and took out a little blue zipper bag of toiletries with a US Airways label. He handed it to Grant.

"Travel survival kit."

Grant looked at the fold-up toothbrush and miniature toothpaste.

"Thanks. I think I can survive this."

He picked up a free map from the display stand and kept the positive thoughts going all the way to the automatic doors. Right until the steaming hot North Carolina night hit him when he stepped outside.

TWO

The Sleepy Nook Inn was only ten minutes away but felt like it was in the middle of nowhere. There were no streetlights. There were no houses. There was no traffic. Just trees and darkness. Anywhere else and the darkness would have helped cool Grant down, but Charlotte in July wasn't anywhere else. Even this close to midnight, the air was hot and steamy. Sweat soaked through his shirt and trousers long before the minibus picked him up at collection point D. Grant lost his sense of direction after the third turn. He had no idea where he was by the time the driver swung into a tree-lined driveway and parked outside a low flat reception block.

Grant got out and swung the rucksack over his shoulder. The driver didn't offer to help. There wasn't any luggage to carry. Grant wiped a finger across his forehead and flicked the sweat to one side.

"The heat always this intense?"

The driver's dead eyes didn't flicker.

"What heat?"

So much for the have-a-nice-flight attitude. Grant closed the door, and the minibus pulled across the parking lot into an angled bay in the corner. He walked under the portico and almost bumped into the automatic door. The door didn't open. Grant couldn't remember the last time he'd used a manual door. He pulled it open and stepped into air-conditioned air. He took a deep breath and let the air cool the sweat on his back.

The single-story building was separate from the accommodation blocks. There was a drinks machine on the right and a conservatory on the left with low bamboo furniture. The reception desk was high wide and handsome, sandy-colored wood that looked like it had been imported from a more expensive hotel. The Sleepy Nook wasn't an expensive hotel. It wasn't even the Days Inn that it used to be before the signs had been changed but the color scheme retained. There was a single light above the night desk. A slow-eyed woman came out of the office behind the desk.

"You the one from the airport?"

Grant didn't ask who else she was expecting. With the knitting circle conference taking all the hotel rooms, he might get the wrong answer. He didn't want to lose the only room he'd been offered. He crossed the lobby and slid the hotel voucher across the counter.

"Yes. Thanks. You're a lifesaver."

The woman took one look at the voucher and slid it back to Grant.

"Sorry, sugar. We off the grid."

She tapped the voucher.

"That only works on database hotels."

Grant put the voucher in his pocket.

"I guess US Airways haven't found you yet."

The woman gave him a stern look.

"Plenty folks found us. You just got the last room."

Grant raised his eyebrows and smiled.

"Lucky me."

The smile didn't work. The night clerk was frosty and all business.

"Passport and credit card."

The woman took a copy of both on an old-fashioned photocopier by the door. She filled in a registration sheet and asked Grant to sign it. The room rate was less than the meal he'd bought at La Guardia, probably another reason the Sleepy Nook was off the grid. It would be hard for the database to siphon commission from such a low price. The woman handed Grant his credit card but kept the passport.

"Room two-fifty-seven. Smoking."

Grant pocketed the passport and credit card.

"Doesn't mean I've got to smoke, though. Does it?"

The woman's stern look wasn't much different from her friendly face.

"Don't mean you got to stay either. I've seen folks sleep under the freeway."

Grant took the plastic key card she'd put on the counter.

"Two-fifty-seven. Yes, ma'am."

He looked around for directions. The woman pointed a finger out the door, then jerked it to the right. Grant got the message and didn't bother thanking her. He didn't think she'd know how to cope with that. He was halfway up the stairs when he found another reason the Sleepy Nook wasn't on the US Airways database.

"You want a good time, mister?"

The slim black girl was leaning provocatively against the balcony rail at the top of the stairs. The accommodation block was a traditional two-story motel with rooms on both sides. There were stairwells at either end with an extra one in the middle. Room 257 was up the left-hand stairs and along the balcony facing away from the reception office. The parking lot extended all the way around the outside. There were only two security lights down there. Everything else was heat and darkness. Apart from the Fire Exit signs at the top of each stairwell. Grant slowed as he reached the landing.

"I'm already having a good time. Can't you tell?"

The girl looked barely twenty. Her smile was trying for seductive but came across shy and embarrassed. Her voice was borderline squeaky.

"I can help it get better."

Grant stood in the pool of light under the Fire Exit sign.

"Thanks. But right now the only thing better is bed."

The girl tilted her head.

"I can help you with that as well."

Grant noticed that the door to the first room was slightly open. Light spilled out through the gap. A shadowy figure stood behind the door. Grant saw him reflected in the mirror on the far wall. Probably the girl's pimp or manager. Grant ushered the girl toward the door and she smiled. Her walk was unsteady on impossibly high heels. The figure behind the door didn't move. Grant nodded along the balcony to room 257.

"Sleep is what I meant."

The girl threw a worried glance toward her door. She changed tack.

"We got pills can get you up or put you down. Anything you need."

Grant smiled.

"What I need is a good night's sleep. I can manage that on my own."

He placed his hand flat on the door.

"But I think you'd be more comfortable in out of the heat."

The girl proved she was acclimatized.

"What heat?"

Grant shoved the door, hard. There was a muffled grunt and a thump. The girl stepped inside and closed the door behind her. A male voice told her she should have tried harder as Grant walked to 257. He struggled to use the key card in the darkness between Fire Exit signs. Once he was inside, he dumped the rucksack and turned on the air-conditioning. Five minutes later he was in bed. Five minutes after that he was asleep. He didn't know how long after that the scream woke him up.

THREE

The darkness was all-encompassing. The scream faded into memory. Grant opened his eyes but could see nothing. For a moment he wondered if he were still asleep and this was some kind of blind-man dream. He'd had dreams before where he was trying to get somewhere but things kept getting in the way. Like losing his keys or going blind in the night.

A door slammed further along the balcony, and something was knocked to the floor. There was a slap and another cry of pain. A female voice that was borderline squeaky. The black girl from the end room. A man's voice told her to shut up, and there was another slap. That's when Grant swung his feet out of bed and pulled his trousers on.

"I guess you didn't see the Do Not Disturb sign on the door."

Grant had put his shoes and T-shirt on but didn't rush to help the girl. In his experience, rushing into the unknown was a recipe for disaster. He walked along the balcony and stopped at the end room. The door was ajar. He pushed it open, gently this time, and saw the girl sprawled across the bed holding the side of her face.

"My door. Not yours."

He was talking to a skinny black man with acne scars so deep they almost went right through his cheek. Dimples up either side of his mouth were etched like knife wounds. Judging from his line of work they could be knife wounds. A pimply white backside disappeared into the bathroom and shut the door. The black man blocked Grant's path and flexed his shoulders. They didn't flex very far.

"Move along, Milk White. Ain't none of your business."

Grant jerked a thumb back toward his room.

"Actually, since my business is getting a good night's sleep, it kind of is."

He waved a hand at the other rooms along the balcony.

"And since all these other people are trying to sleep as well, I'd appreciate it if you'd keep your noise down."

Grant looked at the girl. Fear saucered her eyes, and she shook her head. The pimp stood as tall as he was going to stand and glared at Grant.

"And I'd appreciate you shift your white ass out of my face."

Grant sighed and let his hands hang loose.

"Now that's the second time you mentioned that."

The pimp grinned.

"Your ass?"

Grant lowered his voice.

"My color."

He shrugged but kept his hands ready just in case.

"This seems like a racially diverse establishment, so how about this?"

He pointed at the pimp…

"You leave the girl alone."

…then jerked his head toward Room 257.

"And I'll take my Yorkshire arse back to bed."

The black guy put his hands on his hips as if that made him look tough.

"Thought this was about the noise."

Grant stepped into the doorway.

"It's slapping her around that made the noise. Stopping every-one from sleeping. And since the Sleepy Nook Inn is in the business of sleep…"

He raised his eyebrows and held his hands out.

The black guy didn't move.

"You work for the motel?"

Grant thought about telling him he was a cop but decided that off duty was off duty. He remembered warning Jamie Hope about charging in without backup. The night Snake Pass hit the shit fan. He didn't feel like explaining it again.

"I'm passing through."

The pimp indicated the girl on the bed.

"Well, we ain't. So mind who you're messing with and fly away home."

He took a step toward the door, and Grant backed off. One step. Two. The pimp was encouraged and kept moving forward. Across the balcony passage until Grant butted against the railing. Just where he wanted to be. The pimp was still coming when Grant reversed direction and grabbed the front of his belt. The pimp doubled over as if he'd been punched, and Grant used the momentum to yank his shoulders up and over the railing. The pimp sailed over the balcony and did a somersault into the warm, dark night.

The girl squealed. The naked white guy stayed in the bathroom. Grant looked over the railing. The pimp was a crumpled mess in the flowerbed, soft earth and straggly flowers having broken his fall. He didn't cry out on the way down. Grant nodded his approval.

The pimp untangled himself and sloped off. There was a rustling sound behind Grant and he spun around. The girl picked up her shoes and padded along the balcony to the middle stairwell. She disappeared into the night without so much as a thank you. Grant closed the door so the white guy could come out of the bathroom. Considering how fast he'd gone in Grant reckoned he'd probably spend the night in the bathtub. That wasn't Grant's idea of getting a good night's sleep.

With the excitement over he walked back to his room and locked the door. It took him longer to nod off this time but he slept without dreaming. Not about blind men or Snake Pass.

DAY ONE

FOUR

The slow-eyed woman wasn't working the desk the following morning. That wasn't the standout difference as Grant crossed the forecourt to reception. It was the two police cars parked under the entrance portico with their radios squawking through closed windows. In this heat, air conditioning was a premium. Nobody was going to drive around with the windows open, and no cop was going to leave his car unattended with the windows down. The two cars were unattended.

Grant was once again amazed how nice American patrol cars were. These were showroom quality and clean as a whistle. Back in Yorkshire, the only time the Ecclesfield cars were this clean was Sunday morning on shampoo day. There wasn't a dent or a scratch on these two, the gleaming white paintwork blinding in the morning sun. Pale blue signage declared them to be CHAR-LOTTE–MECKLENBURG POLICE.

Grant looked around. There was no sign of the Charlotte–Mecklenburg Police, so he went through the door to ask the slow-eyed woman. The man behind the counter wasn't slow-eyed or a woman. Youssef Khan was Indian, not the Native American kind, and hailed from round the back of Ecclesfield Police Station. Five hundred yards from where Jim Grant had worked uniform patrol.

* * *

"Patel's? On Ravenscliffe Avenue? I remember that shop."

Khan sat opposite Grant on the bamboo furniture in the conservatory. Both had a Pepsi from the vending machine. Khan leaned back but kept his knees together.

"And that's why you are in America?"

Grant shrugged.

"Freddy Sullivan's why I came to America. Other stuff is why I stayed."

Khan waved a hand in greeting.

"I feel blessed that you are staying at my hotel. It is always good to see somebody from back home."

Grant rolled the can across his forehead. Condensation cooled his brow.

"Your family not here with you?"

Khan glanced through the windows at the covered swimming pool.

"I bought this business three months ago. There is much to do before my family can join me. Much badness to clean away."

Grant indicated the paint peeling off the walls.

"You talking decorating or low life?"

Khan raised his eyebrows.

"There is low life wherever you go. The trick is for it not to affect business."

Grant nodded at the patrol cars out front.

"Unless low life is your business."

Khan followed Grant's gaze.

"Their business is to remove the low life from my business. I want to run a clean establishment. Not only with the paintwork."

Grant took a drink and let the coolness settle inside him.

"Is that what they're doing right now?"

Khan gave Grant a sad little smile.

"What they are doing is responding to an anonymous call. Apparently, there was a disturbance in one of the rooms last night. You didn't hear anything, did you?"

Grant shrugged. He didn't want to get involved. He was off

duty and in transit and intended to spend a couple of days enjoying North Carolina's legendary climate.

"I could have done with it being a bit quieter."

He rolled the can on his forehead again.

"I've slept through worse."

Khan turned to look at the accommodation block. Grant looked at the staircase up the far end. The noisy room was round the other side, but there was no doubt that was the one the police were searching. There was no noise. There didn't seem to be any resistance. Grant wondered if the pimply white backside was still in the bathroom. He doubted it. Curiosity got the better of his desire to remain off duty.

"I could take a look if you like."

Khan indicated the police cars.

"The police are already taking a look."

Grant put the Pepsi on the coffee table.

"Fresh eyes."

He stood up.

"Like a security consultant. Since we're both from Bradford."

Khan stood, keeping his knees together in a strangely old-fashioned way. Like an Imperial lackey from The Raj. He held his hands clasped in front of him and almost bowed.

"That would be very kind of you."

Grant nodded.

"Once a cop, always a cop."

Khan tilted his head to one side.

"But you are still a police officer."

Grant smiled.

"Not here."

The older cop looked at Grant's badge and waved it aside.

"That don't cut no ice around here."

Grant wiped sweat from his forehead and flicked it over the balcony. The Fire Exit sign was off, but the heat was just the same.

It didn't seem to matter the time of day; Charlotte was hot and steamy the whole time. Clear blue sky and bright green foliage shone under the glare of the sun. Ice would be nice, but he didn't think making jokes was the way to go.

"I know. Just doing a favor for Mr. Khan."

The cop stepped aside to let Grant in.

"What you want to know?"

The other cop was searching the bathroom, part of a tag-team deployment of youth and experience. The senior cop was doing the talking. Grant stood in the doorway and scanned the room before answering.

"Just what kind of shit they were up to in here."

The cop watched Grant's face for clues.

"You got any kind of opinion on that?"

Grant knew what the cop was doing. He'd have done the same thing himself if the position were reversed. Cops have a hard enough job as it is without visiting officers getting in the way. Grant met him halfway to the truth.

"Saw a young girl and a black guy hanging about when I checked in last night."

The cop waved a hand at the messed up bedclothes.

"Then you know what kind of shit they were up to."

Grant stood at the foot of the bed and checked the fixtures and fittings. All the drawers were closed. The mirrored wardrobe was partly open but empty. The bedside cabinets and lamps were clean and tidy. Almost. There was some staining on the right-hand cabinet, a screwed-up strip of tinfoil on the floor. Grant could smell the residue. The cop followed Grant's gaze and nodded.

"That too. Didn't leave anything else behind."

Grant smiled at the older cop.

"More exciting than the knitting circle conference though, huh?"

The cop folded his arms across his chest.

"We're Freedom Division. Northwest. They'd be mainly Metro. Heard some of them ladies can be a handful."

Grant chuckled.

"Blue rinse brigade."

The cop almost cracked a smile.

"They can be opinionated."

Grant nodded at the tinfoil.

"I doubt they're into sex and drugs though."

The cop unfolded his arms.

"Or people getting thrown off the balcony."

Grant feigned surprise.

"That what happened here?"

"So I'm told."

The younger cop came out of the bathroom and stalked to the door. He didn't look happy checking bathrooms or being chaperoned by a retiree. He ignored Grant and jerked a thumb toward the bathroom.

"Nothing. This is wasting our time. I'll be outside."

He put a pair of mirrored sunglasses on and leaned over the balcony rail. The blue-tinted lenses would have looked good at the knitting circle conference. The senior cop gave a sad little smile at the impatience of youth then turned his attention back to Grant.

"He'll be checking where the guy landed. You know anything about that?"

Grant avoided the question.

"What did the caller say?"

The cop let it slide.

"Disturbance. Raised voices. Smell of drugs."

Grant glanced toward the door.

"Who called it in?"

The cop watched Grant's face again.

"Anonymous. Some black guy, dispatch reckoned."

Grant turned to the cop.

"They can tell that? Over the phone?"

The cop frowned.

"Intonation. Speech pattern. Not exactly racial stereotyping."

Grant didn't mention the white guy with the pimply backside. It would suggest more knowledge than he wanted to admit. Throwing the pimp over the balcony rail was something else he'd rather keep to himself, but it did beg the question why the pimp dropped a dime to the police about the room. He looked in the bathroom and noticed the bathtub and shower curtain, not a comfortable place to spend the night. He came back out and scanned the room one last time. From a different angle. He spotted something sticking out from under the bed, bent down, and pulled the length of black wire.

"They usually charge their phones while pulling tricks?"

The cop looked at the charger.

"Could have been a lap dancer."

Grant examined the bulky plug and the broad flat connecter and knew where the cop was going with this. He let out a sigh and shook his head.

"You know, laptop jokes aren't really all that funny."

The cop took the charger and tossed it on the bed. The room wasn't a crime scene, and there was no complaint apart from the noise. This was going to be an intelligence report and nothing else.

"That's why I'm a cop and not a comedian."

He moved to the open door and made a diving motion over the balcony.

"Or an acrobat."

He ushered Grant out of the room and closed the door.

"You haven't seen any acrobats, have you?"

FIVE

Grant had breakfast at Hardee's Diner across the road from the motel. Back when the Sleepy Nook used to be a Days Inn, the hotel had on-site dining, but Pepino's Restaurant & Bar closed down long before Days Inn moved their franchise elsewhere. Mr. Khan apologized for any inconvenience, but Grant was glad to stretch his legs. In Yorkshire, across the road meant just that. In America, it meant hiking down the wooded driveway and half a mile along Little Rock Road. Trees marched up the hills on either side of the road. The sun blazed out of a clear blue sky. Steamy heat plastered his clothes to his back.

"You from the inn?"

The waitress wasn't as slow-eyed as the night clerk, but they could have been related. There were two cars in the dusty parking lot and one sales rep sitting in the corner. The other car must have been a pool car for the staff because Grant didn't think Hardee's was on the bus route. There weren't any mailboxes on Little Rock Road and only two businesses: Hardee's and the Sleepy Nook. Process of elimination meant the waitress got it right.

"That's right. You got room for a tall one?"

The waitress took out her order pad and waved a hand around the diner.

"You just missed the breakfast rush."

She smiled.

"All three at once. Almost blocked the kitchen."

The smile transformed her face from surly insolence to twinkly-eyed pixy. Grant smiled back and indicated a booth at the window. The waitress nodded and stood over him as he slid into the bench seat.

"Can I get you a drink?"

Grant remembered American tea.

"You do latte?"

The waitress didn't write it down.

"I can do coffee with lots of milk."

Grant nodded.

"Just like my mum used to make."

An exaggeration since Grant's mother had died in childbirth, but an icebreaker. The waitress took it in the spirit it was given.

"Your momma not being from around here."

Grant smiled.

"You guessed."

The waitress became all giddy schoolgirl.

"I love the English accent. Ain't missed a single episode of Downton Abbey."

Grant never thought he'd be mistaken for anyone off Downton Abbey but was beginning to get used to the accent thing. A woman asked him once to give the "My name's Bond. James Bond" line. She didn't seem to mind the Yorkshire accent. The waitress slid a menu across the table then stepped away.

"One coffee coming up. Momma style."

Grant thanked her and opened the menu. He was busy figuring the smallest portion when the patrol car pulled into the parking lot. On its own this time. The senior cop, not the young one. The cop saw Grant through the window and nodded. Dust puffed around his feet as he got out of the car.

"He's into healthy eating and mirrored shades."

Explaining why the cop was alone.

"And a ton of hair product I can't even pronounce."

Grant leaned back in his seat.

"You get a lot of trouble at Hardee's, do you?"

The cop looked across the table.

"I take my break when I can. Never know when the knitting circle might spread out here causing trouble."

Grant waved a hand toward the door.

"You just missed the breakfast crowd. Apparently, they can get a bit rowdy."

The cop ignored the menu.

"My time of life. I try and avoid rowdy."

Grant nodded.

"I always avoid rowdy."

The cop turned a level stare at Grant.

"You'll appreciate this piece of advice then. Try not to get mixed up with the colored element around these parts."

Grant returned the look.

"As opposed to the white element?"

The cop laid his hands flat on the table.

"This isn't as much a color thing as a group rivalry. The groups don't mix. They don't like each other. And whatever your sympathies, you aren't ever going to pass for black."

Grant frowned.

"I can get really dark in the summer."

The cop sighed.

"You're a cop. You know what I'm saying. You don't want to get caught one side or the other."

Grant lowered his voice.

"By throwing black men off the balcony."

The cop smiled.

"That would be my advice."

He slid out of the booth and stood up.

"Enjoy your breakfast."

Grant watched the cop walk out just as the waitress brought his coffee. She followed his gaze, then took out her order pad.

"You in trouble, mister?"

Grant held the menu up.

"Only if you've stopped serving the all-day breakfast."

The waitress smiled, pen poised.

"No trouble there. That's why it's called the all-day breakfast."

Breakfast set him up for the day. The heat drained him. He went back to his room and freshened up. A cold swill and a quick brush of his teeth. He looked at the fold-up toothbrush and miniature tube of toothpaste, then glanced in the mirror at the rucksack on the bed. All his worldly possessions until he was reunited with his suitcase. That wasn't going to happen until Manchester in two days. The toothpaste wasn't going to last that long.

Grant hung the rucksack in the wardrobe and put his travel documents in the bedside drawer. There wasn't much—just his itinerary and boarding pass and a film magazine to read on the plane. Hotel reception had his passport. Grant took the map out of his back pocket and considered checking it, then decided local knowledge was the best way to go. In a hotel, the best local knowledge was the concierge.

"A toothbrush? That's all you've got?"

Mr. Khan was in his office behind the check-in desk. Sleepy Nook Inn didn't employ a concierge.

"Like the big man in those books?"

Grant leaned against the doorframe.

"I'm not Jack Reacher."

Khan looked up from his desk.

"No. You're too short and not wide enough."

Grant plucked at his T-shirt to unstick it from his chest.

"And I miss my luggage. This isn't going to last three days."

Khan glanced at his watch, then stood up.

"I've got to get some building supplies. Why don't I take you to Walmart over at Westerly Hills?"

Grant pushed off from the doorframe.

"If it's not too much trouble. That'd be great."

Khan picked up his car keys.

"No problem. Even Jack Reacher needs more than a tooth-brush."

SIX

Grant had been to a Walmart before but never anything like the Wilkinson Boulevard Shopping Center. It was huge. A gigantic square hangar of a building that housed a CVS Pharmacy, Smart Style Clothing, Walmart Tire & Lube Express, and a Vision Center. There was a food court the size of Times Square, a branch of Woodforest National Bank and a Home Entertainment Center with more TVs than Sony. When he stepped inside, after Mr. Khan dropped him off with a promise to pick him up in an hour, he peered into the distance and couldn't see the far end.

It took him fifteen minutes just to find the menswear section. It didn't take much longer to pick some clothes and move to toiletries. Grant was a fast shopper. He toyed with the idea of buying shorts for the heat but didn't know any cop who looked good fighting crime with his legs showing. Even though he was only here in transit, he still thought of himself as defending the peace. So, he bought two pairs of lightweight cargo pants, four T-shirts, two packs of underwear and a whole bunch of socks. After that, it was a proper toothbrush, shower gel and body spray. A pack of disposable razors. And a small tube of toothpaste he'd never heard of. This wasn't a Jack Reacher throwaway moment. Grant planned on keeping everything he bought. Total package came to less than forty dollars.

At the checkout, he grabbed an iced tea from the cooler and

was back outside in fifty-five minutes. The heat made him thankful he'd bought the iced tea. The sun glaring off the parking lot made him wish he'd bought a pair of sunglasses. The four-door pickup came round the corner from the gas station like a tank, Mr. Khan driving, his handyman riding the backseat. Half a dozen tins of outdoor paint and two rolls of roofing felt were strapped to the load bed.

"Did you get what you wanted?"

Grant got in the passenger side and held the bag up.

"Got what I needed. Thanks."

Mr. Khan pulled away from the Drop & Collect lane toward the exit. He jerked a thumb over his shoulder at the building supplies.

"I have to get this back."

He glanced at Grant's shopping bag.

"Any plans after you've put that in your room?"

Grant shook his head. Mr. Khan nodded.

"Okay then. I'll drop you at the South Park Mall."

He indicated the heat baking off the tarmac.

"You can spend all day there and never have to step outside."

At least that was the plan.

Mr. Khan was on the phone when Grant came back into reception from his room. He didn't sound happy. A day girl had taken over the desk. She saw Grant come through the door and waved him toward the bamboo chairs. The conversation was getting heated, but Khan noticed Grant and shrugged. He closed the office door for privacy. Outside the conservatory windows, the handyman was busy unloading the paint and roofing felt. The girl at the desk leaned over the counter.

"Car will be here in five minutes."

Grant nodded but didn't speak. He was wondering why a car was coming for him when Mr. Khan slammed the phone down and came out of the office. He came over to Grant wringing his hands.

"I am very sorry, but something has come up. I have arranged for a local man to take you to the mall."

Grant stood up.

"That's okay. Thanks for the lift, before."

Khan bowed his head.

"You are most welcome. Thank you for your help also."

Grant got the feeling that was more for throwing the pimp over the balcony than asking the police what happened in the room. He wondered how many people knew about that. Mr. Khan went back into his office, and the girl busied herself behind the reception desk. A big American car pulled under the portico, and a black guy got out. He came in and walked straight to Grant.

"Sorry I'm late. So, you're the guy threw Leroy off the balcony."

South Park Mall was a long way south of Charlotte on the I-77. To Grant, it felt like they were driving to another town. To Bruno Morris, it was a short cab ride around the corner. It was the cab ride part that caught Grant by surprise. The big, ugly car looked more like private hire than a taxi, but when Morris handed Grant a business card outside the Sleepy Nook, he realized a taxi is what it was.

PROFESSIONAL TRANSPORTATION
And Taxi
Long Distance Services
B. MORRIS XO
AUTO LOCKSMITH 24/7

There was a contact number and an email address. Morris was maybe fifty years old with a face as lived in as Sid James. Grant doubted Morris knew who Sid James was, the *Carry On* films not being big in the States, but if Sid James had been black, then Bruno Morris was him. The lines on his face were carved by smiling. The eyes laughed when he spoke.

"I bet he didn't bounce too well. Him being full of shit like he is."

Grant sat up front but didn't answer. Morris pulled out of the Sleepy Nook and began the long drive around the southwest of Charlotte like circling the outside of a clock from nine o'clock to six.

"Weren't no great shakes as a paratrooper neither."

He glanced at Grant and smiled.

"Chute not deploying and landing like a sack of shit."

Grant raised his eyebrows and shrugged.

"Roll on impact or break your legs. I heard he rolled on impact."

Morris kept his eyes on the road.

"Heard?"

Grant watched the scenery drift by.

"Story seems to be going around. You're not the first person to get me mixed up with somebody else."

Morris took a left and then a right, then eased up through the gears.

"Deputy Dawg?"

Grant looked at Morris.

"You know about Hardee's?"

Morris was comfortable in his own skin. He looked calm and confident and hard as nails behind the smile.

"I know about everything. Part of being a Professional Transportation contractor."

Grant nodded.

"And executive officer."

Morris laughed.

"The XO part is for effect."

He glanced in the mirror, then changed lanes ahead of the next exit. Grant checked the map in his head, based on the one he'd picked up at the airport. He hadn't given it a lot of attention but guessed he was somewhere around seven o'clock on the circle.

"Army or Navy?"

Morris followed the exit ramp, then headed through a residential area, no doubt cutting a corner that Grant didn't know existed. Grant had lost the map in his head. Morris knew exactly where he was going. Tree-lined streets and expensive houses were bathed in sunshine. Morris's smile dialed down a notch.

"Does it matter? Long time ago."

Grant looked at the locksmith and taxi driver who had once been so much more.

"Long time but never far away."

Morris followed his route.

"You?"

Grant shrugged.

"Same."

Neither spoke for a few minutes. The silence was peaceful, not awkward. Both men at peace with what they'd done in the name of country. Neither of them feeling the need to big it up or brag. Eventually, Morris changed the subject back to where he wanted it.

"So? Did Johnny Law warn you not to get in the middle of this?"

Grant let his eyes drift. Taking in the green of the trees and the blue of the sky and the glorious brightness the sun bestowed on them both.

"Must have been an Eastwood fan."

Morris smiled.

"The rival gangs in that Dollar movie?"

Grant nodded.

"A bit of friendly advice. One cop to another."

Morris glanced at him.

"You went from the military to the police. Tried that. Prefer my own company."

He steered the cab out of the housing estate and onto the main road. Another long straight thing heading south.

"He's right though. You don't want to get caught between Leroy's black army guys and those white supremacists down by the river."

Being told not to do something was the wrong approach to take with Grant. Being warned off twice only piqued his interest.

"Unless I wanted to go all *Fistful of Dollars*. Play one off against the other."

Morris took one more exit, then followed the signs for the South Park Mall. They were close now. And not just to the shopping center.

"From the inside you mean? Join both. Work from the middle."

Grant shrugged and didn't answer. Morris slowed past the Zebra Restaurant & Wine Bar, then turned into the shopping complex. He glanced at Grant one last time, then echoed the senior cop's sentiments.

"Might work with the white supremacists."

He shook his head.

"But you ain't never gonna pass for black."

SEVEN

The cab fare cost almost as much as the clothes Grant bought at Walmart. By the time he added the tip, it came to forty dollars straight. When he walked into the South Park Mall, he reckoned that was the cheapest thing he'd be buying all day. The walls were polished marble. The floors were smooth and shiny tile. The customer service desk at the intersection of the four shopping wings was carved wood and leather. This was a seriously expensive place to shop. It was a good job Grant was only browsing.

One thing Mr. Khan was right about: the mall was cool and air-conditioned and far more pleasant than the steamy heat outside. Grant checked the mall directory just to get his bearings. He wasn't looking for anywhere in particular. He wasn't looking to spend any more money. That wasn't going to happen. He spotted the two things he could never resist. A sports shop and a department store. Dick's Sporting Goods store was out through the West Wing. Grant headed north to Macy's, because you could never have too many socks. If he'd spent longer searching the bargain rails, the day might have turned out different. As it was, he decided to visit the food court to grab some lunch, and the day took a different turn.

* * *

"You still having a good time?"

Grant was standing out front of the Chick-fil-A concession, trying to decide between that, Cucina Italiana or Firebirds Wood Fired Grill. The glossy photos above each service counter made all the food look the same: bright, colorful, and plastic. The voice was low and close behind him, not as squeaky today. The slim black girl stepped back when Grant turned around. He waved a hand to indicate all the food outlets.

"What do you recommend?"

The girl was wearing figure-hugging leggings, a bright yellow crop top that showed her bare midriff, and high heels that she still hadn't mastered. The crop top was ideal for the heat outside, but the air conditioning brought out goose pimples on her arms and stomach. She tried for sultry but came across as bored.

"Big Easy Cajun is good."

She nodded across the mass of tables in the middle of the food court.

"Pasta and pizza if you're into Italian."

The jerk of the head made her wince, and Grant noticed the swelling for the first time. Around her right eye and cheek. He couldn't tell if she was bruised, but the eye was bloodshot.

"What do you prefer? My treat."

Her eyes opened in surprise. At someone being nice to her, Grant reckoned.

"I always wished I was Italian. Or French."

Grant moved away from Chick-fil-A, and the girl followed.

"Cucina Italiana it is then."

The girl shivered and hugged herself. Grant slipped off his windcheater and draped it over her shoulders. The yellow went with her crop top. The girl's eyes considered him again. Not trying to sell herself this time. Grateful for the jacket. They both turned toward the seating area—Cucina Italiana was on the other side—then Grant heard an electric hum come up behind him.

"Excuse me, little lady. None of that business in the mall."

Grant thought that short, dumpy mall cops were a cliché

perpetuated by that Kevin James movie. The parallel-wheeled Segway was the icing on the cake. The uniformed lawman even had a crash helmet with "Security" written on both sides in case nobody recognized his authority. Authority was the last thing he exuded. A two-wheeled hobby-bobby playing at being a cop. Still, he was an offshoot of law enforcement. Grant gave him credit for that.

"Oh, she's with me. We're neighbors."

The mall cop swung his Segway right then left, just to show he could. He looked at the girl, then back at Grant.

"You sure she's not bothering you?"

Grant smiled.

"Do I look bothered? She's beautiful."

The mall cop didn't look convinced but wasn't prepared to argue with a man taller than him, even on the Segway. He scrutinized the girl and gave Grant one last stare. He nodded...

"Okay then. Have a nice day."

...and spun the Segway back toward the main hall. The electronic hum faded into the hubbub of the food court, and Grant turned back to the girl. She looked shrunken and embarrassed. The jacket clung to her like a shawl. Grant walked her toward Cucina Italiana.

"How's Leroy doing?"

Nona Hartley went for pasta. Grant ordered pizza that came in separate slices the size of oriental fans. He bought two slices so he had a choice of toppings and knew he wouldn't finish either of them. Nona glanced at the tables. Grant indicated an alcove near the windows between a potted palm and some creeping vine. Nona took the drinks while Grant brought the food. Despite the plastic photos, the food smelled nice. He put the tray on the table and pulled out a chair for Nona, something else that surprised her. Nobody had ever pulled a chair out for her. Grant sat opposite and passed Nona her plate.

"I don't want to sound rude, but have you got a black eye?"

Nona looked across the table.

"You mean because I'm dark complected?"

Grant looked at the bloodshot eye.

"It is kinda hard to tell."

Nona sighed.

"That's one good thing about being black, I guess."

Grant leaned forward.

"Shouldn't have to put up with black eyes. No matter what color you are."

Nona shoved a straw through the top of her gallon of Pepsi.

"I'll tell him next time I see him. See how that works out."

Grant did the same with his Pepsi.

"Why don't I tell him for you?"

Nona snorted a laugh.

"Oh yeah. Like you haven't caused enough trouble already."

Grant took a cool, refreshing suck on his straw.

"I didn't cause anything. Leroy should learn how to fall better."

Nona twisted some pasta around a plastic fork.

"He didn't fall. You threw him off the balcony."

Grant shrugged.

"Land better, then."

Nona paused with the fork in front of her mouth.

"You're passing through, remember? I've got to live here."

Grant wasn't a handheld pizza man. He cut a piece off and forked it.

"You don't have to live like that."

Nona had to wait until she finished the mouthful. The only reason she didn't snort another laugh was that she didn't want to spray this strange man with pasta and sauce.

"What planet you from, mister? I'd like to live there."

Grant spoke between chews.

"You wouldn't like it. It's cold all the time."

Nona raised her eyebrows to show she was being facetious.

"But black hookers got choices there, right?"

41

Grant paused cutting the next piece of pizza and thought about Lumb Lane in Bradford. The red-light district and the streetwalkers and the girls with few choices and no prospects. Black or white. Dirt poor. Nona had a point, but he couldn't let it stand.

"Everybody's got choices."

This time she did snort the laugh again.

"Not around here. It's between a rock and a hard place for me."

Grant smiled, his mind running over Clint Eastwood and the rival gangs of *A Fistful of Dollars*. He looked her in the eye.

"The black Paras and the white supremacists?"

Nona looked shocked that Grant knew so much.

"You should keep one eye out front and the other over your shoulder. Keep out of this, then fly away home. This ain't your fight."

Grant watched her face.

"So, there is a fight then?"

Nona ate more pasta to avoid answering. Grant took the opportunity to sample both toppings and half the pizza. He barely made an impact on the Pepsi and he hadn't even asked to go large. Grant was thinking about ex-military black men and pseudo-military white supremacists. The food was good, the company pleasant, but his focus was on an untidy hotel room and a pimply-arsed white guy. It wasn't the drugs or the sex that held his attention; it was the charging lead under the bed.

They finished eating at the same time. Nona managed all of the pasta. Grant gave up halfway through the pizza slices. He swilled it down with one last swig of Pepsi, then pushed the carton away. He looked at the slim black girl wearing his light-weight windcheater.

"Cab fare's extortionate. I can spring for a bus ticket if you need it."

Nona shrugged the jacket off her shoulders and stood up.

"I got that covered."

Grant stood and put the windcheater on.

"Leroy?"

Nona didn't answer. Grant smiled.

"The battered pickup that followed us, two cars back."

Nona softened her eyes as she looked at Grant.

"I told you. One eye out front and the other over your shoulder."

Grant nodded.

"I'll bear that in mind."

The girl seemed reluctant to leave.

"Thanks. For being so nice."

Grant sighed.

"That's how it works on my planet."

He thought about Lumb Lane again.

"Mostly. You stay safe now."

Nona balanced on the high heels then clip-clopped toward the exit. She threw him one more glance and spoke over her shoulder.

"I've got that covered too. You're the one needs to watch out."

EIGHT

Grant checked the mall directory at the customer service desk. He considered asking one of the uniform assistants, but they were so smartly dressed he didn't want to crease their tunics. The illuminated directory stood in the middle of a seating area dotted with soft leather easy chairs and potted plants. It was color-coded for the separate wings, and the shops were listed by type. He found three that dealt with cell phones and computers and dismissed two straightaway. The Apple Store would only stock their own products instead of a broad spectrum of laptops, and RadioShack was more for parts and spares.

Connect was in the South Hall between Chico's and Bare Essentials. The hall widened into another rest area opposite Nordstrom with more plush leather furniture and potted palms. Grant looked through the window to make sure it carried what he wanted. The store looked like a cross between PC World and US Cellular. Backlit display tables held working models of everything from laptops to cell phones to various size tablets and e-readers. Staff mingled with customers. Customers tapped on keyboards. Grant tried to picture the charger connector and stepped inside.

He had absolutely no idea what he was looking for. The charger didn't have a brand name—just a serial number. If he'd been thinking of checking up on it, he'd have gone back in the room and brought it with him. As it was, he was reduced to navigating the display tables, looking at the connectors jutting out the back of the phones and computers.

"You look a little lost there, sir. Maybe I can help you."

The woman was smartly dressed but casual. A name badge on her left breast read EVELYN COVER. Grant tried not to look like he was staring at the badge. He shrugged.

"I've barely mastered texting."

He indicated the array of technology around him.

"So this is all a bit over my head."

The woman looked up at the six-foot-four Yorkshireman.

"You don't look like much goes over your head."

Grant brushed a hand across the top of his head and made a whooshing sound.

"Oh, you'd be surprised. I'm more hands-on than technical."

The woman looked him in the eye.

"Well let's help you get hands-on."

Grant's mind did its usual man thing and misread the signs. He reminded himself he was only here for three days and focused on business.

"I'm looking for a hole that fits a certain plug."

He knew it sounded wrong as soon as he said it.

Connect was a bright, shiny oasis of white and silver. Everything looked clean in here. The laptop charger had been half-hidden under a motel bed. The very opposite of bright and shiny. Grant doubted he'd be able to identify his own phone if it were on display at Connect. After three attempts, Evelyn Cover tried a different approach.

"Are you sure it was a laptop?"

Grant looked around the store.

"I'm not sure it was electric."

Evelyn turned steady eyes on Grant. Grant gave an embarrassed nod.

"Sorry. Trying to sound cool."

Evelyn watched his face.

"You're English. You'll always sound cool."

Now he was embarrassed. He shrugged.

"On the laptop thing. I'm not sure."

Evelyn moved away from the main displays toward the back wall. Heat-sealed plastic packages hung from adjustable hangers. There were headphones and external hard drives and a variety of cables and extensions. Some had bulky transformers and rolled-up wires. Replacement chargers. There weren't many customers perusing the accessories wall. Evelyn turned to face Grant.

"Why would the English police be interested in a Charlotte laptop?"

Grant looked at the saleswoman.

"I work Boston PD now."

Evelyn's expression didn't change.

"Why would Boston police be interested in a Charlotte laptop?"

Grant thought about that for a moment. Why was he interested? He was only passing through, and any trouble the Sleepy Nook Inn had was none of his business. He settled on the only answer that came to mind.

"Something smells wrong. Doesn't matter where I work. It smells wrong here."

Evelyn leaned against the display wall and crossed her ankles. Casual.

"So you're a gut-instinct kind of cop. Hunches and such. Like on TV."

Grant was acutely aware that there was nobody standing near them, but he lowered his voice anyway.

"I'm nothing like on TV."

He shrugged.

"Well, maybe *The Sweeney*."

Evelyn looked puzzled.

"The demon barber?"

Grant smiled and shook his head.

"Not Johnny Depp in *Sweeney Todd*. An English cop show

back in the seventies."

He leaned forward as if telling a secret.

"Although Sweeney Todd is rhyming slang for *Flying Squad*, which is where *The Sweeney* got its name."

Evelyn raised her eyebrows.

"They were flying police?"

Grant shook his head.

"Fast. Mobile. Responded wherever they were needed."

A hint of a smile played across Evelyn's lips.

"And you reckon you're needed here?"

Grant shrugged.

"It can't do any harm."

Evelyn didn't look convinced.

"Which motel are we talking about? So I can avoid the trouble."

Grant looked in her eyes.

"You think I'm trouble?"

Evelyn looked straight back.

"I think you go poking about in Charlotte, trouble's what you're going to get."

Grant frowned then smiled.

"Sleepy Nook Inn. Out on Little Rock Road."

Evelyn nodded.

"Over near the airport. Well, at least they'll get a good signal."

"The laptop?"

She nodded again.

"Laptops. Cell phones. Whatever. Best signal in Charlotte."

Grant tilted his head to one side.

"How come?"

Evelyn was back on safe ground. Local knowledge and expertise.

"Most powerful booster tower in North Carolina. In the woods over past the runways."

She turned her eyes to the ceiling.

"You could uplink to the space station."

Grant considered the beautiful woman in the business suit and the three days he had to kill before his flight. He put added friendly into his voice.

"Should be good if I wanted to call you about dinner then?"

Evelyn looked at the Englishman who would always sound cool in North Carolina. She gave the faintest of nods.

"Or you could ask me now."

She shrugged then held a hand to her ear in the universal telephone symbol.

"But yes. Signal. So good even the airport uses it."

NINE

They arranged to meet downtown at 8 p.m. That left the rest of the day and part of the evening to kill. Grant killed some of it wandering around South Park Mall and a bit more soaking up the heat in a landscaped plaza between the California Pizza Kitchen and Dick's Sporting Goods. Dick's was a separate building west of the mall across terracotta tiles and through tastefully arranged conifers. An ornate fountain sprayed water like it was auditioning for a Busby Berkeley musical.

Grant used the outside seating for California Pizza Kitchen but only had an iced tea. The drinks bucket was as big as the Pepsi but less gassy. He watched the world go by from his position in the shade. There were a lot of women wearing not very much, a benefit of the steamy climate, but the woman in the business suit kept his mind off the rest of them. Evelyn Cover was intelligent and beautiful, a winning combination that was augmented by her confident manner and no-nonsense approach. She liked Grant, and Grant liked her. There was nothing else to discuss. So she agreed to meet him for dinner. Grant wasn't going to be around long enough for the relationship to progress, but pleasant company and a smile was good enough for him.

There shouldn't have been anything else to distract him until 8 p.m. That was the case until he got off the bus just south of the I-85 and walked along Little Rock Road under the interstate.

* * *

They were waiting for him on the service road from the I-85 that ran behind the Sleepy Nook Inn and cut a corner opposite Hardee's. The motel was hidden behind the trees that formed the woodlands north of Charlotte. Hardee's was too far for anyone to see him even if they were looking this way. Nobody was looking. Sunlight glinted off the diner's windows as it dipped low in the evening sky.

Grant performed a casual threat assessment as he entered the underpass. It was second nature, but he wasn't expecting trouble. The six-lane highway meant that Little Rock Road became a tunnel of darkness on an otherwise sunny day. Any threat would come out of the dark. Grant stayed away from the buttress and the concrete pillars and scanned the shadows as he walked. Traffic thrummed overhead like rolling thunder. His footsteps echoed under the bridge. Even in the shade, it was warm and humid. A shower and a change of clothes was the order of the day.

The heat intensified when he came out of the tunnel. The danger was behind him. He glanced across at Hardee's, then took the service road shortcut. Trees crowded the hard shoulder. He was squinting through the trees to find the motel when it happened.

The dry twig snapped like a gunshot. Grant spun to his right in time to see three men come out of the trees. Leroy folded the twig over and snapped it again for effect. The noise wasn't as loud now that Grant was expecting it. The other two men weren't as black as Leroy, but they were a long way past being suntanned. This was black America showing a united front. Grant concentrated on Leroy.

"It's like the trees just came alive. Same as in that Schwarzenegger film."

Leroy stood at the side of the road. The other two hung back on either side of him. Showing they had his back without forcing the issue. Grant stopped three paces from the pimp.

"Except in that, the hunter had dreadlocks and a spaceship."

Leroy put his hands on his hips and puffed his chest out.

"You're the alien around here. All the way from England."

Grant leveled a hard stare at Leroy.

"But you're the predator. Is that how it works? Prey on the weak, then turn them out on the street. Or have them turning tricks at the motel."

Thoughts of the Sleepy Nook Inn seemed to remind Grant.

"How's the leg?"

He bent his knees and feigned a sideways roll.

"I heard you learned to roll at jump school. Airborne, was it?"

Leroy flexed his neck.

"It's different without a chute."

Grant held his hands out.

"Sorry. You didn't leave me much choice."

The other two men came forward and spread out, making it three men on a wide front. Good attack formation. Grant could only engage one at a time, and whichever he chose, the other two would get behind him. This wasn't a fight he was going to win. Leroy indicated his partners.

"We learned more than that. Landing only gets you there. After that, you got to know how to fight."

Grant nodded.

"I never did parachute training. We deployed from helicopters."

He relaxed his arms and flexed his knees. Ready to attack or defend.

"Thing about fighting. Even when you win..."

He took a step toward the trio.

"You've got to be prepared to take casualties."

He braced his shoulders.

"You willing to go to hospital over this? Maybe two of you?"

Leroy didn't flinch, but his colleagues looked less confident. Grant shrugged.

"But like you said. I'm passing through."

He smiled.

"I'll be out of your hair in a couple of days. So why don't we call it a draw."

Leroy found his voice.

"A what?"

Grant watched Leroy but kept the others in his peripheral vision.

"A tie. Honors even."

He waved a hand at the three of them.

"We all know you're going to win."

Then turned both hands palms up.

"So why get hurt proving it?"

He smiled again.

"It's a win-win situation. Everybody's happy."

Leroy appeared to consider the suggestion. He flexed his wiry frame and jutted his chin out. It was time to save a little face.

"Couple days?"

He lowered his voice for added menace.

"Don't mess with my business."

Grant held a hand out to shake.

"Don't keep me awake."

Leroy shook it, then waved his men back.

"Enjoy your stay."

The two men melted into the trees and disappeared. Leroy followed suit. Grant stood at the side of the road, and it was as if they'd never been there. He waited a few moments, then turned toward the motel. With the release of tension, his hands began to shake. That surprised him. His hands didn't usually shake after a confrontation. They'd calmed down by the time he climbed the stairs to his room. Nona Hartley was waiting at the top of the stairs.

"Leroy is coming for you."

Nona was shivering despite the heat. She followed Grant to room 257 and hugged herself as he used the key card in the door.

She looked frightened.

"He's got friends."

Grant opened the door and ushered her inside. He didn't turn on the air-conditioning and left the door open.

"With his sparkling personality, I'm not surprised."

Nona grabbed his arm.

"I'm serious. He's going to hurt you."

Grant patted her hand and sat her on the edge of the bed. The first one nearest the door.

"And why would that worry you?"

She tried to show a hard front.

"He's not a bad man."

Grant tilted his head but didn't speak. Nona shrugged.

"Not really."

She looked Grant in the eye.

"But he never pulled a chair out for me."

Grant met her stare.

"I hold doors open for ladies as well."

Nona lowered her eyes.

"You think I'm a lady?"

Grant softened his tone.

"I think you can be anything you want to be."

He didn't really believe that. He knew that some people were dealt a bad hand at birth and had to live with it, but he did believe you could make choices that mitigated how bad that hand was. Moving away from people like Leroy would be a good place to start.

"I think it's your choice."

Nona shook her head. Her shoulders sagged.

"I'm all out of choices, mister."

Grant patted her hand again.

"Start with small ones, then. Go stay somewhere else."

She turned sad eyes on him.

"I ain't got nowhere else."

Grant wondered if she was playing him. He decided she wasn't.

"I've got a couple more days. You can stay here until then."
Nona yanked her hand back. Grant made a placating motion.
"I've got a date. Could be late back. I won't wake you."
He pointed at the other bed.
"Just remember that one's mine."

TEN

Despite the heat, Grant had a hot shower then dialed it down to lukewarm. It was the nearest he'd ever get to having a cold shower. He didn't like the cold. It reminded him of Operation Snow Queen and the diner at Snake Pass. Neither of them were good memories. He would happily never see snow again.

After the shower, he dried off and stood naked in front of the mirror. He ran hot water into the basin and lathered up to shave with the disposable razor. The ambient temperature meant the mirror hadn't steamed up. When the door opened and closed, it didn't cool him. The quiet voice behind him combined shyness and experience.

"You're in pretty good shape for an older guy."

Grant looked at Nona through the mirror. He didn't cover himself but didn't turn to face her either. He paused with the razor halfway to his face. Nona looked him up and down.

"Looks like you've been in the wars though."

She reached out and ran soft fingers over the scars on his back. Grant didn't pull away. The touch was electric but wrong. Nona was half his age. In another life, he could have been her father. As much as he liked women, he wasn't a cradle snatcher. He locked eyes with her reflection. She held his gaze for a few seconds, then crossed her arms and pulled the crop top over her head. She was a woman. Her body was lithe and toned and developed in all the right places. Small firm breasts with hard black nipples. A flat stomach that was all muscle and no stretch marks. She hooked her thumbs into the top of her leggings and began to slide them down.

Grant turned and stopped her, his grip firm but gentle.

"This isn't one of the choices you should make."

Nona stood firm, not hiding her breasts.

"You don't want me?"

Grant sighed.

"Twenty years ago, yes. Not now."

Her voice was confident.

"I've had older."

Grant looked in her eyes and softened his gaze.

"That doesn't make it right."

Nona looked him up and down again, then nodded. She looked into his eyes, still confident, still not embarrassed.

"Is this a gentleman thing? Like pulling out chairs and opening doors?"

Grant smiled.

"This is bigger than that."

Nona dangled the crop top at her side.

"You think?"

"I know."

"Why?"

Grant couldn't resist one more look at what she was offering.

"Because pulling out a chair isn't turning down a seat."

He indicated the razor in his hand.

"And I still have a date."

Nona opened the door.

"Then she's a lucky woman."

Grant turned back to the mirror and began to shave. He spoke to Nona's back as she left the bathroom.

"Don't forget. Yours is the bed nearest the window."

Nona glanced over her shoulder.

"I know. And you won't wake me up."

* * *

Grant met Evelyn Cover at the Cowbell Burger & Whiskey Bar on West 5th, just behind the Fifth Third Center and next door to the Capital Grille. Evelyn guessed right that Grant was more of a burger man than into posh steaks. The Cowbell was the perfect choice.

"You're not psychic, are you?"

Evelyn stepped through the door Grant held open for her.

"You don't have to be psychic to read a man."

Grant stood beside her and scanned the interior.

"I'm that obvious, am I?"

Evelyn smiled at him.

"You're wearing cargo pants."

Grant tugged at his trouser leg.

"I can explain that."

Evelyn shook her head.

"Doesn't matter. Capital Grille frowns on cargo pants."

Grant surveyed the interior and nodded his approval. The Cowbell presented itself as a rock and roll–themed gourmet burger restaurant. The wood-framed panels of the right-hand wall displayed giant headshots of John Lennon, Twiggy, and Elvis. There were some other psychedelic posters Grant didn't recognize; he was more into movie posters. An L-shaped bar took up most of the back wall, and the floor space was neatly arranged with single tables and leather-backed chairs. Curved booths extended along both sides. Fifties' rock and roll music played just loud enough to give atmosphere but not so loud you couldn't hear yourself talk. Half the tables and three of the booths were vacant. Grant waved a hand for Evelyn to choose.

"Ladies first."

Evelyn looked at him.

"I noticed that about you. When you held the door open. I bet you give up your seat to little old ladies on the bus as well."

Grant shrugged.

"I would if they hadn't taken all the hotel rooms."

Evelyn feigned concern.

"That makes a difference, does it?"

Grant jerked his head toward the door.

"It's why I'm out in the sticks."

Evelyn gave him a questioning look, but Grant swept a hand around the empty tables again.

"Take your pick. I'll tell you all about it."

They both had soft drinks, Evelyn explaining she was driving, and a plate of shared starters. Nibbles and bite sizes for them both to pick at while they talked. Grant had his back to the wall under a pair of cow horns in a booth on the left. He'd given Evelyn the choice, but she seemed to know Grant preferred to watch the room and not the wall. Maybe she assumed all cops protected their backs, but Grant just liked people watching. Right now, he was watching the beautiful woman in the business suit, Evelyn having come straight from work.

"So that's my excuse. I don't normally wear cargo pants."

Evelyn toyed with some kind of chicken nugget.

"A knitting circle convention?"

Grant dragged a nacho through the dip tray.

"Conference. Apparently, they can get a bit rowdy."

Evelyn took a bite out of the nugget.

"And they take up a lot of room."

Even talking with her mouth full, Evelyn looked classy. Grant paused his nacho dipping.

"They took up *all* the rooms. Between them and the delayed flights before mine."

Evelyn wiped her lips on a napkin. They were nice lips.

"So, that's how you came across this laptop charger."

Grant finished eating the nacho and nodded.

"At the Sleepy Nook, yes. Got me curious."

"Because you're a cop and something smells wrong."

Grant took a deep breath through his nose.

"Not in here. Everything smells great."

He lowered his head and raised his eyebrows.

"The food doesn't smell bad either."

Evelyn shook her head.

"Oh no. And you were doing so well."

Grant winced.

"That was a bit cheesy, wasn't it?"

Evelyn nodded at the sharer plate.

"Worse than the nachos."

Grant reached across the table and took Evelyn's hand. He drew it slowly toward him and patted it with his other hand.

"Sorry. I blame the heat."

He squeezed her hand.

"I promise I won't kiss your hand."

Evelyn laid her other hand over his.

"Oh, don't promise to stop everything."

Grant looked her in the eye.

"The hand?"

Evelyn met his gaze.

"The kissing."

Grant tilted his head to one side.

"Is that part of Connect's after-sales service?"

Evelyn kept her eyes on him.

"I didn't make a sale."

"So this is just customer care?"

She squeezed his hand and slipped hers out of his grip.

"This is dinner. Let's see how much we care after that."

Grant saw the waitress coming over with their main courses, balancing a huge tray on one shoulder. The waitress set up a folding trestle and put the tray on it. The burger was still sizzling. The fries overflowed a plate the size of Texas. Grant looked around the side of the waitress and nodded at Evelyn.

"As long as you don't start knitting."

Evelyn even made the sly wink look classy.

"As long as you don't talk with your mouth full."

That got his mind racing. He didn't think she was talking about the Cowbell Ranch Burger and fries. The waitress left with an "Enjoy your meal." The Yorkshire cop and the sales manager exchanged a smile, then started to eat.

It was dark when Grant walked Evelyn to her car, parked at a meter opposite First Presbyterian on North Church Street. A short walk from The Cowbell but long enough to feel like a romantic stroll. Hand in hand at first, then arm in arm. She smelled nicer out here than she did in the restaurant. There were fewer smells to distract him. It was still warm and steamy.

"Doesn't it ever get cold here?"

Evelyn stopped under a tree and a One-Way sign five cars along the street.

"You don't like the heat?"

Grant turned to face her.

"I love the heat. It's just different. Than Texas, for instance."

She rested her back against a car Grant guessed was hers.

"Everything's different than Texas."

Grant rested his hands on her hips.

"You're a lot friendlier. That's for sure."

She brought her arms up and draped them around his neck.

"That's why it's named after a woman."

Grant moved closer.

"Sounds better than Mecklenburg."

Evelyn looked up into Grant's eyes. She had to crane her neck.

"Thanks for dinner."

Grant lowered his head.

"Thanks for not being a little old lady."

Evelyn drew her head back.

"A little old lady that took your hotel room."

Grant smiled.

"Oh, I've got a hotel room."

Then he thought about Nona Hartley sleeping in the bed near the window. He hoped the thought didn't show on his face. Maybe he'd have to settle for pleasant company and a goodnight kiss. Evelyn looked into his eyes.

"And I've got a house."

Problem solved. A siren began to sound in the distance. Grant stroked the side of her face, then took her chin in his hand. He tilted her face up to his and kissed her gently on the forehead. She closed her eyes and sighed. A second siren joined the first and then another. He kissed the lips she'd wiped with the napkin, and she kissed him back. Her arms tightened around his neck. An air horn joined the sirens, a fire truck on an emergency run. Somewhere northwest of town.

Grant stopped the kiss and raised his head. A worm of doubt knotted his stomach. Evelyn saw the worry on his face, then looked toward the noise before looking back at Grant.

"You don't think…"

Grant stepped back and tried to get his bearings. The map in his head was dulled by the pleasant evening. North Church Street ran down to the Andrew Jackson Highway and the Andrew Jackson ran parallel to the I-85. Out past Charlotte Douglas International and just south of Little Rock Road.

ELEVEN

The fire was out by the time Evelyn dropped Grant at the Sleepy Nook Inn. She parked on the service road near the rear exit with a view overlooking the back of the motel. Firefighters had thrown everything from the burned-out room over the balcony and were busy damping down so it wouldn't reignite. Secondary units were checking the rooms on either side of it to make sure the fire hadn't spread. It hadn't. The only room burned was room 257.

"Nona."

Grant didn't explain who Nona was nor thank Evelyn for the lift. He was out of the car and racing across the parking lot before she'd fully stopped. Steam drifted across the tarmac. Grant ran through it and came out the other side like a wraith, trailing tendrils of smoke and mist. He took the steps of the central stairway two at a time and reached the landing just as a firefighter came out of Grant's room.

"The girl?"

The firefighter took his facemask off and waved toward the front of the motel.

"Better ask them. They were here first."

Grant didn't ask who "them" was. He went back down the stairs and out past the swimming pool. Two police cars and an ambulance with flashing blue lights were parked out front of the reception lobby. As Grant came round the corner, the ambulance pulled away, then sped off toward the freeway. A cop noticed Grant approaching and turned toward him, the cop a blurred silhouette against the flashing lights. Grant stopped and let out a sigh to calm his nerves. Bad news was always upsetting. Being responsible for that bad news made it worse. The senior cop from this morning gestured Grant to one side.

"Looks like you pissed Leroy off more than you thought."

The cop took Grant's explanation sitting in a bamboo chair in the conservatory. He wrote it down in his notebook together with Grant's description and contact details, which here in Charlotte were his cell phone number and email address. Since Grant hadn't mastered emails on his phone, he suggested using the phone number. He was impatient to get to the hospital.

"You got enough? Can I go now?"

The cop closed his notebook.

"For a guy who tossed a pimp over the balcony, stole his girl, and had his room torched, you're in an awful hurry."

Grant pushed forward in his seat, ready to get up.

"You got some bad information there. I didn't toss anybody."

The cop put the notebook and pen in his jacket pocket.

"The hooker was in your room."

Grant sat on the edge of his seat, thighs straining.

"She needed somewhere to stay."

The cop fastened the pocket.

"Because you tossed her pimp over the balcony."

Grant had had enough. He stood up and looked down at the cop.

"Can I go now?"

The cop stood as well and stepped close to Grant.

"You've got some balls on you. A hooker in the bedroom—" he jerked his head toward the parking lot, "—and out to dinner with a woman from South Lake Mall."

Grant didn't back off but didn't front the cop either.

"Am I a suspect?"

The cop stepped sideways away from his chair.

"If you were, you'd be face down and cuffed right now. But you've got yourself an alibi, haven't you? Dinner with the other woman."

Grant stayed where he was.

"I don't need an alibi. Why would I torch my own room?"

The cop watched Grant's face.

"Maybe it wasn't the room."

Grant saw where this was going but repeated himself anyway.

"The girl needed somewhere to stay."

The cop took a step back toward Grant.

"In bed next to the window where the petrol bomb came in."

Grant remembered telling her to use that bed. Something else to feel guilty about.

"Then she might have seen who threw it."

The cop held back from prodding Grant in the chest, but it was all over his face that he wanted to.

"She might have seen who threw Leroy over the balcony too. But she ain't telling nobody now. Convenient, ain't it?"

Grant felt cold for the first time since he'd arrived in Charlotte.

"She's dead?"

The cop shook his head.

"She might wish she was when she comes round. They've got her sedated for the pain."

He glared at Grant.

"Burn scars are the worst."

Grant ignored the intimidation tactic and started thinking like a detective.

"Petrol bomb?"

He searched the map in his head.

"Where's the nearest gas station?"

The cop was way ahead of him.

"Citgo, other side of the underpass. Don't worry. We'll be checking if that's where you bought the fuel."

Grant looked at him.

"Cameras?"

The cop gave Grant a sarcastic look.

"I never thought of that."

He shrugged.

"It's a two-pump backwoods joint. They've barely got a phone."

Grant remembered some of the smaller petrol stations back in Yorkshire. Franchised out from the big companies. They didn't spend a lot on security because it was cheaper to write off the occasional drive-off without paying.

"You'll check though. Yes?"

The cop finally set off toward his car. He paused halfway to the door and threw Grant a final comment.

"I'd be more worried about checking they'll still give you a room."

He nodded at the reception desk.

"Motel like this. In the airport buffer zone. They can't afford trouble."

He turned his eyes skywards.

"Coming in to land. Last thing you see out your window before you hit the tarmac. It's the Sleepy Nook Inn."

He smiled.

"They don't like fires in the flight path."

TWELVE

"So let me get this straight. You've got a girl in your room while you're out for dinner with me. And you want me to drive you to the hospital to see her? Have I got that right?"

Evelyn had brought the car round to the parking lot and was parked in an angled slot away from the reception building. They were standing next to the open driver's door. Grant held his hands out in surrender.

"I can explain."

Evelyn didn't look convinced.

"Like you explained about the cargo pants?"

Grant kept his eyes soft.

"More like how I explained about the laptop charger."

Evelyn watched his face.

"Because of the guy you threw off the balcony?"

Grant nodded.

"Because of that."

He leaned forward and rested his arms across the top of the open door. The sigh he let out almost emptied his lungs. His face was guilty, sad, and angry all at the same time.

"She got burned because of me. I need to make this right."

He didn't have to say more. Evelyn waved him to the passenger side, then got in and started the engine. There were no more blue lights behind them as she pulled out onto Little Rock Road and turned south.

CMC-Mercy took up a wedge of land between Vail Avenue and East 5th Street two and a half miles southeast of downtown Charlotte. Evelyn came off the Andrew Jackson Highway at Little Sugar Creek, then took surface roads to the Presbyterian Medical Center and the emergency department at Mercy round the back. She dropped Grant beneath the big red EMERGENCY letters that blazed from the portico over the ambulance delivery bays and said she'd look for a parking space. Grant took her hand and gave it a gentle squeeze.

"You've done enough. Thanks."

He wanted to kiss her but didn't think this was the time.

"Sorry to mess up dinner."

Evelyn looked at his face, tinged with red from the sign.

"Dinner was fine. This is…"

She shrugged as she tried to find the words.

"Unfortunate."

She leaned over and kissed his cheek. Grant was glad for that.

"You've got to be up for work. Can I call you tomorrow?"

Evelyn pointed at the clock on the dashboard. It was almost 1 a.m.

"Today. Yes, of course."

She nodded toward the emergency department entrance.

"I hope she's okay."

Grant squeezed her hand again, then got out. The car disappeared into the one-way system as Evelyn tried to find the exit. Grant turned toward the oasis of light and sliding doors. One thing he was certain of, Nona Hartley was a long way from being okay.

Once you've been in one hospital waiting room, you've been in them all. Whether they call it Accident & Emergency or the ER or the emergency department, the sharp end of emergency medicine was always the same. Antiseptic, shit, and rush-rush-rush interspersed with periods of calm and overlaid with the sounds of pain and sadness. Screams and groans and low wailing moans.

When Grant walked through the sliding doors, the emergency department was experiencing a lull. There was the constant background noise of hushed conversations and occasional groans, but there were no panicked bursts of activity or rushing gurneys. There was less of a shit smell too. It was the cleanest and least frenetic emergency department he'd ever been in. And he'd been in a lot.

There was some kind of corporate logo on the wall next to the doors with a brief mission statement underneath.

CAROLINAS MEDICAL CENTER
Mercy
Uncompromising Excellence. Commitment to Care.

It was the kind of thing business managers dreamed up as a form of advertising but frontline doctors and nurses did as second nature. Emergency services worked in the trenches. When lives were at stake, they didn't need reminding about commitment to care or uncompromising excellence. Grant found the nurses' station and went in search of answers.

"Nona Hartley? Burn victim. Just brought in?"

He held the Boston PD badge wallet up, but it was his body language that told the nurse he was a cop. She didn't ask where he worked or query his foreign accent. Half the people in America were from somewhere else. She checked her clipboard, then turned sympathetic eyes on him.

"She's being examined now. Take a seat. We'll let you know."

Grant knew better than to press for more information. First thing would be to stabilize the girl, then examine her injuries. Telling the investigating officer about that was a long way down the list of priorities. Grant found a vending machine and bought a hot chocolate. Another thing he'd learned over the years was that vending machine coffee was terrible and American tea was worse. Safe option was to buy a drinking chocolate with added sugar. He stirred the drink with a pen he'd taken from the counter and prepared for a long wait.

There was only one emergency arrival and two walk-in casualties during the next two hours. Grant drank three hot chocolates and bought a Hershey's Bar to keep his energy level up. The sugar rush didn't make the time go faster, but it broke the wait into manageable chunks. It was the sort of thing cops learned from doing endless hours of surveillance in parked cars. Break the monotony with little distractions. The nurses triaging the casualties gave him something to watch. Hot drinks and a chocolate bar gave him something to do.

"Are you the cop here for Nona Hartley?"

The doctor was young and clean and wearing casual clothes. He looked like a computer nerd, not a doctor—the only clue being the stethoscope draped loosely around his neck. Grant stood up and shook his hand.

"How is she?"

The doctor led Grant away from the waiting area to somewhere more private: a corridor leading to the examination rooms. His demeanor was calm and professional and totally in keeping with Grant's experience of people at the sharp end.

"Burns are extensive down one side. Most of her hair has gone. She's stable but weak."

Grant felt the weight of responsibility.

"She say anything?"

The doctor shook his head.

"We've got her sedated to contain the shock. And the pain, of course. She won't be saying anything for a while."

Grant was thinking if there was anything that would help him find out more about her. The only thing he knew was that she was a prostitute pimped by Leroy and that she had nowhere else to go. That implied there was no family she could stay with or that her family had disowned her. He'd seen that before in situations like this. One thing he was certain of was that every girl he knew of Nona's age had a mobile phone.

"Did she have any possessions with her?"

The doctor thought back to the paramedic's report.

"She was in bed. Found sheltered down the side. Only had the clothes she was wearing."

Grant thought as much. When the shit hits the fan, the last thing you've got time to do is gather your things. Phones tended to be different with girls though.

"She didn't have a phone?"

The doctor shook his head again, then waved along the corridor.

"You want to see her? I'll check with the nurse who cut the clothes off."

Grant nodded and followed the doctor to a curtained cubicle. He paused at the opening and took a deep breath. The doctor pulled the curtain open, and Grant fought back a gasp. He'd seen injured people before, some of them with gaping wounds and amputations, but looking at the fragile girl he'd last seen as a beautiful young woman was hard to take. Most of her hair had gone, and what was left was singed beyond recognition. Half of her face and one arm and shoulder were wrapped in burns dressings and ointment to calm the inflammation. The rest of her was hidden in a hospital gown and raised bedsheets to keep the weight off the burns. The only good thing was she wasn't tubed up to a breathing machine, so her lungs must have been okay.

The doctor went in search of the admitting nurse. Grant sat on a chair in the corner of the room. The heart rate monitor beeped its steady pulse. The antiseptic smell was corrupted by the smell of burned hair and flesh.

Running feet and raised voices signaled an end to the lull, and for the next hour and a half it was all hands to the pumps after a pile-up on the I-85 brought six casualties and a hoard of friends and relatives. Grant listened to life on the front line while concentrating on the girl he'd first met offering sexual favors on the balcony of the Sleepy Nook Inn. Once again, he thought about the choices he'd made. If he'd shown more restraint, Leroy wouldn't have been sent flying, and Nona wouldn't have been sleeping in Grant's room.

He moved the chair to the side of the bed and sat down. Her good hand rested across the top of the sheets, hooked to an IV drip hanging nearby. Careful not to disturb the needle, he laid his hand over hers and whispered in her ear.

"Come on, girl. You can do this."

He leaned closer.

"You can be anything you want to be. Remember?"

The nurse he'd met at the triage desk swished through the curtain, and Grant sat back as if caught being inappropriate. She nodded her understanding.

"It's good to talk to her. Sometimes they know what's going on around them. Even when sedated."

Grant patted Nona's hand, then got up. He went to the nurse. "Thanks."

She looked at him.

"You were asking about her possessions?"

"Yes."

The nurse pointed to a plastic bag under the bed.

"Her clothes are in there. Had to cut them off, obviously."

Grant looked at the bag, then back to the nurse.

"Anything in her pockets?"

The nurse shook her head.

"No. And no phone either. I heard you asked about that."

She pulled a hospital envelope out of her smock.

"But her hand was balled in a fist. Didn't notice at first. Clamped tight."

She held the envelope up.

"Had to prise them open to get this."

DAY TWO

THIRTEEN

Dawn was feathering the horizon when Grant got off the bus downtown. He needed time to think, and using public transport always gave him plenty of that. He considered having breakfast at Burger King in the bus station but decided to wait until journey's end at Little Rock Road. Between waiting for the change of bus and the meandering journey, it was half past eight by the time he walked under the I-85 toward Hardee's.

Grant paused at the side of the road where Leroy had come out of the trees. The black Para was his priority now, then talking to Nona when she came round. Talking to the girl would have to wait though. Finding Leroy was his first goal. There was something else he should look into as well. He took the thick plastic disc out of his pocket; the token Nona had felt was so important that she'd kept hold of it even when she was on fire. The ninety-day token of being sober or drugs-free for three months.

He ignored the Sleepy Nook Inn and crossed the road to the diner. He wouldn't meet any of his targets if he didn't have something to eat. That was something he'd learned in the army that was just as important in the police. You never know when you'll get the chance to eat again, so fuel up whenever you can. That thought reminded him of the cop who'd fronted him at Hardee's. *"I take my break when I can."* And that got him wondering how the cop knew Grant had met a woman at the South Lake Mall.

He put the token in his pocket and walked through the parking lot. When he pushed the door open, he walked right into the middle of the breakfast rush.

"I told you it can get pretty busy."

Grant stood with the waitress just inside the door.

"They had to close the kitchen yet?"

The waitress pointed to a name badge on her chest. Tilly waved a hand across the seating area. There were four customers this morning, an even bigger rush than yesterday.

"I can always find room for a tall Englishman."

She took out her order pad.

"So long as the cops don't come and drag you away."

Grant thought about the fire and impersonating an investigating officer and stealing evidence from Nona Hartley. Being dragged away by the Charlotte PD was a distinct possibility. He smiled at Tilly.

"I'm sure they'll let me finish breakfast."

Tilly snorted a laugh.

"You've got more faith than I have, then."

She pointed to the same booth Grant sat in yesterday.

"Mom's milky coffee?"

Grant walked toward the booth with Tilly in tow.

"If I ever start a coffee shop franchise, I'm going to patent that. Latte sounds so..."

He turned to the waitress.

"Un-American."

Tilly wrote on the order pad.

"I blame Starbucks. You having the all-day?"

Grant slid into the booth with the window facing the parking lot.

"If the kitchen can cope."

Tilly wrote it down and smiled.

"For you, sugar, I'll give him a prod."

She walked to the kitchen to motivate the chef and left Grant looking out of the window. The parking lot held more cars this morning, but it was still mainly empty space and dust. In the distance, over the top of the trees, a dull smudge stained the clear blue sky where the Sleepy Nook Inn bore the scars of the night's excitement. The fire was out, but the residue hung in the air like a thundercloud. Grant thought about his room and knew he'd have to face Mr. Khan and get a new one. He felt bad for the man from Bradford who had come here to make a better life for himself and his family. To Grant, it seemed like he was feeling guilty about everybody. Except the man he'd thrown over the balcony.

Leroy whatshisname.

He began to take stock of how many people knew about that. Mr. Khan had implied he knew when he thanked Grant. The older cop suspected Grant had tossed the pimp. Bruno Morris not only seemed to know about it but also had knowledge of the rivalry Grant was supposed to avoid getting in the middle of. So the taxi driver was Grant's best shot at finding out more.

That was Leroy taken care of. Fleshing out Nona Hartley was something else. He took the thick plastic token out of his pocket and examined it. The disc looked like a poker chip only thicker, more like a playing piece from a game of draughts. Checkers in America. There was a zigzag crack etched across the face, presumably to denote something broken made whole again, and some letters embossed around the edge. A.E.L.T.C. Whether that stood for some kind of affirmative saying or the group it came from he didn't know. A big red "ninety" was emblazoned on the top face. Three months sober, or more likely for Nona, ninety days drugs-free.

"I didn't think you'd been here long enough to get your ninety-day chip."

Tilly put Grant's coffee on the table.

"I'm guessing old man Brubaker didn't give that to you."

* * *

77

Tilly promised to come over after a late rush of two more customers: a salesman and his assistant who was too attractive not to be having an affair with him. Their closeness over coffee looked to be more than talking sales strategies, and she failed to hide the hand on his leg under the table. Grant waded through the all-day breakfast and gave up halfway through again.

The crowd thinned. Tilly cleared tables. Grant ordered another coffee as he picked at the remnants. He turned the ninety-day chip in his fingers while he stared through the window. The parking lot had emptied somewhat, but there were still two cars in the far corner. The sun had climbed the pale blue sky and blazed down on another hot, steamy day in North Carolina. An eighteen-wheeler drove north off the I-85 toward Paw Creek and the clutch of refineries beyond the woods. A dusty pickup came the other way and drove right past Hardee's, the breakfast rush almost done. No police cars pulled into the parking lot. No cops came to drag Grant away.

"You'll be joining the magic show, doing tricks like that."

Grant looked up at Tilly, then down at his hands. He'd been absentmindedly rolling the token across the top of his fingers, turning it over at each knuckle.

"Prestidigitation."

Tilly stood at Grant's table.

"Did you just make that up?"

Grant smiled.

"Conjuring. I can do card tricks as well."

Tilly nodded.

"Sleight of hand. I always knew the English were tricky."

Grant waved for the waitress to sit down, then held the token up between finger and thumb.

"This guy Brubaker. He run the meetings?"

Tilly slid into the booth opposite Grant.

"Local chapter. Alcoholics and narcotics."

Grant put the token down and pushed it across the table.

"What do you know about this?"

Tilly looked at it but didn't pick it up.

"I know it isn't yours."

Grant sighed. The weight of responsibility showed on his face. Tilly noticed.

"The girl in the fire?"

Grant tapped the token with one finger.

"Would he know where she lives?"

Tilly looked at the Englishman.

"It's called anonymous for a reason."

Grant smiled a frown.

"Private things don't seem to stay private around here."

Tilly smiled back.

"Like you throwing Leroy over the balcony?"

Grant nodded.

"See what I mean?"

He tapped the token again.

"Think he can help?"

Tilly fluttered her eyelids.

"I don't think he watches Downton Abbey."

Meaning Brubaker wasn't as big a lover of the English as Tilly. Grant rested his elbows on the table and leaned forward.

"But he looks out for troubled souls."

Tilly looked into his eyes.

"Is she a troubled soul?"

Grant lowered his voice.

"She's under sedation at Mercy. What do you think?"

Tilly sighed and nodded slowly.

"I think that's a terrible thing."

Grant took a deep breath.

"I've seen her. It is. And I want to find the bastard who did it."

Tilly fidgeted under the table.

"Leroy, you reckon?"

"He'd be my best bet."

"Because you threw him off the balcony?"

"Because she was with him. I don't think he likes being made a fool of."

"Thought he'd have come after you, then."

Grant's tone hardened.

"Burning her is coming after me."

Tilly fell silent for a moment. She brought her hands up onto the table. Grant reached over and placed his hand over hers.

"Where does Brubaker hold his meetings?"

Tilly looked down at her hands, then up into Grant's eyes. She made a decision and nodded through the window.

"Just down past the highway. Uses a room round back of the station."

Grant felt a shiver run down his spine despite the heat.

"The gas station?"

Tilly looked back at Grant.

"Yes. Two-pump joint. Citgo."

FOURTEEN

Grant was sweating before he left the parking lot at Hardee's. By the time he'd walked the half a mile or so to the filling station, his body had adjusted and he was just pleasantly warm. He reckoned he must be acclimatizing. Next thing, he'd be asking, "What heat?"

The forecourt was clean and traditional, the Citgo signs and canopy over the gas pumps freshly painted and modern. The building itself was a throwback to darker times, not exactly a log cabin but close. Once you looked round either side of the façade, the gas station was all faded wood paneling and a sagging roof. Little Rock Food Mart took up most of the front half together with the pump controls and sales counter. A driveway curled round to the back where the repair bays used to be. Nobody brought their cars here for repair anymore. The shutter doors were boarded shut. The windows were cracked and dirty.

Grant stood on the sidewalk to get his bearings. The Little Rock Citgo and Food Mart filled a parched clearing cut into the woods at the side of the road. The steady hum of traffic drifted down from the I-85 just past the bus stop where he'd got off from the hospital. Beyond that, through the underpass, was the Sleepy Nook Inn on the right and Hardee's on the left. Everything within walking distance. A circle of trouble that included throwing Leroy off the balcony, being fronted by the police over breakfast, and having his room destroyed by a petrol bomb. It didn't surprise Grant that the circle of life brought him to an AA meeting hall behind the gas station where the petrol was probably bought.

A car pulled away from the pump and paused at the exit before turning south. It was the sales rep and his assistant from Hardee's. Lovers getting back to business. In the vastness that was America, Grant felt like he'd wandered into a small-town drama. Charlotte wasn't a small town per se, but this neck of the woods was definitely interconnected. It wouldn't surprise Grant to learn that Nona lived two houses down the street, if there had been any houses on the tree-lined road.

The car picked up speed and left a swirl of dust on the forecourt. There were no other customers. Grant took one last look at the sight lines, then walked between the pumps to the front door.

"That badge don't make no never mind around here."

Grant wondered where they taught people to mangle the English language like they did in great swathes of backwoods America. Sometimes not even backwoods. There were parts of Boston where he couldn't understand a thing they said.

"This is more of a friendly enquiry."

The old man behind the cash register scratched his chin.

"Don't need no badge-flashing to be friendly."

Grant closed the door and entered another world. From outside, the frontage portrayed modern efficiency. In here, a time warp changed the gas station into a roadside convenience store that just happened to sell petrol. The shelves looked pre-war, the paintwork older than that. The false ceiling sagged almost as much as the pitched roof, and two out of the four fluorescent lights hanging on chains blinked but stayed dark. Faded sports photos hung in frames around the walls. Grant looked at the old man, who needed a shave and a haircut.

"That is absolutely correct. I apologize."

He put his badge wallet away.

"I'm trying to be friendly to a girl got injured last night."

Brubaker came out from behind the counter.

"Burned at the Sleepy Nook?"

Grant nodded.

"She needs a friend right now."

Brubaker's voice sounded like a grumbling bear.

"Lots a folk be trying to friend that girl."

He beetled his brow and turned a hard stare on Grant.

"Half the problem that brought her here in the first place."

Grant held his hands out, palms up. Coming in peace.

"Too many people have taken advantage of her. She needs to know what real friends are. Real friends try and help. If we get it right, she can start a better life away from here. I understand you help people who need helping."

Brubaker considered Grant for a moment that stretched into an awkward silence. He scratched his chin again out of habit because up close he didn't look as dirty as he first appeared. When he spoke again, the folksy vernacular disappeared, replaced with a calm steady tone that reminded Grant of Henry Fonda.

"It isn't where she lives that's the problem, it's who she chose to spend that life with. You threw one of them over the balcony. I'm hoping you don't turn out to be just as bad."

Grant relaxed, his instincts proving correct. You don't run a meeting hall for the disadvantaged if you're a cranky old man. He nodded at Brubaker and let out a sigh.

"Does everybody around here know about that?"

Brubaker played it deadpan.

"Around here, we know about everything."

Grant took the ninety-day chip out of his pocket.

"Good. So, what do you know about this?"

The meeting hall round the back could only be accessed from a door next to the boarded-up repair bays. Citgo had insisted there was no connecting door into the gas station. Brubaker hung a

BACK IN A WHILE sign in the window and walked Grant round the outside. The door was sprained and hung crooked off rusty hinges. The letters painted over the door were as faded as the woodwork.

MEETING HALL

That was all. There was no description or welcome or timetable, just the bare minimum so people knew what the door was for. Brubaker unlocked it and ushered Grant into the dark. When the lights came on, they were dirty yellow bulbs in faded canvas shades. There were more sports photos framed on the walls of the corridor leading from the door. Grant turned right at the end into the workshop that had been turned into a meeting hall. There were three rows of wooden pews from an old church and a lectern for guest speakers. A table along one side for refreshments. A notice-board on the wall had A.E.L.T.C. across the top, then each letter down the left with the inspirational message attached.

Add
Everything
Lots
To
Close

It didn't make much sense, but the initials looked familiar, and not just from the edge of the token. Grant waved a hand around the hall.

"You use this a lot?"

Brubaker came in behind him.

"I use it all the time."

He indicated the false wall that cut off the far end of the hall.

"I live back there."

Grant nodded.

"Resident counselor."

Brubaker shrugged.

"Can't help if I'm not around. You help people, right?"

Grant surveyed his surroundings.

"I prefer not to live among the people I'm arresting."

Brubaker looked at Grant.

"I don't arrest people."

Grant tapped one of the pews with his fist. The noise echoed around the room.

"Drink turns some people nasty. Drugs too."

Brubaker stood behind the lectern and rested his arms across the top.

"All the more reason to be handy if they need me."

"Did Nona need you?"

Brubaker raised one shoe onto the footrest.

"That would be private."

Grant stood in front of the lectern.

"Because she needs you now."

Brubaker's voice took on that bear-like grumble again.

"She was doing good until you showed up."

Grant felt the weight of responsibility. To a certain degree, he knew the old man was right, but Grant hadn't forced her into the lifestyle she'd chosen. He opened his palm to show the token.

"Ninety-days is doing good?"

The bear growled.

"One day is doing good. Ninety is excellent."

Grant shook his head.

"Excellent isn't what I'd call hanging out with the likes of Leroy."

The growl softened.

"I can't argue with you there."

Grant closed his fist on the token.

"I'm looking for her family. You know where I might find them?"

Brubaker's shoulders sagged.

"No father. Mother abandoned her to the system."

He shook his head.

"Nobody."

"She must have stayed somewhere."

"Around. With Leroy mostly. And some others."

"Where'd she keep her stuff?"

"What little she had, from being a kid. She had a room couple of houses down the road."

Grant remembered thinking that when he arrived. Circle of life.

"I didn't see any houses."

Brubaker pushed back from the lectern.

"It's a long road."

A car horn sounded from the forecourt. Somebody wanting to fill up. The old man came around the lectern and past the refreshment table. The noticeboard looked like it needed dusting. Everything did. Grant looked at the inspirational saying and couldn't resist asking.

"Does that make sense if you stop drinking?"

Brubaker looked at the sign.

"Thought you were supposed to be a detective."

Grant shrugged.

"I'm detecting deep and meaningful."

Brubaker waved toward the sports photos.

"You walked past all the clues."

Grant looked at the images more closely and was surprised at the lack of any American sports. No baseball players. No big American football stars. They were all faded pictures of tennis players from days gone by. Rod Laver. Bjorn Borg. Jimmy Connors. Some newer but nobody later than Pete Sampras and Andre Agassi. Everyone playing on the grass of the All England Lawn Tennis Club. A.E.L.T.C. The old man smiled.

"I love tennis."

The horn sounded again.

"Let me sort this out, then I'll give you her address."

* * *

The horn-blower turned into three cars and a customer wanting something to eat. Grant perused the shelves while Brubaker served them. General groceries. Brand names that Grant had never heard of. Some that had been changed from the English versions. Frosted Flakes instead of Frosties. Stuff like that. He turned his attention to the warped ceiling. There was a large mirror high up on the back wall giving Brubaker a view down the shopping aisles, but there were no CCTV cameras. The cop who'd fronted him over breakfast at Hardee's had been right. If the petrol for the Molotov cocktail had been bought here, there'd be no footage to prove it.

The bell above the door pinged as the last customer left. A car door slammed and the engine roared, the driver impatient to get somewhere else. Grant understood how he felt. He'd spent enough time here finding out not very much about Nona Hartley and was no closer to tracking down any family to step up and help her. There was one other thing he could ask Brubaker about though.

"You work this place alone or you got staff?"

The old man finished with the cash register and came round from behind the counter.

"I've got staff."

Grant waved toward the pumps on the forecourt.

"Can you ask if any of them sold a bottle of petrol last night?"

Brubaker rubbed his hands as if washing them.

"Don't have to ask. I was working the late shift."

"Did Leroy come in? Any of his guys? And buy the petrol?"

Brubaker looked at Grant.

"For the fire, you mean?"

The old man shook his head.

"Wasn't Leroy, bought the gas."

Grant waited. The old man frowned.

"Damnedest thing. Never thought much of it at the time. But

now you mention it. Damn."

"Well?"

Brubaker turned sad eyes on the English cop.

"It was Nona came in. Bought it herself."

FIFTEEN

Brubaker's idea of a couple of houses down the road was as broad as Alan Street's description as a street. What it really was was twin tracks in the grass that could loosely be described as a dirt track but was barely a spoor leading to nothing. The nothing, in this case, was a rundown shack that used to be a roadside grocery back when people still bought fresh vegetables. Now it was the end of the line for whoever lived there. According to Brubaker, that somebody was Nona Hartley.

Alan Street was on a bend in Little Rock Road two and a half miles north of the Citgo gas station, past the Sleepy Nook Inn and Hardee's and just over the crossroads with Tuckaseegee Road. If Brubaker's meeting hall was in a clearing cut out of the trees, Nona's shack wasn't even in a clearing, just a natural glade in the woods with a view of nothing but distant tarmac and tree trunks.

Grant stood in the twin tracks and surveyed the approach.

Sun baked down from a clear blue sky and painted the foliage a lush green that extended to the trees surrounding the shack. The dirt track ran straight for ten yards, then stopped at the front door. Trees crowded the back and sides, but the front was open with good site lines to Little Rock Road. A good view of anybody approaching along the trail. It didn't look like anybody had been looking out of the windows for a long time. They were so dirty they didn't even glint in the sunlight.

Grant walked halfway to the shack, then stopped. The angle changed. He could see down one side. The windows there didn't look any cleaner, the curtains no less faded and still. He'd been in cemeteries with more life. He'd been in desert townships that looked less dangerous. The danger bristled the short hairs up the back of his neck. This was a bad place.

Grant squinted against the glare of the sun and checked the two sides of the shack he could see. The front door was plain wood painted green a century ago. The paint was peeling and faded. There were two windows along the front, both curtained and closed. One had a crack running across it but was otherwise whole. The pitched roof sagged more than the meeting hall and had a crooked metal chimney with a cone on top like a Chinaman's hat. The side of the shack that he could see had one window, but Grant couldn't tell anything except it wasn't open. The trees crowding the back and the other side were so close that the roots warped the wood-planked walls. Several planks had sprung and pointed outwards.

There was no movement. There was no sign of life. Grant approached with caution. Whenever he saw somewhere that looked empty, it was best to assume it wasn't. Whatever life Nona had made for herself with Leroy, it wasn't here. So why keep her belongings in the back of beyond?

A muffled noise came from inside.

Grant's senses sparked, and he was instantly alert. He walked quickly down the track and stopped at the angle of the two walls. He could see both sides. Anybody inside would have to move the curtains to look out. Nobody looked out. There was another noise inside. Grant approached the door and examined the lock. The dull metal tongue was bent, and the frame was splintered. The hinges weren't clean and oiled. The door would creak if he opened it.

Grant picked up a stone from the driveway and hefted it in his hand. It was heavy enough. He looked down the side of the shack, then along the frontage. The door and two windows. Not big enough to have separate rooms along the front. Not likely to have an entrance hall. The door would open straight into the main room. Inwards, not out. He took one step back to open the angle, then threw the stone at the far window.

The breaking glass sounded loud in the clearing.

Grant yanked the door open and went inside.

The man rummaging through the cupboard spun toward the broken window. He stood at the far side of a room so dark he almost blended in. He was a black guy, maybe a little younger than Leroy, with short-cropped hair and dark clothes. The light was bad even with the broken window and open door, but it was bright enough to see that the furniture had been upended and the drawers trashed.

Grant kept to the shadows near the door.

"Don't move. Keep your hands where I can see them."

The man had his back to Grant.

"Hold your hands out to the side."

Not behind his head like they did in the movies. Grant didn't want the man reaching for a weapon in his collar or up his sleeve. Grant left the door open to let some fresh air in. The room smelled of dust and rot. It was hot. The man obviously thought Grant was armed, and Grant didn't enlighten him. He stepped over debris on the floor and grabbed one arm. He pulled it back and down, then did the same with the other. When the arms were pulled tight behind his back, Grant yanked the guy's jacket down off his shoulders to handcuff him, then pushed him to his knees. A quick pat-down showed he was unarmed. That made Grant feel better. He stood over the man, two paces back.

"What you looking for?"

The man kept quiet. Grant stepped in and slapped him up the back of the head, then stepped away, maintaining a safe distance. The man instinctively hunched his head down into his shoulders.

Despite the slap, Grant kept his voice conversational.

"You lose your keys or something?"

The man slowly brought his head out of the hunch and turned a wary eye on Grant. Scars down the side of his face made it look like melted chocolate. Burn scars but not recent. Not last night.

"Ain't no balcony here. How you gonna work that?"

Grant remained alert in case the man tried to stand up.

"There's alternatives to balconies."

The man didn't turn more than halfway. The single eye slitted, and the mouth twisted into a sly smile.

"You think I can't tuck and roll if you throw me out the window?"

Grant jerked a thumb toward the front door.

"How about you tuck and roll into a police car? For breaking and entering."

The slyness left the smile, becoming almost friendly.

"Last I checked, this ain't your house."

Grant shrugged.

"Found committing. A police officer has the power to arrest anyone found committing an arrestable offense, or anyone suspected of committing. You look pretty damn suspicious to me."

The man twisted his shoulders so he could turn further. Both eyes stared at Grant. Only half the face was melted.

"Nona asked me to come get some stuff."

Grant ran the timeline the doctor had given him. *"She won't be saying anything for a while."* Mid-morning of the day after wasn't a while. This guy was full of shit with half a face. Grant pointed at the scarring.

"With burns like that, you know what she's going through."

The man wasn't moved.

"I know she ain't making no complaint of breaking and entering."

Grant kept with the scarring theme.

"I guess you weren't so careful last time. Bottle slip and blow up in your face?"

The man kept steady eyes on Grant.

"You ain't no idea what blowed up in my face."

Grant lowered his voice.

"And you ain't no idea what I'll do to the guy put her in hospital."

The man's eyes watched Grant but couldn't help flicking them over his shoulder at the rest of the room.

"Maybe you want to spend some time in there with her."

Grant spun around a fraction too slow. The second man came out of the shadows near the kitchen door, swinging a rolling pin in one hand. Grant had just enough time to raise a protective arm and notice that the attacker didn't have a second hand.

Grant had become sloppy. Maybe it was the heat or the circumstances, but he'd completely ignored his own rules of engagement. Scout the location and gauge the enemy strength and choose your battleground. The litter-strewn floor was a terrible battleground, and the enemy strength had just doubled.

The rolling pin came down from an overhead swing aimed at driving Grant into the ground. A full swing with maximum effort and minimal control. Grant stepped forward inside the fighting arc and took the blow on the back instead of the head. He pushed upwards from flexed knees and lifted the attacker off his feet. That was the good part. The bad part was the unsure footing and cluttered floor. Grant stood on the edge of a drawer and his foot went from under him. He crashed sideways onto the couch and bounced onto the floor.

The one-armed man swung sideways with the rolling pin and caught Grant a glancing blow on the cheek. Grant saw stars. His eyes popped and blinked, but he had enough awareness to roll over and kick upwards between the attacker's legs. He got lucky. No man can handle having his wedding tackle crushed. The one-armed man dropped the rolling pin, but the first man wrestled his jacket loose and freed his arms. He got up off his knees and pressed an elbow down on Grant's throat. The tag team switched out.

Grant's vision was becoming blurred. The room dimmed. He was wedged between the discarded drawer and the couch and couldn't roll out of the chokehold. He tried to force the elbow off his throat, but the first man was in a good position straddling the prone Yorkshireman. Grant couldn't kick between his legs because he was too far up Grant's torso. He tried anyway, slamming his knee into the guy's back but couldn't dislodge him.

Lights sparked in the corners of his eyes.

The smell of sweat and dust became stronger.

The room began to fade.

Grant reached up with both hands and clamped them on the man's face. He drove his thumbs into the soft flesh of the eye sockets and heard rather than saw the man scream. The pressure came off Grant's throat as the man tried to prise his fingers free. Grant obliged, releasing one hand, but drove his elbow into the man's face. Blood and snot spread from his nose across his cheeks. Grant rolled from under him and knelt up, gasping for breath. Both men were down but at great cost. Grant struggled to his feet, his head swimming until he regained his balance.

Scout the location.

Gauge the enemy strength.

Choose your battleground.

Grant had failed on all three. The ramshackle cabin looked to be a one-room dwelling no bigger than a bedsitting room, with separate bathroom and kitchen. He hadn't checked the layout when he'd come in because he was too busy with the melted man. He'd missed the second intruder in the kitchen. He didn't realize until it was too late that he'd also missed the bedroom at the rear of the shack.

"Can't you two do anything right?"

The third man was bigger and stronger than the first two. He picked up the heavy coffee table as if it were matchwood and swung it fast. The swing weight doubled. The table caught Grant on the back of the head and the lights went out for real.

SIXTEEN

The rules of life and movies are completely different. In life, one punch doesn't knock you out. Hit somebody hard enough to render them unconscious, and you're probably looking at brain damage and a fractured skull. There is never just that simple tap on the head followed by half an hour of darkness and a headache. The only thing that crossed both worlds was the headache, but in real life, coffee tables don't knock you out. It did stun Grant long enough for the trio to escape though.

There were raised voices and some complaining, but mainly Grant heard the noise of scrambling to get out of the shack. A car sped down the dirt track to pick them up, and then the intruders were gone in a cloud of dust. Grant saw the dust when he struggled to the broken window. There was no point giving chase— he was on foot and they were in a vehicle, so he turned his attention to the ransacked living room. Not just the living room.

Nona Hartley's home had been turned upside down. Every cupboard and drawer had been emptied. Every cushion and mattress and pillow had been ripped open. This wasn't burglars wanting to steal the TV. It was intruders looking for something specific. Judging by their hasty retreat, Grant didn't think they'd found it. He straightened the couch and put the drawers back in, then sifted through the clothes and ornaments as he cleared some space on the floor. He did the same in the bedroom and kitchen.

There wasn't a lot to clear up. Nona didn't have a lot.

Twenty minutes later, he sat in front of the coffee table with a cold compress held against the back of his head: a folded towel he'd soaked under the faucet. The only things of note he'd salvaged were a high school yearbook for some place he couldn't pronounce and a six-by-four flip album with creased photos and torn pages. There were only three photos in the album: a young black girl sitting on a swing and the same girl grinning at the camera. The girl was obviously Nona aged five or six. It didn't look like her childhood had generated any more memories worth keeping.

He turned his attention to the high school yearbook. He'd heard about such things but had never seen one outside of the movies. It was a hardbound book with good-quality paper and less-good-quality photos of the students of that particular year. Grant half expected Nona to be registered under a different name, but there she was, Nona Elizabeth Hartley, staring blank-eyed at the camera and not looking like the girl most likely to do anything except fail. The beautiful young woman who had stood in Grant's bathroom was nowhere in sight. He wished he could have told her back then that she could be anything she wanted to be. Maybe her life would have gone down a different track than the one called Alan Street.

Without knowing what the men had been looking for, there was no point spending any more time searching the shack. Grant sat amid the ruins of a life turned to rat shit and felt an overwhelming sadness come over him. He knew that some people had bad upbringings; he'd served with some of them in the army and the police force. Childhood was just the starting point for the rest of your life. It could shackle you or set you free. Soldiers and policemen he'd worked with had used it to spur them on. Nona Hartley had sunk under its weight, dragged down by the likes of Leroy and his cohorts.

Leroy. That was the place to start. Everybody seemed to know him. Nobody had told Grant where he lived. It was time for that to change. He opened his phone, then took the business card out of his pocket.

PROFESSIONAL TRANSPORTATION
And Taxi
Long Distance Services
B. MORRIS XO
AUTO LOCKSMITH 24/7

Bruno answered on the second ring. Grant closed the yearbook. "How d'you fancy showing an Englishman the sights?"

The taxi crossed the Catawba River on the Andrew Jackson Highway. Sun glinted off the water either side of the four-lane crossing, and a speedboat knifed along the river heading south. A FedEx van passed them going the other way, and a family saloon kept pace fifty yards behind them. There was no other traffic. A heat haze simmered up ahead. The dashboard was too hot to touch beneath the windshield even with the air conditioner on full.

"You think this is a good idea? Seeing as how you threw him off the second floor and stole his girl?"

Bruno kept loose hands on the steering wheel and watched for their exit. Leroy lived in a trailer park just across the river near the railroad bridge to Belmont. The shortest route was the Andrew Jackson, then cutting south on surface roads toward the railroad tracks.

"Not to mention his three guys giving you what-for at Nona's."

Grant watched the world go by on the long, flat bridge.

"One thing you should know about me. I don't hold a grudge."

He glanced across at Bruno.

"But I won't be put off."

Bruno slowed as they passed T&T Auto Repair at the end of the bridge. He flicked his turn signal and eased into the left-hand lane at the lights.

"If those boys are with him, you might want to rethink that."

Grant looked straight ahead.

"I don't rethink my decisions either."

Bruno nodded.

"Oh, a straight-ahead kinda guy. Look how well that's worked out so far."

Grant touched the back of his head.

"Bumps in the road."

Bruno turned left and drove along the wooded riverbank.

"A bigger bump for some than others."

Grant clenched his jaw at the accusation. He thought about Nona lying sedated in the hospital with a face that would never look the same again. He thought about the part he played in her downfall and sighed.

"All the more reason to carry on."

Bruno nodded but didn't speak. He already knew that Jim Grant wasn't somebody who changed his mind. He concentrated on negotiating the network of residential streets beyond the woods until they crossed the railroad tracks and took a final left past the container depot. They were heading back toward Catawba River. The trestle bridge was just ahead. The railroad tracks went straight. The road dipped and curled into the trees. When the taxi came out of the trees, it pulled into the Greenway Circle Trailer Park and stopped. Bruno took his hands off the wheel.

"Last chance."

Grant nodded.

"For somebody."

Bruno turned the engine off and pointed along the row of trailer homes.

"Third on the left. I'll listen out for gunfire."

Until Grant got out of the car, he hadn't realized how many mobile homes you could fit onto one patch of grass. The ones initially visible lined the dirt road that circled the green, but the majority of them were hidden in the trees. It was like looking at a housing estate in the fog—until you got close, you couldn't see much, then the houses came out of the mist at you. What caught Grant by surprise wasn't the decay and peeling paintwork so much as the fact that every single one had a Stars & Stripes hanging outside. These people might be down at heel, but they sure were patriotic.

The third house on the left was slightly less run-down than the rest.

The flag hanging outside was the biggest on the block.

Grant stopped one house before the target premises and surveyed the approach. He'd already made that mistake once; he wasn't going to repeat himself. There were no cars parked out front or along the sides. The mailbox was a battered green box on a stick. The number had faded off. A freight train rattled across the trestle overhead and just kept going. There must have been fifty carriages. The trees absorbed some of the noise, but the rattle and creak were constant. Grant waited for the train to pass. He wanted to be able to hear what was waiting for him.

The windows were clean and open. The curtains had more color than the faded paintwork. There was nobody looking out. There was somebody moving inside. Grant took a deep breath and let it out slowly. He walked past the house to look down the other side. Same thing. Clean windows and nice curtains. Nobody watching. If Leroy had really been in the Airborne, some of the cleaning habits must have stuck with him.

The movement inside was slow and methodical. One person. Nothing agitated. Not the three guys from Nona's. No getaway car parked nearby. Grant made his decision and stuck with it. He walked up to the front door and gave it his copper's knock. Loud and insistent. He stood back so he could see the windows on either side of the door.

Nobody answered. Nobody came to the door. Nobody moved. Grant was about to knock again when the door opened. A woman so small he hadn't seen her approaching came out and stood on the porch.

"Whatever you sellin'. Ain't no call for tryin' to deafen me."

SEVENTEEN

Mothers always did the same thing when Grant came a calling. They put the kettle on and broke out the cookies. Evangeline Holmes was no exception. Grant didn't even have to flash his badge. She knew he was a cop and she knew why he was here. The same reason the cops always came. Grant doubted she made tea and cookies for them. Coffee in this case. Milky like his mother used to make. If he'd known his mother.

"You ain't with the regular po-lice."

She set the tray on the table in the bay window up front.

"You're not from around here by a long way."

Grant sat on a worn dining chair at the table.

"No, ma'am. I'm not."

Mrs. Holmes sat opposite and passed the coffee.

"You with the military?"

Grant stirred two sugars into his cup.

"Used to be. Not now."

Mrs. Holmes looked out through her front window. Her eyes took in the peaceful setting and the run-down trailer homes, then looked at the Stars & Stripes hanging out front. It flapped in the gentle breeze coming off the Catawba River.

"I've been around military types all my life. Whole family served at one time or another. Can spot one a mile off. Way you hold yourself. It speaks volumes. Says a lot about a man. Serving his country."

Grant nodded toward the other homes.

"Seems a lot of people agree with you."

Evangeline snorted a laugh and waved a dismissive hand.

"Don't pay them no never mind. Half them folks just fitting in. Around here, you *don't* have a flag in the window, you in big trouble."

Grant smiled and held out his cup in salute.

"Well, thanks for the sentiment. Country above everything."

He thought he might be laying it on a bit thick but kept going.

"Except family and God."

Evangeline held her cup out too. The clink sounded loud in the quiet room.

"Amen to that."

Grant ignored the cookies and took a swig of coffee. His eyes wandered around the living room, taking in the clean and tidy floor and the dust-free environment. Like most women her age, Mrs. Holmes cleaned twice a day whether it needed it or not. There weren't many ornaments, but the walls were loaded with photos.

"Family is important."

A lot of the photos were of men in uniform. Different ages. Different eras. It looked like the Holmes family had been providing cannon fodder for decades. Grant even thought he spotted an old daguerreotype from the civil war. He remembered that movie with Denzel Washington so he knew that blacks had served even then. It was the more recent photos he was interested in. A teenage Leroy in full dress uniform proudly displaying his wings and beret. Another of him standing with a taller black guy, different uniform but same grin. All teeth and acne.

"It's family why I came to see you."

Evangeline put her cup down.

"I figured no different."

Grant cast his eyes around the room again. It was clean and well-appointed. Mrs. Holmes wanted for nothing, and Grant had no doubt that was down to her son. Drug dealers and pimps usually had plenty of disposable income. At least this one was looking after his mother. One thing Grant was certain of though, Leroy was looking after her from afar. There was no sign that he was living here.

"Your boy takes care of the bills?"

The old lady swelled with pride.

"He's a good boy. A landowner now. Him and the military look out for me."

She pointed a quivering finger across the room. In the corner, partly hidden by a high-backed chair, was a glass display frame containing a folded Stars & Stripes. The traditional offering to families of the fallen.

"I still get the allowance. It helps."

Grant let out a long, slow breath. Death in the services was an acceptable risk, but it was always the families that carried the weight. There was no greater sacrifice for your country than giving up your children. Grant nodded gently.

"I'm sorry for your loss."

He toyed with his cup while he decided how to approach the delicate issue of her son being a petrol-bombing lowlife. Some people came out of the military and used the experience to step up and take the weight. Others bucked the system and let the weight take them down. Leroy was hitting bottom. Grant needed to find him.

"Your boy might be involved in something I'm looking into."

Mrs. Holmes turned stern eyes on him.

"My boy ain't done nothing wrong. He's only looking out for his own."

Grant pushed the cup aside.

"I'm sure he is. But maybe he's slipped a bit. Serving can bring its own burden."

Mrs. Holmes shook her head.

"No. Not my boy. I won't believe it."

Grant leaned forward.

"Somebody got hurt."

The mother threw her hands up in protest.

"That girl, got burned? Oh my. You got it all wrong there, mister. My boy done nothing but try and help that poor child."

Grant didn't mention that Leroy had been helping Nona into other men's beds. There are some things a mother will find hard to swallow and others that are darn right impossible. No mother can accept that her son turned from a military hero into a woman burner.

"Well, she's hurting now. And Leroy knows something about it."

That shocked Evangeline to silence. She stared at Grant as if he'd come from another planet, the words he was speaking an alien tongue. Grant spoke quietly.

"I need to find him."

Mrs. Holmes found her voice.

"Leroy?"

Grant nodded.

"That's who I'm looking for."

Mrs. Holmes stood so suddenly Grant thought she was going to fall over. She waved his assistance away and crossed the room to the high-backed chair. The glass display frame looked heavy, but she carried it over to the table with care approaching reverence. She laid it in front of Grant.

"Then you're looking in the wrong place."

Grant looked at the neatly folded triangle behind the glass, then read the citation on the polished brass plate.

LEROY ELWOOD HOLMES
On Behalf of a Grateful Nation

EIGHTEEN

The car hadn't cooled when Grant got in despite being parked in the shade. Bruno had turned the engine off to save fuel, and the North Carolina heat took no prisoners, even under the trees. Grant sat with the door open and one leg outside. Bruno kept his face deadpan.

"They didn't shoot you then."

Grant twisted in his seat to face the ex-marine.

"You ever have any of that big-brother stuff growing up?"

Bruno frowned.

"Big Brother is watching you? That kind of stuff?"

Grant shook his head.

"Kid brother looking up to big brother."

Bruno wiped sweat from his forehead.

"I had sisters. All older."

Grant let out a sigh.

"Well, it turns out big brother is dead. And Leroy isn't Leroy."

Bruno looked confused and was about to ask what Grant was talking about when Grant's phone began to vibrate in his pocket. The ringtone was muffled until he took the phone out and looked at the caller ID. Unknown number. He brought the phone to his ear and clicked "answer."

"Grant."

He listened for a moment, then nodded as if the caller could see him.

"Okay. Thanks. I'll be right over."

He hung up and looked at Bruno.

"Nona woke up."

Bruno started the engine.

"Mercy?"

Grant swung his leg in and closed the door.

"Yes."

Bruno followed Greenway Circle all the way round until they were back on the access road heading toward the container depot.

"It's gonna be cheaper, you pay me a retainer."

CMC-Mercy was quieter during the day, and the Emergency Department had gone into a lunchtime lull that was just asking to be broken. It still smelled of antiseptic and shit, but there was no rush-rush-rush. Not yet.

"She's been asking for you since she came round."

It was a different doctor and a different nurse. The day shift looked less frazzled than the night crew, something Grant could relate to. Even working uniform patrol there were two distinct modes of operation: fire brigade policing at night, when you chased emergencies, and investigative work during the day, when you cleaned up after the shit storm. The day staff at Mercy was in clean-up mode, with an occasional emergency. The doctor was leaning against the nurses' station and waved toward the ICU.

"She's still in Intensive Care. We'll be moving her this afternoon."

He turned concerned eyes on Grant.

"She's not strong enough to give a statement yet."

The concern turned into exasperation.

"But she insisted on talking to you."

The doctor pushed off from the nurses' station to lead Grant toward the ICU, but Grant put a hand on his arm.

"Straight talking. Is she going to be okay?"

The doctor wasn't offended. He saw the concern in Grant's eyes.

"Depends on your definition of okay. She's out of danger. There's nothing life-threatening."

The sad look on his face showed more than just professional courtesy.

"But she's a long way from being okay. It's a long road. Most of the scarring will be hidden. The face…"

He shrugged.

"She'll be able to smile again. Eventually."

His own smile was less than convincing.

"Try and keep her spirits up."

Grant followed the doctor along the corridor past the emergency cubicles. The antiseptic smell clung to his clothes but the shit didn't smell as bad during the day. He took a few deep breaths anyway to prepare himself. Grant knew that keeping Nona's spirits up was one thing, but keeping his own up was something else altogether.

"You'll be okay if you stay on the left."

In answer to Nona asking Grant about the burns down one side of her face. Grant didn't know any other way to get through the bad times than to employ gallows humor and a shrug of the shoulders. It's how cops coped with life in the bottom of shit valley. He wasn't sure if Nona had the same defense mechanism, but it was the only thing Grant could think of. He thought a smile feathered her lips. On the other side of her face. Grant continued to keep things light.

"I remember this sitcom set in a prison. Young inmate saying he sat next to Ann Podmore in junior school. She was left-handed. His cellmate gives him a wink and says, 'I bet you got on the right side of her.'"

This time she did smile. It looked painful. Grant rested a hand over hers.

"So, stick to the left. Until they make you beautiful again."

Nona looked at him through one eye. The other side of her face was swathed in burn wraps.

"You think I'll be beautiful again?"

Grant nodded then shook his head.

"Not today. Give you something to look forward to though."

Nona let out a sigh.

"Is that like, I can be anything I want to be?"

Grant squeezed her hand.

"Might have taken a couple options off the table. Until your hair grows back."

Nona's voice quivered on the edge of tears.

"I loved my hair."

Grant was struggling to hold it together.

"I should have given you the other bed."

Nona looked at Grant, her voice becoming stronger.

"They burned both beds."

Grant leaned forward in his chair. This was what he wanted to talk about but hadn't been sure she could cope with the fire. Nona was proving herself to be stronger than she looked.

"Did you see who did it?"

Nona couldn't move her head much but gave an almost imperceptible shake.

"The breaking window woke me up. After that. No."

Grant kept his voice low and calm.

"What about voices. Did he shout anything? Call a name?"

Again the imperceptible shake.

"Nothing I could make out. Maybe some shouting."

Grant remembered the police dispatcher recognizing the caller's color from the voice on the original disturbance call. When Grant first met Nona and her pimp. He stuck with the name Nona knew him by.

"Was it Leroy?"

He didn't want to ask her about buying the petrol herself. Not in her condition. But even allowing for that, she certainly didn't throw it through the window. Whoever she gave it to did that.

"Did Leroy use the petrol?"

Nona showed commendable loyalty and circled the wagons around the man who'd turned her out on the streets.

"Leroy would never hurt me. He looks out for his own."

The same thing Mrs. Holmes said. Grant wasn't convinced by either of them.

"That why he beat you up the night I threw him off the balcony?"

Nona looked nonplussed, which wasn't easy with only half a face.

"The balcony?"

Grant leaned closer and softened his voice.

"The first night. In your room. The disturbance."

Nona fell back on her old argument.

"He looks out for his own. He wouldn't hurt me."

Grant didn't push it. If she didn't see who threw the petrol bomb, then so be it. Misplaced loyalty was still loyalty. It showed character. He reckoned she'd be strong enough to come through this. He was about to stand up when she blew the Leroy theory out of the water.

"Leroy was protecting me. It was the white dude who beat me up."

NINETEEN

Bruno Morris dropped Grant at the South Park Mall, and Grant paid him off. Bruno was right; it would have been cheaper to pay him a retainer, but Grant didn't want him hanging around while he took the next step in tracing the petrol-bomber. White guy with a pimply arse. Likes slapping hookers about. Not the best description to go house to house with. Enquiries would need some high-tech input. Like finding who he connected to the internet with, having uplinked at the most powerful cell phone tower in Charlotte.

"Did you get any sleep yet?"

Evelyn Cover stood next to a potted palm outside Connect in the South Hall. The rest area smelled of cracked leather and freshly watered flowers. Nordstrom dwarfed the technology store and made the seating area feel like it belonged to the chain store alone. Grant leaned against a plush leather easy chair.

"I don't have a room. Remember?"

Evelyn proved she didn't hold a grudge about dinner.

"How's the girl?"

Grant felt the weight of guilt press down on him again. The doctor had cut short their interview before Grant could get to the meat of the description. Like, what the white guy's name was and where he lived. The laptop didn't come up at all. There'd be a longer conversation to be had about that but not until the burns eased and Nona was out of danger.

"She's a tough kid."

Evelyn rested a hand on Grant's forearm.

"Even tough kids need a guardian angel."

Grant thought about all the people he'd failed to protect. From the dusty streets of a foreign township to a coffee shop at Beacon Hill via Snake Pass and Jamaica Plain. Some of them put in harm's way by him. None of them qualifying him as a guardian angel. He pushed the thoughts aside and looked at Evelyn.

"You got time for a coffee? I want to pick your brains."

Grant bought two lattes in takeaway cups from Starbucks and walked Evelyn to the food court. He didn't want to sit in the alcove near Cucina Italiana where he'd eaten pizza with Nona, so he chose a table opposite Chick-fil-A with good sightlines back into the main hall. The mall cop didn't tell Evelyn there was, *"None of that business in the mall."* The business suit was classier than the figure-hugging leggings and the crop top. Grant felt guilty even thinking that.

"So, every cell phone, laptop, and iPad has its own signature?"

Evelyn sipped coffee through a slot in the top of her lid.

"Unique and individual to itself. Like DNA or a fingerprint."

Grant had peeled his lid off, preferring to drink his coffee like a man, not through that pissy little hole. He'd taken the lid off carefully, having fallen foul of that once in Texas, and was taking slow sips because the latte was too hot.

"Kind of a locator beacon?"

Evelyn pointed at the ceiling.

"CIA can track your phone anywhere in the world."

Grant looked doubtful.

"If it's turned on."

Evelyn shook her head.

"Doesn't matter. Background signal's on the whole time."

Grant took a bigger swallow and immediately regretted it. He sucked cool air into his mouth to ease the burn. Once he'd got his voice back, he spoke just loud enough to be heard above the food court hubbub.

"So you can find where this guy is. With the laptop."

Evelyn put her coffee down.

"I'm not the CIA."

Grant raised one eyebrow and smiled.

"You're the manager of the biggest technology store in Charlotte."

Evelyn lowered her head, then looked up as if looking over a pair of glasses.

"Not the biggest."

"Big enough."

"Big enough for what?"

Grant made typing movements on the table.

"To track his laptop."

Evelyn sighed at Grant's ignorance.

"You ever tried phoning someone without their number?"

Grant held his hands out, palms upwards.

"Can't do it. Without the number."

Evelyn gave him a *there you go then* smile.

"Same thing. Can't look for a laptop if I don't have its details."

Grant considered that for a moment but wasn't giving up that easy.

"I heard one time, some kid in his basement hacked the Air Traffic Control network and caused chaos for half an hour. Like that Korean hacker, almost screwed Sony Pictures."

Evelyn took another sip of coffee. She resigned herself to the fact she was talking to a techno-moron. Grant could see it on her face and wouldn't argue against it. He still wasn't much past knowing how to send a text message, never mind track somebody's phone. The techno-wizard gave him a sad little smile.

"That's like a needle looking for a haystack. Bigger target. And you know where the haystack is. If you've got the knowhow, you can hit your target. Try that the other way. Haystack looking for a needle."

Grant shrugged.

"CIA can do it."

Evelyn frowned.

"CIA is a bigger haystack."

"What about the kid in his basement?"

"He'd need to know the laptop's details."

Grant thought about that for a moment.

"What about sales records? Subscriptions? Like that?"

Evelyn tried not to sound pissed off.

"Under what name? Address?"

Grant gave an exasperated sigh.

"That's what I'm trying to find out."

Evelyn put soothing calm into her voice. The "I'm talking to an idiot" voice.

"Then you're coming at it from the wrong end."

A hum sounded over Grant's shoulder and the mall cop drifted by on his Segway. He gave Grant a sideways look, then glanced at the woman Grant was with today. The look said, *Is she a neighbor as well?* A stray thought crossed Grant's mind as he remembered sitting here with Nona Hartley. He wondered if it was the mall cop who'd told the Charlotte PD about Grant meeting the woman from Connect, then discounted that theory. The only person who'd been following Grant was Leroy. That suggested a connection that wasn't beyond the realm of possibility. The local cop ignoring a bit of motel prostitution for a financial consideration. It would explain why he hadn't made much effort at the motel room. Grant waited for the pocket cop to move away, then got back on track with Evelyn.

"Which end do you suggest?"

Evelyn leaned forward.

"The motel room."

It was strange how sometimes everything centered around one thing. Grant leaned forward too, and their faces almost met in the middle of the table. He smiled at the attractive woman in the business suit.

"What about it?"

Evelyn looked into his eyes.

"Not yours. The laptop. If it's a dedicated charger, I can run the serial number. Find the owner that way. Start from there."

Grant leaned further and gave her a little kiss on the lips.

"I knew there was a reason I liked you."

Evelyn smiled and kissed him back. A peck.

"More than being psychic at the Cowbell?"

"More than being the most beautiful computer guru I've ever met."

"You've met a lot, have you?"

Grant pretended to count on his fingers.

"I've met enough."

Evelyn held out a hand.

"Give me the charger and I'll run a check."

Grant sat back too.

"Ah. A slight problem there."

Evelyn kept her eyes on him while she took another sip of coffee. She was relaxed. At ease with his company. Grant wished he had more than three days. Only one left after today. He watched her lips clamp on the rim of the cup.

"You know, if they're going to make you drink through a hole, they really need to make it big enough to get a proper mouthful."

TWENTY

Grant took the bus back to the Sleepy Nook Inn after he bought replacement clothes at Macy's. Lightweight cargo pants again but better quality this time. They were more expensive too despite getting them from the sale rail. Two pairs in khaki and a couple of dark T-shirts. Basic underwear and socks. He kept the wind-cheater zipped this time, proving he was acclimatizing.

There was no welcome committee in the trees near the underpass. There was no smoke cloud hanging over the motel. The sky was as clear and blue as his first day, but everything else had changed. Now he had responsibilities. It's not every day you get to be a guardian angel. He checked the parking lot as he walked up the tree-lined driveway. Part of him hoped Mr. Khan would be out, but the better part of him wanted to apologize. The better part won. The four-door pickup was parked in a slanted bay in the corner.

"Is he in the office?"

The slow-eyed woman from the night Grant checked in looked up from her magazine. She was working a double shift today.

"Uh-huh. And we even more off the grid now, since your smoking room went up in smoke."

Grant almost told her it was the risk you took when you let pimps and drug dealers use the end room but couldn't ignore the fact it was also the risk you took if you threw said pimp over the balcony. There was no hiding the part he played in this. He lifted the hatch in the counter and knocked on Mr. Khan's door.

"Come in."

He did, closing the door behind him.

After the apologies were over and the platitudes given, Mr. Khan showed he had as big a heart as Evelyn Cover.

"How is the girl?"

Grant gave the same answer.

"She's a tough kid."

Mr. Khan widened the scope of his concerns.

"And how are you?"

At first, Grant thought the owner believed Grant had been caught in the fire but then realized it was a deeper question. Everybody seemed to know Grant had thrown Leroy off the balcony. It wasn't a stretch to think that's why Grant's room had been petrol-bombed. The girl's injuries were on him. Grant shrugged.

"Without a room."

Mr. Khan leaned back in his chair.

"I can help you with that."

He placed both hands on either side of his forehead.

"But this. You must deal with yourself."

Grant leaned back against the door and sighed.

"My way of dealing with that is to find the bastard who did it."

Mr. Khan placed his hands in his lap.

"Isn't that for the police?"

"I am the police."

"Not here. You said so yourself."

Grant folded his arms across his chest.

"Way I see it, that's not a bad thing."

Mr. Khan looked down at his desk and clasped his hands. He tried not to show it, but his eyes looked different when he looked up again. A little heavier. He spoke slowly and deliberately.

"There are some aspects of this business that I want to clean up. I am having the place redecorated and rebranded. Certain arrangements will change, but it might take a while. Some of those arrangements are at a local level and involve turning a blind eye to minor transgressions."

Grant looked at the motel owner.

"Petrol-bombing isn't a minor transgression."

Mr. Khan shook his head.

"No, it is not."

He turned sad eyes on Grant.

"But the trade they were plying has been around for centuries. People will find purveyors of those pleasures. Customer care. The law of supply and demand. The other law made sure there was no trouble."

Grant kept his voice nonjudgemental.

"Except there was trouble."

"Not until you arrived."

Grant wasn't taking the blame for that one.

"There was a disturbance in the room. The girl was hit. That was before I stepped in. Where was the customer care for her?"

Mr. Khan shrank back in his chair.

"I know. And that will change. I promise."

Grant believed him. Mr. Khan was on a roll.

"He was going to move soon anyway. Expanding to a place of his own."

Grant thought about Mrs. Holmes saying Leroy was a landowner now. That was something else to look into. He nodded at the motel owner.

"Who paid the cop?"

Mr. Khan felt on safer ground.

"That was a private matter between both parties."

He still seemed smaller behind his desk.

"I merely looked the other way. That is my everlasting shame."

Grant took a deep breath and pushed away from the door.

"Well, I'm not without blame either. So let's make it right."

Mr. Khan looked hopeful.

"Whatever I can do."

Grant linked his fingers and flexed outwards until the bones cracked.

"Assuming the fire brigade didn't toss the bathroom, I'd like to get my toiletries and change rooms."

Mr. Khan stood up and came round the desk.

"Of course. Some of the delayed flight guests have checked out."

Grant nodded toward the accommodation block.

"Then I'd like to take a look in the end room again."

The lock clicked, and Grant removed the key card. He opened the door but stayed on the balcony for a few moments while he gathered his thoughts. He'd already recovered his things from 257 and moved into a new room at the far end of the same floor. Now it was time to collect the laptop charger, providing it was still in the room.

Grant looked at the door where he'd first met Nona Hartley, corner room at the top of the stairwell. He glanced over the balcony rail at the flowerbed where Leroy had landed. Despite the revelations at Greenway Circle Trailer Park, he still thought of the skinny black pimp as Leroy. He'd have to work on that as his investigation moved on. The door opened inwards onto darkness.

The smell of petrol wafted out of the room.

Grant's senses went on full alert. His first thought was, don't turn on the lights. The heat from a light bulb often triggered explosions in fume-filled rooms. His second thought was, this was just a residual smell, not the main source. The room wasn't going to be filled with petrol, but somebody in it had certainly been handling the flammable liquid. Grant's list of suspects on that score was Leroy, Nona, or the white guy with the pimply arse. He took one step into the room. The smell was strong but dissipating. He took another step, then closed his eyes. After a count of ten, he opened them again and the room was no longer dim but bright. He scanned the room in more detail than the first time he'd been in here. With the senior cop who'd been paid to look the other way. Grant didn't look the other way. He looked everywhere.

The room was identical to Grant's. Room 257, not the new one, which was a corner suite. Two double beds, a built-in wardrobe, and a long, wide chest of drawers. There were no clothes in the wardrobe. The chest of drawers was empty. There was nothing in the bedside cabinets. This was a room of business, not residence. The bedsheets were still ruffled. The room hadn't been cleaned or emptied.

The laptop charger was on the bed where Grant had left it. He picked it up and uncurled the plastic-coated wire. There was no writing on the cable or the small connector. He looked at the charging unit and plug. Nothing on the top. He turned it over in his hands and felt a spark of triumph.

"Eureka."

An embossed label was fused to the side with writing so small he'd need a magnifying glass to read it. One thing he did recognize, though, was a very long number interspersed with dots and dashes. The serial number for the laptop and its dedicated charger. Evelyn had been right.

Grant sniffed the air. The petrol smell had thinned, but there was a lingering trace at this end of the room. The bathroom door was closed. No light shone under the door. He put the charger into his jacket pocket and moved to the door. He placed a hand flat against the woodwork as if testing it for heat. Like in a fire. This was North Carolina. Everything felt warm to the touch. He reached for the handle.

The room was quiet. There was no sound from the bathroom. Grant turned the handle slowly, then paused. Still no sound. He opened the door six inches at a time, pausing at every stage to listen at the opening. The bathroom had no windows. The light was off. The smell of petrol was stronger but still only a trace element, more vapor than liquid.

He opened the door wide and stood in the opening for a moment to let his eyes adjust to the gloom. The smell weakened. The room was safe. Grant turned the light on and stepped to one side. Female toiletries and makeup lined the shelf above the washbasin. The shower curtain hung limp above the bath. Grant pulled the curtain back.

The naked body in the tub was curled in an awkward position with its feet in the air, the head twisted at an impossible angle. Grant let out a sigh. Mrs. Holmes might have been given a folded flag for the real Leroy, but she wasn't going to get anything for his little brother.

TWENTY-ONE

There were more police cars this time than the morning after the disturbance and about the same as the night of the fire. Plus one ambulance and no fire trucks. Blue lights and sirens to get here. Just blue lights now that they were parked under the portico outside the reception lobby. Grant watched the circus from his seat on the top step of the stairwell next to the target room. The cops didn't turn their blue lights off even though it was early afternoon. That seemed to be an American thing. Grant had been taught that the use of emergency warning devices such as sirens and lights were to clear a path, warn the public, or protect a crime scene. The Sleepy Nook Inn didn't need protecting at two thirty on a sunny afternoon. The pale blue signage stood out against the white of the cars in the sun.

CHARLOTTE–MECKLENBURG
POLICE

The senior cop was the first one up the stairs. He looked hard at Grant, then went round the corner into the room. Three more cops followed. The last one stayed with Grant. Should have been the first one. Securing the prime suspect.

The paramedics waited at reception—another breach of protocol. Just because somebody phoned in to say they had a dead body didn't mean the body was dead. That was for the medical examiner to decide. Grant wondered how many other rules were going to be broken or missed. There was one he was certain would be adhered to. The senior cop came out of the room and proved Grant right.

"You really messed up this time. Guess the balcony wasn't enough, huh?"

He nodded to the cop standing beside Grant.

"Search him and cuff him. He's coming with us."

Grant held his hands out to the sides like Jesus on the cross and thought about the crime scene inside the room. And his little detour before asking the receptionist to call the police.

Grant looked at the body for a full five minutes before moving. He scanned the scene with soft eyes, not focusing on any one thing but taking in everything. Then he focused on individual components.

The first was the body itself. If Leroy had slipped in the shower, he hadn't done it this morning. Blood had settled in the lower parts and turned the skin darker than his already dark skin. It had pooled and settled against the bottom of the bath, distorting his face and hips like a melted candle. Grant touched him gently. The body was cold and hard. He'd been dead more than twenty-four hours. There were no obvious injuries and no broken skin. There was no blood other than what had pooled under the skin to form distorted bruises. There was no knife sticking out of his back and no gunshot wound. There was no noose around the neck to indicate suicide. That pretty much covered all the bases.

The second thing was the pile of clothes on the floor next to the bath. A scruffy heap of intermingled clothing, shoes, and property. The shirt and trousers were inside out. One shoe lay on top of them and one underneath. A black-faced watch had slid across the floor into the corner near the toilet.

Grant dropped to a crouch and checked the pockets. The wallet had over two hundred dollars and a VA blood donor card.

The watch looked expensive. A heavy-linked gold chain looked even more so. There were no weapons and no dealer baggies. Leroy had died in the shower, and nobody had robbed him. That made that part simple.

Except it didn't. The timing was all wrong and the coincidences too obvious. Grant throws Leroy off the balcony. Unknown person, probably Leroy, petrol-bombs Grant's room, causing injury to a girl Grant had taken from Leroy. Then said unknown person slips in the shower and breaks his neck. No cop was going to believe that chain of events. It was the VA donor card that swung it for Grant. And the untidy pile of clothing.

Returning veterans had one of two reactions after leaving the service. They either reacted against the discipline and lifestyle by letting themselves go and turning into longhaired scruffs, or they kept up appearances, dressed smart, and maintained contact with the VA and their family. Leroy looked after his mother and was a registered donor for fellow vets. Somebody like that didn't throw their clothes on the floor to get a shower. They folded them neatly, ready to put them on again. This looked like somebody had pulled them off after he was dead to make it look good. It didn't look good to Grant.

The last thing Grant found was a set of car keys. Probably the battered pickup Leroy had followed Grant to the South Park Mall in. He tried to remember if he'd seen it parked outside the motel but didn't think he had. If Leroy was running illegal business from the motel room, the pickup was probably parked somewhere else for safety. Grant pocketed the keys for later, then stood up.

That was the crime scene examined from his point of view. Now he could hand it over to the professionals but not before he dropped the keys and the laptop charger off in his room. Rule of thumb for murders was that if it was a husband-and-wife thing, the spouse usually did it, and if somebody reports finding a body, it's an eighty percent possibility that person killed the victim. Once he'd done that, he returned to the scene and called reception on the house phone.

* * *

The paramedics confirmed that Leroy was dead and left him in situ for the detectives and the crime scene techs. The detectives didn't arrive until half an hour after uniform patrol confirmed the body was a known felon and therefore warranted a closer look. The detective didn't look happy at being called out to a man who slipped in the shower.

"Really? You got me out here for a domestic accident?"

The detective was alone, showing how thinly spread Freedom Division was today. He looked like he wanted to wrap this up quickly and get back to more serious cases on his workload. He stepped into the shade of the portico and spoke to the senior uniform cop.

"Run it by me."

Grant watched from the backseat of the lead patrol car while the cop ran the timeline that Grant had already considered. Disturbance involving Grant and Leroy. Petrol bomb on Grant's room injuring a girl Grant had taken from Leroy. Then Leroy is found with a broken neck by the man he had the disturbance with. The detective did what any cop would do.

"Search him. Take him to the office. I'll be down to see him shortly."

The senior cop couldn't hide the smile as he got in the car. He looked in the mirror at his prisoner.

"You get all that?"

Grant shuffled into a more comfortable position so the handcuffs didn't bite his wrists. He looked at the cop through the interior mirror and spoke before his partner joined them.

"Losing Leroy is going to put a dent in your extracurricular income."

He locked eyes.

"Guess you forgot to mention that."

When his partner got in the car, the senior cop wasn't smiling anymore.

TWENTY-TWO

Freedom Division police station was at 4150 Wilkinson Boulevard opposite NAPA Auto Parts and covered 46.1 square miles in the southwest section of Mecklenburg County. It was a long, low building with a central rotunda forming the main entrance and reception. It looked like an office building, and nowhere on the signage did it call itself a police station or Freedom Division. The sign on the main wall read:

CHARLOTTE
MECKLENBURG
POLICE
DEPARTMENT
West Service Area Center

The smaller blue sign on the entrance driveway read:

P O L I C E
&
GOVERNMENT SERVICES
4150
Wilkinson Boulevard

It was just half a mile from the Walmart at Westerly Hills where Grant had bought his first clothes and, as such, felt like he'd come full circle. Right back where he'd started from: Sleepy Nook Inn to Walmart via a Charlotte PD interview room. He doubted they'd let him out to buy a change of clothes today.

They didn't fingerprint him or take his property. They didn't put him in a holding cell. It wasn't until Detective Yates arrived that Grant realized why it wasn't called a police station.

"Place isn't staffed twenty-four hours a day."

Detective Yates closed the interview room door and sat at the table.

"They do have voicemail though. If you call out of hours."

Grant sat in a chair that wasn't bolted to the floor at a table that looked like an office conference table. There was no recording equipment and no soundproofing. No matter how much Grant changed his position, the handcuffs still dug into his wrists behind his back. The detective noticed Grant's discomfort and waved for him to stand up. He unfastened the cuffs and laid them on the table.

"But it seemed like a good place to talk."

Grant noticed the detective said talk, not interview. This felt a bit surreal, being brought to a police station as a suspect but not being under arrest. A casual visitor was the best Grant could come up with. He decided to wait for the detective to explain before saying anything.

The detective sat back down. He smiled but didn't offer to shake hands.

"Danny Yates. I've done some checking on you."

The bottom line was that Yates knew Grant was a UK cop transferred to the Boston PD and that he was delayed in Charlotte en route to England. He knew Grant was due to give evidence about Snake Pass in Crown Court and even had the flight number and seat allocation. That was the good news.

"You're not going to make the flight."

That was the bad. Grant still didn't say anything. He reckoned Yates would get to the point in his own good time.

"We've contacted your Crown Court Liaison and told them you'll be delayed. They said they can put you on last."

None of that explained why Yates was talking to him in a glorified office building with no custody suite or dedicated interview rooms, or why Grant hadn't been read his rights and arrested. That was all good, including the fact that Yates had told Crown Court Liaison that Grant would be delayed. If he'd been a genuine suspect for murder, Crown Court would have been canceled and a new court date arranged. Grant watched Yates to see where this was going. Yates crossed his legs and rested an arm across the chair next to him.

"Has that Resurrection Man tag faded yet?"

Grant shrugged.

"Nobody's mentioned it this week."

Yates gave an embarrassed smile.

"Until now. Sorry. It must be a pain in the ass."

Grant kept his tone light, if not quite friendly.

"Not as big a pain as having your room torched and the suspect killed."

Yates nodded and swung his leg down. He leaned forward and flicked open a brown manila folder on the table.

"Yes. Let me tell you what we've got on that."

He leafed through the papers until he found his overview notes.

"Thomas Armstrong Holmes. Formerly of the 101st Airborne. Lately of the small-time pimp and drug dealer brigade. Goes by the name of Leroy in memory of his big brother, killed in the line of duty. Medal of Honor. Folded flag. The whole nine yards."

He looked up from his notes.

"I'm not quite sure how using his brother's name to become a small-time pimp honors his memory."

He continued where he'd left off.

"Runs his girls out of the end room at the Sleepy Nook Inn with the help of a blind eye from the manager and local police."

He looked up again.

"Not our finest hour, but…"

He shrugged.

"Not uncommon at the fringes. Best we can tell, turning a blind eye is as far as it went."

Grant rumbled into life.

"We're supposed to be in the business of protect and serve. Honesty and integrity. Turning a blind eye lets everyone down."

Yates' tone grew harder.

"The truth, the whole truth, and nothing but the truth. Is that right?"

He laid his hand flat on the folder.

"But you didn't throw Holmes off the balcony. Did you?"

Grant knew Yates had got him there. The trouble is that once you've told a lie, you're tied into it for the duration.

"I asked him to keep the noise down."

"And did he?"

"I slept like a log the rest of the night, so I guess, yes. He did."

Yates considered Grant for a long pause before continuing. He glanced at his notes but knew them off by heart.

"Well, here's where it gets tricky for you. The main reason you looked good for this in the first place. You had a discussion with Holmes over noise abatement. The following day, the girl he was pimping is staying in your room instead of his. The same day your room is petrol-bombed and the girl rushed to the hospital."

He looked at Grant.

"Given your history of protecting wayward girls and Resurrection Man stuff, that's the kind of thing might make you angry."

Grant stared back at him.

"I try and keep anger out of it. Clouds your judgment."

Yates kept his eyes on Grant.

"Well, judge this. Day after the fire, the prime suspect—the guy you asked to keep the noise down but did not throw off the balcony—turns up dead in the shower."

He tapped the manila folder for effect.

"And the guy who finds the body is..." He held his hands out to Grant. "The guy who stole his girl."

Grant let out a sigh.

"The girl was trying to get her life in order. She needed somewhere to stay."

Yates raised an eyebrow.

"That's all she needed?"

Grant lowered his voice.

"It's all she got."

Yates lowered his voice too.

"No. She got a lot more than that. And we both know that's down to you."

Once again, Grant knew Yates had got him there. He'd been harboring similar thoughts himself but having started with a lie there was only so much Grant could admit without digging himself a deeper hole. Yates didn't take his eyes off Grant.

"Judging by lividity and rigor, Holmes didn't die when you found him, but that doesn't rule out yesterday. So, you're not out of the woods yet. Until we get a time of death from the coroner."

He took a sheaf of blank pages from the folder and slid them across the table. He slapped a pen on the paper.

"So, help me get the timeline straight. Write down everything you've done since you landed in Charlotte until now."

Grant took the pen and looked at the blank pages. The same as throwing Leroy off the balcony had set this whole thing in progress, lying about it set the path for the lies he was about to tell. He could hardly admit to visiting Nona's cabin or Leroy's mother, and he certainly wasn't going to mention the laptop charger and the man with the pimply arse. He decided to keep it simple and began to write.

The room grew quiet apart from the scratching of the pen. Yates watched Grant time and date each entry on the page. Silence worked its magic. It was good for interview technique but sometimes worked against the interviewer too. Yates filled the silence with small talk that wasn't small at all.

"You've seen corpses before. What's your take on it?"

Grant paused with the pen in mid-stroke. He looked across at Yates.

"Showers are dangerous places."

Yates frowned.

"What do you reckon?"

Grant shrugged and raised his eyebrows.

"Could have slipped on a bar of soap."

TWENTY-THREE

"Okay, tell me a story."

Grant sat in the dusty pickup that wasn't dusty at all. On the inside. Everything in North Carolina was dusty on the outside; that's what constant heat and sunshine did to you. Dried you out and shit all over you. Humidity just added a film of moisture like standing in a tumble dryer with a damp towel. The outside was dusty because of where it was parked. The inside was as clean as a paratrooper's bunk.

It hadn't taken a genius to find the pickup after Grant had been released. There were only a couple of possibilities within walking distance of the Sleepy Nook Inn, and Grant discounted Hardee's straight away. He'd eaten breakfast there two days in a row and even round the back there was nowhere to hide the big, ugly flatbed.

Grant's biggest problem had been deciding how much he could trust Danny Yates. The detective's casual acceptance of the blind-eye turning troubled Grant. If something like that was "Not uncommon at the fringes," he wondered what else was deemed acceptable in the Charlotte-Mecklenburg Police. As such, Grant decided to play his cards close to his chest until he had something concrete to show. Concrete would be finding who else could have thrown the petrol bomb, because he was starting to think it wasn't the man formerly known as Leroy. Some of that was based on Nona Hartley's insistence that Leroy had protected her on that first day and the way he looked after his mother. The rest was what he'd learned at the other place Grant had looked for the pickup.

Brubaker was alone behind the counter at the Citgo gas station when Grant pushed the door open. The last customer had driven off ten minutes ago, while Grant was checking the parking bays round back of the meeting hall. Having drawn a blank, Grant decided to pick Brubaker's brains since he'd already admitted to knowing just about everything going on around here.

"Damn. You've been busy the last couple days. Feel like I should shut up shop and lock myself in the restroom."

Grant closed the door and crossed the room.

"Why? You don't have a balcony, do you?"

Brubaker rested his elbows on top of the cash register.

"Balconies aren't your only preference. If what I hear is true."

Grant stopped beside a display of Frosted Flakes and looked at the old man.

"Well, if you heard it from Officer Blind Eye, I'd take it with a pinch of salt."

Brubaker gave a short, sharp laugh.

"You mean I can't trust the local po-lice? I am in shock."

Grant drummed his fingers on the familiar packaging with the unfamiliar name. Tony The Tiger grinned at him from the cereal box. Grant stopped drumming.

"Is that Standard Operating Procedure around here?"

Brubaker pushed back from the cash register and stood up straight.

"It's SOP everywhere. Cops can't stop everything. They have to prioritize. Around here, a bit of low-level prostitution is no big deal."

Grant considered the resident counselor.

"That as far as it goes, you reckon?"

Brubaker came around the counter to stand with Grant.

"You get shot, robbed, or butt-fucked. Ain't no better police."

Grant unzipped the windcheater and put his hands in the pockets.

"What about if you slipped on a bar of soap?"

Brubaker noticed the weight in the windcheater pockets.

"Depends who did the slipping."

Grant toyed with the charger and car keys he'd collected from his room.

"What about Leroy?"

The old man raised his eyebrows.

"You mean, will the police dig in or take the easy option?"

"I mean what do you think of him?"

Brubaker frowned.

"I think he's a low-life piece of shit who loves his mother."

That didn't help Grant much. He looked out of the window at the gas pumps. Backwoods America had its own value system, even if the backwoods were only on the outskirts of a city the size of Charlotte. Brubaker didn't stop there.

"On the other hand, it seems like he cared for Nona more than his behavior suggests. And I heard he's been trying to build a community for returning black veterans. Bought an abandoned neighborhood and plans to rebuild it. I guess you can do a lot with pimp money."

Grant remembered Mrs. Holmes saying, "He's only looking out for his own," and Nona's assertion that, "Leroy was protecting me." He thought about all the ex-servicemen he'd met in the police, people who had turned their military service to good use. Maybe Thomas Armstrong Holmes wasn't all bad despite having a sharp way with strangers. Grant was beginning to regret throwing him off the balcony.

"You sure he wasn't just going to build his own little pimp empire?"

Brubaker sighed.

"There's always that possibility, I guess. But if that helps fund soldiers who were damaged in service of their country, I can turn a blind eye to that."

Grant looked at the old man.

"Seems this blind-eye turning thing is spreading."

Brubaker stared back at him.

"People do what they need to. To survive."

He waved toward the meeting hall round back.

"That's what ninety-day chips are all about."

Grant waved the other way, out through the front window.

"So, where was he building his ninety-day chip?"

Brubaker looked in the same direction.

"I heard he bought the old Notebook Trail development. Out past Paw Creek. Been empty since they tore the houses down."

Grant consulted the map in his head.

"Paw Creek? Near the refineries up north?"

Brubaker shook his head.

"West. Along the railroad cutting toward the Catawba River."

Grant left the pickup's door open and shuffled across the driver's seat. Walking back toward the Sleepy Nook Inn through the underpass, he'd stopped at the side of the road where Leroy and his friends had come out of the trees, seemingly from nowhere. There is no such place as nowhere. The overgrown fire road was barely visible from Little Rock Road. The pickup was hidden behind a wall of trees and undergrowth. Close enough to all the places Leroy might want to visit. Far enough that nobody was going to look for it here.

The interior was gleaming, the upholstery as smooth and clean as a car showroom new sale. A shiny Satnav was mounted on the dashboard. A plastic bottle of spring water stood in the cup holder on the central console. The water was warm. Grant opened the glove box.

"Okay, tell me a story."

There was an owner's manual and manufacturer's booklet

inside, half-covered by a folded yellow duster and a chamois leather wash rag. There was a duplicate VA blood donor card with Leroy's real name on it. Grant looked for a road map or street atlas but couldn't find one. Modern technology had consigned the good old-fashioned map book to the waste bin. Grant always preferred a map. You could get an overview of what you were looking at instead of street-by-street directions with no clear idea of where you were.

There were no weapons, drugs, or condoms. There was nothing untoward at all. The pickup could have been owned by a teacher, a doctor, or a member of the clergy instead of a drug-dealing pimp. There was a 101st Airborne Division screaming eagle transfer in the window. A bumper sticker at the back read:

I believe in a better world,

Where chickens can cross the road,

Without having their motives questioned.

It seemed like an appropriate sentiment for somebody looking to build a better world for returning veterans but using questionable means of funding it. Grant closed the glove box and had a quick look under the seats and in the door pockets. There was nothing here the police could pull him in for. There was nothing going to get him arrested if the blind eye was revoked.

So where did that leave him? There was nothing incriminating here. No hints pointing to the other possibility for the petrol-bomber, Mr. White Guy with the pimply arse. Grant thought about going to ask Nona a few more questions but doubted the doctors would give him enough time to go deep for the answers he needed. He shifted in his seat and the windcheater pocket banged against the door. He took the charger out and looked at the serial number again.

Plan B.

Grant shut the door and started the engine. His mind was wrestling with the directions to South Park Mall when the Satnav came on automatically. It was time to put his trust in technology. He found the search function and typed the address.

TWENTY-FOUR

Grant missed the guys following him this time because they were better at it than Leroy had been. They used three cars and alternated their positions from lead car to trailing cars. It was made easier for them because Grant's Satnav took him on a more conventional route instead of the shortcuts that Bruno Morris had taken. It was fairly obvious where he was going by the time he was halfway there. Even so, if Grant had spotted them things might have turned out different.

Evelyn slapped Grant across the face, standing beneath the potted palm out front of the Connect technology store. The shock sparked his senses and made his eyes water. As soon as the swing finished its follow-through, she wrapped her arms around him and held him tight. The tears in her eyes spoke volumes, the slap an involuntary reflex to shock and relief.

"Why didn't you call?"

Grant was still stunned to silence by the slap. Evelyn stepped back and looked up into his face.

"The news just said one man found dead. It didn't say who."

She let out a sigh that made her tremble.

"I knew it was your motel. And after the fire, I thought…"

She didn't need to say what she thought. The slap explained it all. The ringing in Grant's ears slowly subsided, and the world around him eased back into the bubble they had occupied since he beckoned Evelyn out of the store. He lowered his head and kissed her on the nose.

"I hope the rest of your customers didn't see how you treat a visitor."

Evelyn gave him a stern look. Grant stopped being flippant.

"I didn't know it made the news. Not being that big of a story."

Evelyn pushed Grant onto one of the soft leather chairs and sat on his knee.

"The fire and the girl made it three strikes."

Grant nodded and put his arms around her.

"Of course. I'm sorry, but the police had me for a while."

Evelyn gasped.

"They arrested you?"

Grant shrugged.

"More like intensive questioning."

"But you're a cop. Didn't they know that?"

"That's why they didn't arrest me. That and the lividity."

Evelyn shook her head.

"I have no idea what that means."

Grant watched shoppers strolling past the rest area. Some went up the escalator to the second-floor shopping gallery. Some went into Nordstrom and Bare Essentials. A couple of men leaned on the gallery rail and looked down. A woman argued with her husband about visiting the cosmetics department. A third man stood window-shopping outside Connect. Grant looked at Evelyn.

"It means Leroy wasn't killed this morning. Probably sometime last night."

Evelyn went all Sherlock Holmes on him.

"That would make it around the time of the petrol bomb."

Grant patted her knee for her to get up.

"Charlotte PD will have a better idea when they confirm the time of death. The room did smell of petrol though."

Evelyn stood up.

"That nails it then. Leroy threw the petrol bomb."

Grant pushed up out of the chair.

"Not so fast, Sherlock. The room smelled of petrol, not Leroy."

"You don't think Leroy did it?"

"I'm beginning to have my doubts."

"Who then?"

Grant put his hand in the windcheater pocket.

"Only other person I saw in that room apart from Nona was the guy she was with. Turns out he was the guy beat her up, and Leroy was just protecting her."

Evelyn blew out her cheeks.

"Retaliatory strike, do you think?"

Grant looked at her.

"Where'd you come up with a phrase like that?"

Evelyn shrugged.

"CNN."

Grant toyed with the charger in his pocket.

"Well, insufficient data. It's all speculation at this stage. Oh, I forgot to mention. Gas station next door said it was Nona bought the petrol. Don't know how that fits in either."

"You asked her?"

Grant frowned.

"I will. When the doctors let me."

He took the charger out of his pocket.

"Meantime, that other thing we talked about."

Evelyn made a satisfied noise and took it from him.

"The laptop guy."

Grant nodded.

"You were right. There's a serial number."

The two guys leaning on the gallery rail moved toward the down escalator. The guy window-shopping moved away from the Connect storefront. Evelyn turned the charger over in her hands, then dropped it in the deep pocket of her business suit jacket. It pulled the cloth down at one side.

"This is going to cost you more than dinner."

Grant smiled at her.

"Really? I kind of liked it at the Cowbell."

Evelyn made sure nobody could see from the store and gave him a kiss.

"Well, cargo pants does limit our choices."

Grant pointed at the charger.

"How long d'you need?"

Evelyn stepped back.

"I'll need to run it on my break. Why don't you grab a coffee?"

Grant took her hand to stop her leaving.

"Thanks for this. And…" He leaned in close and lowered his voice. "Looks like I'm going be around a few days longer."

Evelyn squeezed his hand and smiled.

"We'd better buy you some proper clothes then."

She turned toward the technology store, and Grant went out the other side of the rest area to the food court. The mall cop hummed around the corner from the crosswalk. The three men converged on Evelyn. Grant was halfway along the south hall when he heard her shout.

TWENTY-FIVE

"Get off me, you frog-faced motherfucker."

Grant wasn't sure if it was the panic in her voice or the fact he'd never heard Evelyn swear before, but the disturbance got his attention and got it fast. He swung round in time to see three white men surrounding her. One man grabbed her in a bear hug from behind while another snatched at her jacket pocket. A third stood under the potted palm where Evelyn had slapped Grant a moment ago. The man stepped forward and repaid the favor with a slap so hard it snapped her head to one side and shut her up.

Evelyn went quiet but didn't stop struggling. She kicked out with pointed shoes and caught the third man on the shins and knees but missed where she was aiming. The bear-hugger stood firm on braced legs. The snatcher's hand became entangled in the jacket pocket as Evelyn twisted to one side. The slapper balled his hand into a fist and leaned into the punch. It came all the way from his shoulder, and this time Evelyn did stop struggling.

Grant covered the distance at a sprint. Evelyn became a dead weight, making it hard for the bear-hugger to hold her up and more difficult for the man rifling her pocket to snatch its contents. Shoppers standing nearby gasped in shock, then somebody shouted for help. The hum of the Segway came from somewhere behind Grant. Grant launched himself sideways over the soft leather chair and brought the potted palm down between the

139

attacker and the struggling robbers.

There were no words, only grunts. There was no noise except punches, kicks, and gasps of surprise. None of the men who'd followed Grant to the mall expected him to attack them with a potted palm.

The man behind Evelyn let go but was trapped between her and a second chair. The pocket-dipper had one hand stuck deep in her pocket and couldn't get it out as her dead weight twisted to one side onto his arm. The attacker was hit in the chest by the palm and pushed backward. The tree roots were yanked out of the terracotta urn, and the plant pot rolled across the tiles. Grant hit the floor in an untidy heap but sprang to his feet. He grabbed the trunk of the palm and slammed it into the attacker's face. Twice. Then a third time for good measure. The heavy palm tree smashed his nose and knocked out two teeth. One eye swelled shut almost immediately, making his wide, flat face look even more like a frog.

Grant sidestepped the fallen palm and stamped on the pick-pocket's leg just below the knee. The leg buckled. He screamed in pain but still couldn't get his hand out of her pocket. Grant used core strength and balance to whip his elbow across the pick-pocket's head, and he went limp. The relaxed state freed his hand, and it came out holding the laptop charger.

The ugly black plug distracted Grant. The man standing behind Evelyn took full advantage. He stepped over the crumpled bodies and picked up the heavy plant pot. He raised it above his head with both hands and brought it down on Grant's head. Grant managed to get one arm up but took the full weight on the side of his head. His face went numb, and warm blood blinded one eye.

The man shoved the uprooted palm tree aside and stood over Grant. He didn't speak. He didn't kick Grant while he was down. He picked up the charger and shook his head. He slammed it to the ground, then picked up the largest piece of broken plant pot. Evelyn stirred beneath the pickpocket. Grant wiped the blood from his eye, but everything was blurred. What he saw would have made him smile if his face didn't hurt so much.

The short, dumpy mall cop leapt off the speeding Segway like a cowboy launching off his horse. He hit the bear-hugger square in the back, and momentum and bodyweight sent them both skidding across the tiled floor. It was a valiant effort and one that saved Grant from more serious injury. Unfortunately, it also knocked out the mall cop instead of the attacker.

Grant tried to push up on one arm, but his head was spinning. Evelyn rolled off the pickpocket. The mall cop lay still amid the twisted palms and damaged roots. The bear-hugger had had enough. He helped the pickpocket up, and they both tugged the third man out from under the palm. The trio staggered into Nordstrom and disappeared toward the west entrance. Grant tried to formulate a Hi Ho Silver joke but settled for patting the mall cop's leg. The offshoot of law enforcement had done good.

"Are you sure about this?"

Evelyn sat beside Grant on one of the leather easy chairs. She held a gauze pad from the store's first-aid kit against the side of his head to stop the bleeding. The mall cop had come round and was filling out an incident report for when the police arrived. An ambulance had also been called and mingled sirens sounded in the distance, muted slightly by the plush surroundings and the gigantic mall. Grant kept his voice down so the mall cop didn't add this to his report.

"Keep it simple. Mugging gone wrong."

Evelyn looked doubtful.

"But don't mention the charger?"

Grant took over holding the dressing against the wound.

"I shouldn't really have the charger. Strictly speaking, it's part of the crime scene at the motel. Not sure they'd appreciate me taking it."

He looked at Evelyn sitting beside him.

"The way he threw it down, doesn't look like it's what they

were after anyway."

Evelyn wanted to touch Grant's head but resisted.

"So what were they looking for?"

Grant shrugged. Easy answer was, he didn't know. The question was, were they looking for the same thing the black guys had been searching Nona's place for? And why follow Grant to the technology store before trying to snatch it? His first thought was that the charger was the obvious choice because the owner could be traced and Evelyn would be doing the tracing. But they hadn't taken the charger. Either they didn't realize its significance or the thing they were looking for was even more important.

"Keep it to yourself. And run the check when you get the chance. I'll call you later."

Evelyn nodded. She looked up when she heard a commotion coming along the south hall. The paramedics beat the police by fifteen minutes. They made a beeline for the man holding a bloody dressing to the side of his head. They went straight into emergency triage. Evelyn was checked and cleared. The mall cop was hustled to one side and questioned about losing consciousness. He said he'd been stunned but had stayed awake. That made Grant the most serious casualty. Cut to the side of the head and possible fractured skull. That meant he was heading for hospital.

Evelyn watched them walk Grant toward the exit. Grant gave her a little wave, then turned his attention to the ambulance crew. They confirmed he was going to CMC-Mercy. What Grant was thinking was, good, because Nona had a couple of questions to answer.

TWENTY-SIX

There's a saying in combat that anything you can think of, your opponents can think of as well. Grant had become complacent since being detoured by the knitting circle conference, so he didn't realize that until it was almost too late. Nona Hartley had a couple of questions to answer, so it stood to reason there were people who didn't want her to answer them. If Grant hadn't been having his head examined, he might have realized sooner. As it was, he didn't.

"How many?"

"Five. Maybe six."

"It was only a plant pot."

"From what I heard, it was a pretty big plant pot."

The doctor peeled off his rubber gloves and dumped them in the clinical waste bin. The same doctor who'd told Grant to "Try and keep her spirits up" when he'd come to see Nona earlier. Telling Grant he was going to need five stitches wasn't doing much to keep his spirits up. Grant hated stitches and always felt faint at the sight of needles. The doctor sugared the pill.

"Be thankful the x-rays came back negative."

He tapped himself on the side of the head.

"You must have a thick skull."

Grant wasn't in the mood for jokes. He swung his feet off the examination table and immediately knew he should have stayed put. His head began to spin and his stomach lurched up into his throat. Shock and head trauma don't make for a settled life. Grant waited for the wave of nausea to pass, then took a drink of water from the paper cup beside the bed. It settled his stomach. It didn't help the ache pulsing through his head. The doctor took his foot off the pedal and the lid dropped shut on the bin.

"Nurse will be in shortly with a suture kit."

Grant tried one last suggestion.

"Can't you just stick it back together?"

The doctor knew Grant's medical history and military service.

"We only glue people shut in combat zones. Back here in civilization..." He made a sewing motion. "We do it the old-fashioned way."

Grant puffed his cheeks out.

"Great. From knitting circle to sewing bee."

At least they hadn't cut his clothes off. Maybe he should be thankful for small mercies. Right now, his head didn't feel like a small mercy. The doctor swished out of the curtained cubicle and gave Grant time to think about what he wanted to ask Nona once his cut was stitched and dressed. Number one was who she'd given the petrol to the night Grant gave her shelter in Room 257. That was interesting enough, but it was numbers two and three where the questions got really intense: what was the scale of Leroy's plans for developing Notebook Trail, and what did she have that both sides of the black and white conflict were looking for? Avoiding getting caught between the two gangs didn't seem like an option anymore. He didn't think this was how Clint Eastwood felt in *A Fistful of Dollars*.

The nurse came through the curtain carrying a sterile suture kit on a tray. She put the tray down and turned a sympathetic eye on Grant. She pointed at the cut down the side of his head.

"Do you want an anesthetic?"

Grant looked at the syringe on the tray then back at the nurse.

"Unless you plan to stamp on my foot as a distraction."

The nurse unpacked the suture kit.

"I once had a guy wrote 'Do Not Resuscitate' on his chart for a joke."

She took the protective tip off the syringe.

"What do you think happened?"

Grant resigned himself to a few seconds of blinding pain.

"You stamped on his foot?"

She tested the flow and came over to Grant.

"Close your eyes and think of England."

The dressing was less bulky than the compress and sterile gauze because it was only protecting the stitches instead of stopping the blood flow. Keeping pressure on the wound wasn't necessary anymore. Grant stripped off the plastic gown he'd been wearing over his clothes, and the nurse bundled it into the clinical waste bin. She had small hands and a steady nerve. Apart from the injection into both sides of the wound, she had been delicate and considerate. Nobody liked having stitches. She was used to people being apprehensive, but it felt wrong for somebody as big and strong as Jim Grant. Grant watched her close the bin.

"Seven?"

She wiggled her fingers.

"I have small hands. Makes for tighter stitching."

Grant was still quivering a bit from feeling the pull of the thread. There was no more pain apart from a headache that would likely last a couple of days. He didn't nod his thanks but gave her a thumbs up. She smiled an acknowledgment and pointed at the dressing.

"Keep the dressing clean. You can take it off in a couple of days."

She wafted a hand up the side of her face.

"It'll heal better if you let it breathe. Any problems, come back in."

Grant drained the paper cup and crushed it in one hand. It didn't make him look strong and tough, but it helped get some of the angst out of his system. The nurse indicated a normal waste bin, and Grant slid off the examination table to throw the cup away. His knees buckled, and the nurse put a strong arm around his waist.

"Whoa. Timber."

She waited until he regained his balance then let go.

"Take your time. Head injuries sometimes affect your balance."

Grant leaned against the tall bed.

"Thanks. I should be used to this by now."

The nurse looked up at him.

"You get banged on the head a lot, do you?"

Grant shrugged.

"If I don't get the banging in first."

The nurse waited until she was satisfied Grant was okay, then drew the curtain back. She picked up the tray and instruments and stood in the opening.

"Well, you got enough first strike in to save the woman getting mugged."

Grant's head cleared and he felt strong enough to walk. He stood up and waited a moment, then followed the nurse out of the cubicle.

"Where's the girl from the fire?"

The nurse stopped in the corridor.

"The one overnight?"

Grant forced himself not to nod.

"Nona Hartley. Can I have a quick word with her?"

The nurse waved toward the ICU.

"Have to be quick. Orderlies just stretchered her out."

She set off toward the nurses' station.

"Let me find out where they're taking her."

Grant followed and watched as she checked the transfer board. Nona Hartley's name was still shown on the ICU section with various annotations and the time and date of her arrival.

The nurse reached under the counter and checked the patient list and disposition sheet. A frown creased her brow, then she looked around for the on-duty doctor. He was talking to an intern at a computer terminal behind the desk. Once he'd finished, the nurse went over to him.

"Nona Hartley, the burn victim. Which ward's she transferring to?"

The doctor glanced up at the whiteboard.

"We're keeping her for now. Until she's stronger."

The nurse looked back along the corridor.

"But I just…"

All three set off together, Grant in the lead. He'd been to Nona's bed before. The nurse overtook him on the bend and pushed into the room. The doctor brought up the rear and stopped dead inside the entrance. The bed was empty, the tubes dangling as if they'd been ripped out. They were still swinging. Grant turned to the nurse.

"Which way they go?"

She waved toward a pair of swing doors, and Grant set off at a sprint.

"Get security."

He barged through the doors and shouted over his shoulder.

"And call the police."

The doors cut off his words as they flip-flapped shut behind him.

TWENTY-SEVEN

There was no problem following the route the orderlies had taken, but it was a big problem trying to keep up with the wheeled gurney and the two men wearing hospital scrubs and facemasks. Grant was dizzy and weak after the first corridor. Startled nurses and cleaning staff pointed the way. Grant took a left at the end and caught sight of the gurney just before it took a right and disappeared.

His feet pounded along the corridor. Forward momentum kept him upright but taking the corners threatened his balance. There was more finger-pointing. There were more gasps of shock at the speed the gurney with the injured girl was being pushed. The fake orderlies turned left and then left again and barged through the double doors into the ambulance bays. Sunlight flooded the corridor. The parking area was bleached out until Grant charged through the doors.

Then an engine started up on his left.

A blood-red panel van burned rubber as it screeched out of the angled bays marked AMBULANCES ONLY. The back end shimmied until it got on track and headed toward the entrance where Evelyn Cover had brought Grant on his first visit to the emergency department. The back doors of the van were shut, but the right-hand door hadn't latched. It swung open as the van swerved past a parked ambulance. The wheeled gurney rolled gently across the parking lane. The fragile figure of Nona Hartley lay bundled on the floor of the van.

An ambulance turned in from East Fifth Street with its blue lights flashing and slammed its brakes on, blocking the entrance. The van skidded to a stop and did a furious three-point turn, then sped back toward Grant. He grabbed the gurney and shoved it in front of the van but the driver didn't swerve or slow down. He smashed the gurney aside and sped into the hospital complex. Grant tried to see the driver's face but the sun glaring off the windshield made it impossible.

The ambulance turned its blue lights off and pulled under the entrance portico. The paramedics began to unload a patient into the emergency department. A second ambulance was parked with the doors closed in the angled bay just past the entrance. A third had the back doors open while the paramedic restocked.

Grant glanced at the disappearing panel van, then looked at the ambulance. The paramedics were inside collecting supplies. Grant ran over and looked in the front. The keys were in the ignition. He slammed the back doors shut and jumped in the driver's seat. The engine started on the first attempt, and he was following the van within seconds.

The CMC-Mercy campus was tight and compact. The internal roads were narrow and functional but not conducive to a high-speed chase. The van had to negotiate the loading dock and the incinerator building before heading toward the turning circle in front of the main reception lobby. Delivery trucks were parked against the loading dock. Administrative staff returning from their afternoon break were coming around the turning circle. The van clipped the rear of a reversing truck and mounted the lawn, demolishing an ornamental fountain and two small trees. Grant came past the incinerator building just in time to see the back door fly open and Nona roll across the load bed. He floored the accelerator and went round the other side of the turning circle to reduce the van's options.

Horns blared as the admin staff stopped to avoid the van. The van tore up the turf as it cut the corner. An outpatient transport minibus turned in from Vail Avenue. The red van came down off the turning circle going the wrong way and almost hit the minibus. There was another squeal of tires. There was more horn blaring. Police sirens sounded coming from downtown. Their point of arrival at the hospital would be Vail Avenue, so the red van took a sharp right toward the Ortho Carolina Foot & Ankle Institute and the Outpatient Parking Lot, aiming for an escape back onto Fifth Street.

A family car slowed at the entrance to the Caswell Parking Deck and the driver struggled with the automated barrier. He wasn't a very good driver, and the rear of his car was angled across the service road. The van caught the rear fender and dragged the car all the way across the road. It mounted the curb and wedged itself against a concrete bollard. Grant came full circle under the entrance portico. The van reversed into him and smashed the ambulance radiator. Steam hissed up the front of the windshield. The van door buckled but didn't shut.

The sirens grew louder, definitely police not ambulance or fire service. Grant was getting used to the difference. The van skidded across the lawn again heading back the way it had come, but the reversing delivery truck now blocked the loading dock. The van veered to the right and smashed through the barrier onto the rooftop employee parking lot. Rooftop because it started on the ground level but became a three-story structure down the hill. Grant spun the ambulance around and sped after the van.

The employee parking lot was a confusing picture of long, wide concrete plains and sloping driveways. Without reading the signs, it was impossible to tell which angle went in which direction, so the red van followed its nose and ignored any moving vehicles. If they didn't get out of the way quick enough, they got rammed aside.

Grant followed the trail of carnage to the end of the top tier, then curled around the continuous ramp into the lower levels. The screeching tires sounded louder in the confines of the concrete circle. Brake lights flared up ahead as the van negotiated the tight corners. The buckled rear door hung open at a permanent angle like a broken wing.

The ambulance scraped the walls going down the ramp. Sparks flared in the dark. Steam obscured the windshield. Grant found the headlights and gave them full beam. The van was going too fast, and Grant had no alternative but to keep up or lose Nona.

The bottom of the ramp leveled out after one last tight left-hand twist. The van shot out of the ground-level exit and back up the hill toward the emergency department. Right back where they started from. Grant hit the gas going into the final turn, losing sight of the van for a split second.

A split second was all it took.

The panel van sideswiped the exit wall and the buckled door was ripped off its hinges. The van bounced off the wall. The door spun across the floor. Nona was thrown across the load bed and, without the door to stop her, tumbled onto the concrete ramp. Grant came around the curve at full speed.

Thankfully, Nona's eyes were closed so she didn't witness her onrushing death. Grant's eyes flew wide open. He slammed the brakes on and yanked the wheel hard over, knowing all the while he was too late.

TWENTY-EIGHT

"And what happened next?"

"You know what happened next."

"Tell me from your point of view."

Grant shifted his position on the examination table, and pain shot through his left arm and ribs. He looked at the young cop taking notes and tried not to come over all grumpy. He knew the uniform cop was only doing his job, getting all the witness information he could before the detectives arrived. Grant settled against the pillows and let out a sigh that creased his ribs.

"From my point of view? It all turned to rat shit."

Steam from the cracked radiator filled the cab. The deployed airbag obscured Grant's view even more. The front of the ambulance was a tangled wreck, all twisted metal and broken glass. Blue lights flashed through the haze. Figures moved like ghosts beyond the screen of smoke and steam. There was urgent movement and raised voices. Somebody shouted for the crash cart. This far from the emergency department, getting a crash cart was going to take a while so the responding paramedics did what they did best. Responded.

Two police cars were angled across the bottom of the employee parking lot entrance. The chase had come down the up ramp. The ambulance that had been parked at the ED was on the grass verge beyond them. It set off at a rush but without flashing lights and siren. It reminded Grant of a hearse going too fast but in complete silence. Next to arrive was the fire department. The pain eased when a paramedic gave Grant an injection, then the firefighters started to cut him out of the wreckage.

Somewhere up the hill past the hospital, the red panel van had made good its escape. It wasn't the van that concerned Grant. It was the figure the paramedics had rushed to the emergency department. A girl who was already in pain and shock from being petrol-bombed. Now she'd been hit by an ambulance as well.

Grant replayed the final moments one more time. Speeding around the concrete spiral. Coming into the final straight. The unconscious figure lying in the middle of the road. The final panicked turn of the wheel and the crunch of the ambulance hitting the outside curve. The wall collapsing. The airbag deploying. And the world going dark.

The young cop wrote that down and did what cops always do: asked for more.

"Did you see where the van went?"

Grant had nothing left.

"No."

"Did you get the number?"

Grant knew that having the number wouldn't get them anywhere. The van would be abandoned by now and would no doubt have been stolen anyway. Knowing that didn't help. He should have noted the license plate. One more failing among a list of failings.

"No."

The cop recognized Grant's disposition and closed his notebook. He clicked the pen shut and put it in his jacket pocket. He did that other thing that cops always do: look after their own. Grant was a cop too. When the shit hits the fan, cops pull together. He nodded and placed a hand on Grant's shoulder.

"Amazing you managed to stop in time."

Grant had a different view.

"Yeah, the wall hit her instead."

The cop nodded and drew back.

"Even so, she's a lucky girl."

Grant knew the cop was only trying to be helpful but couldn't help seeing things differently. He sighed again despite the pain in his ribs.

"I doubt she's feeling lucky right now."

The young cop showed his maturity.

"You've got to be alive to feel anything at all. She's alive because of you. Give yourself that. The rest will take care of itself."

Grant nodded his thanks, then lay back against the pillows. The curtain drew back, and Danny Yates came into the cubicle.

"Very moving."

He indicated the uniform cop's notebook. "Leave a copy at the triage desk." Then looked at Grant.

"I've got this."

Despite the chase not happening in Freedom Division, the kidnapping was folded into the motel bombing case and given to Detective Yates. The detective felt like it was raining shit since he also inherited the attempted mugging at South Park Mall. It seemed that anything Jim Grant touched these days turned to rat shit, and that was foremost in Grant's thoughts. Yates looked at the battered Yorkshireman.

"I'm gonna need a bigger folder to keep up with all the shit you're involved in."

Grant only had one question.

"How's Nona?"

Yates acknowledged Grant's concern and decided to cut him some slack.

"Broken arm. Fractured skull. They've got her whacked out

on meds for the pain. But from what I hear…"

He shrugged and softened his tone.

"If you hadn't stopped the kidnappers, she'd be gone. And if you hadn't been so quick, she'd be dead. So, congrats on that."

Grant didn't feel like taking compliments. He knew there was a "but" coming.

"But we've got a shitload of stuff here. And it all centers on you."

Grant dipped his head instead of shaking it.

"It all centers on her. I just happen to be around when it centers."

"And when Leroy got thrown off the balcony."

"And that."

Yates sat beside the bed.

"Do I need to recap?"

Grant took a sip of water from a paper cup.

"You need to cut the crap. Because you've got the time of death now, haven't you?"

Yates considered how much to tell the English cop, then decided to come clean.

"Ambient temperature being pretty much the same across North Carolina, the ME can be fairly accurate. He died sometime between eight and ten the night before you found him."

Grant looked at Yates.

"No later than ten?"

"No."

They both knew what that meant, but Grant felt the need to confirm it.

"So he didn't throw the petrol bomb."

Yates extrapolated from that.

"And you were having dinner at the Cowbell Burger & Whisky Bar."

Grant sighed.

"I'm in the clear then?"

Yates nodded.

"You were always in the clear."

Grant sensed another "but" coming and kept quiet.

"But all this other shit. It's a concern."

Grant looked at the detective and wondered how much he could trust him. There were still things Grant couldn't admit to since he'd lied about throwing Leroy off the balcony and even more now he'd stolen evidence from the crime scene. Even so, he decided he could share his thoughts about the investigation, except he didn't have anything close to an idea what this was all about. Since Leroy hadn't thrown the petrol bomb, that put the crosshairs firmly on Mr. Pimply Arse, but the only person who knew who he was was Nona. That brought up the question of what the black guys were looking for at her house and what the white guys were after at the mall. Add in the red van guys, who could be black or white, and you had more questions than answers. In fact, Grant didn't have any answers at all, so there was nothing else to tell Yates.

"I'm as concerned as you are, but..." He shrugged. "I don't know what to tell you."

He decided to share the only thing he could admit to.

"Only thing I know is, more than one person has warned me about getting caught between rival factions over there near the Sleepy Nook."

Yates leaned forward.

"One faction being Leroy and his boys?"

Grant nodded.

"I don't know who the others are."

There was no point being diplomatic.

"Except it's some kind of black and white thing."

Yates didn't look shocked.

"This is North Carolina. Everything's a black and white thing."

He stood and went to the curtain, then turned back to Grant.

"You know anything else about the girl?"

Grant threw him a bone.

"I know she's a recovering addict. Ninety days clean. Been

going to meetings behind the Citgo, down past the I-85 underpass."

Yates nodded his thanks and opened the curtain.

"You get well soon. I'll keep in touch about the girl."

Grant held up a hand and watched Yates disappear down the corridor. He was wondering what Nona could be mixed up in that made her so important. That line of enquiry was on hold until she was able to talk. That was going to be some time, and after the kidnap attempt, Grant wasn't going to be the one allowed access. She'd be under guard from now on.

That left Plan B. The other question he wanted to ask her about. Leroy's plans for Notebook Trail. More importantly, where the hell the housing estate that had its houses removed was? He considered asking Bruno Morris or Brubaker, then remembered Leroy's Satnav. He felt in his pocket for the pickup keys. Now all he needed was a lift back to South Park Mall.

TWENTY-NINE

Grant needed more than just a lift back to Leroy's pickup at the mall; first, he needed treatment and medication. The treatment was more x-rays and dressings for minor cuts and grazes. The medication was antiseptic and painkillers. Even then, the doctor wanted to keep him in hospital for a while under observation following a second bang to the head. Grant argued the thick-skull theory and signed himself out. Against medical advice. That last bit in case his head fell off and he decided to sue the hospital.

The uniform cop who'd told Grant to give himself a break was finishing up at the crash scene. The debris from the wall had been cleared away and a local garage had recovered the ambulance. The tire marks where Grant had skidded across the ramp would last a good while longer. Between the blue of the sky, the green of the trees, and the brilliant sunshine it looked like the accident never happened.

Grant knew better. So did the young cop. Their eyes met as Grant crossed the scarred grass verge. Grant gave him a cautious nod and pointed at the patrol car.

"Don't suppose you're going anywhere near South Park Mall, are you?"

The cop took the keys out of his pocket.

"Sure. Jump in."

He indicated the skid marks where Grant had saved the girl.

"You can give me some driving tips."

Grant glanced at the damaged wall, then opened the passenger door. He spoke across the roof.

"Keep your speed down. And don't go down the up ramp."

It was supposed to be gallows humor, every cop's release valve for the pressures of the job, but it carried too much weight to be funny. Grant looked at the skid marks one last time, then got in the car.

The pickup was in the narrow parking lot behind Dick's Sporting Goods and The Container Store. On the west side of the mall between the bigger parking lots to the north and the south. It had been parked in the shade of an ornamental tree when Grant left it, but the late afternoon sun had moved across the sky heading west.

Grant considered calling in to see if Evelyn had managed to trace the laptop but didn't want her to see him looking like a war refugee. There'd be time for that later. Mr. Pimply Arse was a big part of the equation. Grant wanted to be able to act swiftly once he identified him. Before that, he wanted to know what Leroy had been doing on an abandoned housing estate.

He bought two bottles of chilled water from Dick's and was thankful when he opened the driver's door. North Carolina had worked its magic and turned the interior into a furnace. He opened the passenger door to let the air circulate and took a few minutes to drink ice-cold water before reaching in and turning the engine on. The Satnav fired up automatically.

Grant climbed in, careful not to bang his arm or ribs, and closed the doors. He turned the air conditioner on full and let blessed cool air wash over him. Once he'd cooled down, he typed in the address. A female voice told him to please wait. The Satnav did its calculations. Grant selected the overview map so he'd have a general direction before setting off. Notebook Trail was way past the Sleepy Nook Inn and the airport over toward the

Catawba River.

Grant fastened his seatbelt and clicked "Start Route." The female voice directed him out of the parking lot, and Grant headed west, into the sun. In all those old war movies like *Twelve O'Clock High*, that was always the danger spot. Grant wasn't thinking about that. The only problem was driving all the way with the sun glaring through the windshield. It wasn't going to be his biggest problem by a long way.

THIRTY

Grant's first thought when he arrived at the scorched patch of earth that was Notebook Trail was that whatever Leroy was doing here it hadn't amounted to very much. He pulled the pickup to the side of Amos Smith Road and looked at the impressive false entrance but wasn't impressed.

There was a ten-foot stretch of concrete sidewalk with wheelchair access on either side of the turn-in, but the sidewalk didn't go anywhere. There was a longer stretch of white picket fence and half a dozen privacy trees that protected the privacy of nothing. A large carved stone took pride of place on an overgrown rockery and proclaimed the development to be:

WILDERNESS ESTATES
Live in the House of the Future
TODAY...

Whatever houses the future had to offer, the ones that had occupied the estate thus far were long gone, leaving scarred land and empty streets. The Satnav had reverted to map mode and showed what the site should have looked like. Notebook Trail was the entrance road and it ran the length of the development. A network of half a dozen streets branched off from it with fancy names like Angel Way Court, Whisper Trail, and Cricket Place

Circle. Grant reckoned that was more to do with grasshoppers than England's contribution to summer sport.

The streets were still there, but the houses had been razed to the ground and the site cleared. Concrete foundations showed where the houses should have been. Scars of bright red earth showed the under soil to be more sand than dirt and, as such, nature was taking its time reclaiming the ground. Bushes and undergrowth had been slow to spring up, and the only grass was the lawns that some enterprising residents had laid before whatever financial crisis forced them out.

There was a manmade embankment between Jeans Court and Angel Way Court, and beyond the hedgerow of McGarry Trail, Woodchip Court sloped away toward the far end of the plot of land. The remaining trees, that had been cut back to form the patch of land, fringed the site to the north and east. The railroad cutting ran alongside Notebook Trail to the south. Scorched Earth policy was a combat strategy where retreating armies laid waste to everything behind them so there was nothing to support their attackers. Adolf Hitler would have been proud at what little was left of Notebook Trail.

Grant pulled into the entrance road and stopped at the padlocked chain that denied access. He turned the engine off and listened to the metal tick as it cooled. It didn't cool very much. He took a drink of the bottled water from Dick's as he looked through the windshield. The place was derelict. Abandoned. Empty. Only it wasn't. It couldn't be. There had to be something here for Leroy to make such a big thing of it with his mother. "He's a good boy. A landowner now." Well, Grant had found the land. Question was, what else was it hiding?

He screwed the lid back on the bottle of water and got out of the cab. You can only see so much from the driving seat. He'd learned that from years of uniform patrol. If you wanted to see what was really going on, you had to walk the beat. Foot patrol was where you got your nose to the ground. Foot patrol today was on the empty streets of Notebook Trail. Grant stepped over the padlocked chain and prepared to walk his beat.

The first thing Grant noticed was the silence. It was complete and all-encompassing and smothered the area like a blanket on a fire. It was suffocating. The only thing Grant could hear was the sound of his breath and the gravel crunching beneath his feet. There was no traffic noise. There was no birdsong. It was like walking into a cemetery or the site of some enormous natural disaster.

Then he heard the freight train coming and listened as it rattled through the cutting toward the Catawba River. It would cross the river on the trestle bridge overlooking Greenway Circle and no doubt rattle Mrs. Holmes' windows. The train seemed to take forever to pass, then the silence returned.

Grant scanned the site, took a slow deep breath of warm clean air, then set off walking the trail. He checked left and right as he passed each intersection, glancing along the stubby cul-de-sacs of Print Court and Jean Court, then followed the curve of Notebook Trail past the manmade embankment behind Angel Way Court.

The stillness was peaceful but unsettling. Grant felt a sadness settle over him at so many homes reduced to flat base and concrete. The foundations were uniform in size and spacing. The houses must have all been about the same dimensions, probably trailer homes like Leroy's mother's. There was nothing left standing, no garages, garden sheds, or outhouses. There were no fences or low stone walls. Angel Way Court had a few shrubs and stunted ornamental trees, but apart from that, the only thing to break the low flat scrubland was the embankment.

Grant walked the site as far as McGarry Trail and peered over the hedgerow down the slope of Woodchip Court. There was nothing at the far end except a pile of rubble that hadn't been completely cleared and the remains of a fire to burn the wood. An airplane droned overhead, too high to be coming into the Charlotte Douglas Airport. Another train trundled past going the other way. Grant headed back toward the entrance, taking the long route through Cricket Place Circle. There was no sound of crickets. Maybe they only came out at night. Grant wasn't up on his grasshopper behavior.

The woods were dense enough along the northern boundary to hide the land outside of the Wilderness Estates, but there was still no sound of birds or wildlife. Grant followed the crescent until it rejoined Notebook Trail. The foundations were a little bigger here, the flat base concrete just as empty. This would have been the premier housing section. Bigger houses. Doublewide trailer homes.

Leroy might have had plans for this place, but he hadn't got around to implementing them yet. If somebody hadn't broken his neck in the shower, he'd have still been just a pimp and a drug dealer. No matter how much he was helping returning veterans, he hadn't got beyond the idea stage. Cheap housing for black ex-servicemen. And no doubt drugs and sex too.

There was nothing more to see here. Grant put a little extra pace into his stride and cut across the red dirt to Angel Way court. He couldn't see the pickup over the top of the embankment but something glinted in the sun. He craned his neck to see if it was the windshield, but it was closer than that. He stopped, then took a couple of steps back. The glint of light came again. Over to his right at the foot of the banking. Something small.

He crossed two crumbling foundations and the tarmac cul-de-sac. The gravel underfoot sounded loud in the silence. The shiny object became bigger as he drew closer. He'd been right about the garages and garden sheds and outhouses. None of the household additions had survived the site clearance. But not everyone had built upwards. Somebody had built down.

The storm cellar or basement was next to the third house from the end. The heavy wooden hatch was solid but flaking at the edges. The paintwork had all but faded away. The padlock was something else. It was shiny and new and built to keep intruders out. Why somebody was worried about intruders in the middle of nowhere was anybody's guess. Grant looked around for something tough and heavy. He didn't like guessing games.

THIRTY-ONE

The hatch creaked as Grant pulled it up. A folding support snapped into place to prop it open. The hole was deep and dark and seemed to run all the way under the adjoining foundations. The bright afternoon sunlight only penetrated halfway along the floor. Grant dropped to a crouch and peered into the cellar. From the lower angle, he could see a bit further but not far enough to identify anything down there. The only way to do that was to go down and look.

The wooden stairs were as solid as the hatch but not as flaky. They were clean and unpainted. Grant wished he'd brought a flashlight but didn't think there was one in Leroy's pickup. That suggested there might be a light switch somewhere down there. He carefully tested the strength of the top step before putting his full weight on it. The wood creaked but didn't flex. Solid. Good. He went down the next two steps, then stopped to reassess. More creaking. Still solid. Even better.

He reached the bottom without incident. The cellar was big enough to give plenty of headroom, even for Grant. He checked either side of the stairs for a light switch and found it on the wall to his right. It was a makeshift affair rigged to a heavy-duty battery, the kind you'd have in a fallout shelter. He flicked the switch and dull yellow lights came on slowly, as if warming up.

The cellar wasn't as big as he thought once it came out of the darkness, but it was solid and well-appointed. The floor had been concreted, the walls brick-built, and the ceiling had solid metal beams beneath more poured concrete. There was a double bunk bed at one end but the rest of the space was for storage. Some of what it was storing surprised him. Some of it didn't.

The walls were lined with Home Depot shelving and Container Store plastic boxes. The boxes were clear plastic with blue lids for one section and red lids for another. The far end, next to the bunk bed, had a wall-mounted gun cabinet of the type used at firing ranges. Tall and narrow, more likely for automatic weapons or target rifles. The padlock matched the one Grant had smashed off to open the hatch. He ignored the gun cabinet and started with the red box section.

Grant pulled one of the boxes out and peeled back the lid. It was neatly packed with military-grade Pakma dry food rations from Lithuania. The heat-sealed green plastic bags were uniform in size and shape but the labels gave a list of contents. Pakma must supply worldwide, because the contents were in English. The main meals were either pork, chicken, or beef with relevant garnish, and the packs included tea, coffee, broth, and dry fuel tablets for the flameless ration heater. They looked pretty much the same as Compo field rations back in England. The last three rows of the red box section held bottled water.

The ground shook as another freight train rumbled by.

Grant checked the blue-box section. These boxes were bigger. When he peeled back the lids, he could see why. If the red section was supplies and rations, then the blue section was clothing and blankets. There was neatly folded bedding, including sheets and blankets—no duvets because they would take up too much room. The rest of the blue boxes had a variety of shirts, trousers, and sweatshirts. There was no footwear or undergarments.

The ground stopped trembling. The train noise faded into the distance.

He put the lids back on and pushed the boxes into place. He examined the firearms locker. It was a standard cabinet designed for secure home storage. Three bookshelves filled the gap between the cabinet and the blue-box section. There was a selection of clean, new softcover books, half a dozen of each. Grant skimmed the titles.

The Wounded Warrior Handbook

Courage After Fire

When Johnny And Jane Came Marching Home

There were several catalogs for local medical resources and two shelves of paperback novels that looked like they'd been well-thumbed. Nothing slushy. No romance. All books featuring strong men taking care of themselves. Some strong women too. Jack Reacher seemed to be a big favorite. Some Zoe Sharp books as well. Half a dozen skin magazines lay on the bottom shelf alongside three boxes of condoms, creams, and lotions, but this clearly wasn't a sex, drugs, and rock and roll bunker.

Grant went back to the gun cabinet. That was the only worrying thing about the entire place, returning veterans with PTSD having ready access to firearms. He knew that injured soldiers were often helped to readjust by visiting gun ranges, but that didn't always work out. Just look at what happened to American Sniper Chris Kyle, shot to death when trying to help a returning veteran. Grant wondered if Leroy and his group used the manmade embankment as a backstop for target practice. He rattled the padlock but didn't try to break it open. It was better staying locked.

The bottom bunk creaked as Grant sat and looked around the storage bunker. It was as neat and tidy as Leroy's clothes had been untidy. On the bathroom floor where he'd supposedly slipped in the shower. If anything it reinforced Grant's belief that somebody had killed the pimp who seemed less pimplike with every new thing Grant learned. Maybe his mother had good reason to feel proud of her son, the landowner. Once again, Grant wished he hadn't thrown him off the balcony.

He let out a sigh and stood up. There was nothing more to learn here, so he turned the light off and climbed the stairs. The wooden structure groaned under his weight. The sunlight blinded him as he came out of the hole. It wasn't until he reached to close the hatch that he realized he wasn't alone.

"Breaking Leroy's neck ain't enough for you, huh?"

One of the black guys who'd been with Leroy coming out of the woods stood with a semi-circle of bigger men.

"You got to go breaking and entering as well?"

THIRTY-TWO

Grant turned to face the threat. The threat was six men fanned out either side of the guy from the woods. They were standing at the foot of the embankment like targets on the firing range that this most certainly was. Now that Grant had seen the gun cabinet he recognized the familiar divots in the parched red earth of the backstop. Fairly tight groupings behind holes where the targets had been jammed into the ground. He hadn't seen the targets down in the cellar; they must have been in the firearms locker.

The embankment gave them cover from the road, good deployment, and with their backs to the sun, even better. Grant squinted into the sun and looked at the not-so-magnificent seven. They all had short hair and a military bearing and looked as if they kept themselves fit. Their clothes were clean but frayed at the edges, not new. The designated spokesman stepped forward.

"Them's Leroy's things down there. Not yours."

Grant let the hatch go. The heavy wood slammed shut, sending clouds of dust flying around his feet. He waved at the cellar.

"Things he put together to help returning veterans?"

He moved two paces to his right to move the sun out of his eyes.

"Well, I'm a returning veteran."

The spokesman shook his head.

"You're not one of us."

Grant moved to his right again, then took one step toward the group.

"Because I'm not black?"

"Because you're not American."

The six men spread out to the sides and began to encircle Grant. Grant kept his eyes on the main man but flexed his knees, ready for action. This was going to turn ugly fast, and when it did, the spokesman was going to be the first man down.

"Leroy isn't Leroy either. Didn't disqualify him."

The spokesman stepped forward.

"Breaking his neck disqualifies you."

Grant braced his shoulders.

"I didn't break his neck."

The spokesman kept coming.

"And I'm not going to break yours."

Grant took another step to his right but changing the angle of the sun only moved him closer to the men circling round his back. It was time to use the policeman's most important asset: his mouth. He put a twinkle in his eye and lowered his voice.

"Is that some kind of cryptic message?"

He held a finger up for the man to stop, and the man did.

"Saying you won't break my neck when you mean that you will?"

Grant wagged the finger.

"You see, that tells me you've got enough smarts to know right from wrong. And if you think about it, I think you've got enough sense to know if I'd broken your friend's neck, I wouldn't have made it look like he slipped in the shower. I'd have said he came at me and I had no choice. Self-defense. A much-overlooked argument in court."

He lowered his hand.

"You do know I'm a cop, don't you?"

The spokesman glowered at Grant.

"Not from around here."

Grant stared back.

"You think that makes me less dangerous, or more? Since I'm not being paid to turn a blind eye."

He shrugged and waved a hand to encompass the seven men.

"Same applies here as what I said at the underpass. I'm going to take a beating. No question about that. But I'm ex-military too, so at least two of you are coming to hospital with me."

He settled a little at the knees and relaxed his shoulders. His arms hung loose at his sides and he flexed his fingers ready to turn them into weapons. Not fists, because punching breaks too many bones in the hand, but open palms ready to deflect blows and strike back.

"Now, I've already got a friend in the hospital."

The spokesman's expression softened. Grant continued.

"And if I thought you'd put her there, we'd be going at it right now. So, it's make-your-mind-up time."

The six men had completely surrounded Grant. The spokesman took a different stance to Grant, not relaxed and flexible but solid and hard. He balled his hands into fists. Grant turned his palms upwards.

"We going to fight or talk?"

It turned out Denzel Washburn was intrigued enough by what Grant said that he decided to talk. At least for now. He ushered Grant over and the group settled into the shade of the embankment, the not-so-magnificent seven plus one. Grant started the conversation with a compliment, always a good opening gambit.

"He must have loved his brother. To go around using Leroy's name."

Washburn sat on an indentation in the sloping hill like a chair. The other six knelt or sat or crouched on the ground. Grant didn't want to sit. This could still turn ugly. He'd given Washburn the opening, now he let the new leader run with it.

"We all served with Leroy. He was a good man. His brother aspired to be like him. The name was a good way to start."

Grant hadn't forgotten the first time he'd met Leroy Junior.

"Turning Nona out at the Sleepy Nook wasn't the best way to honor that."

Washburn rested his elbows on his knees and looked up at Grant.

"No doubt. But these are hard times."

He waved to include the surrounding land.

"You can't buy all this on a disabled pension and handouts."

Grant looked at the scorched earth.

"All this hasn't amounted to much except a hole in the ground and a firing range. Is that the legacy his brother had in mind?"

Washburn's eyes looked tired.

"You can't build until you've got something to build on."

He indicated the concrete foundations up and down Angel Way Court.

"We can put twenty-four houses on this street alone. No groundwork. Just bring 'em in and set 'em down. That's twenty-four vets can bring their families and start to rebuild their lives. There's too many didn't make it back. Even more didn't make it out of the shit in their heads."

Grant sighed.

"I know. More U.S. servicemen have died at their own hands than were killed in the conflicts. I heard that."

Washburn nodded.

"And some made bad choices trying to drag themselves up."

He looked at Grant.

"You telling me you never made any bad choices?"

Grant softened his stare.

"I don't think throwing him off the balcony was my best move."

Then he hardened it again.

"Because putting Nona in the hospital is down to me."

Washburn stood up and brushed dirt off the seat of his pants.

"That wasn't Leroy. And it wasn't us."

Grant nodded.

"I'm going with the pimply-arsed white guy she was tricking.

You got any ideas about that?"

Washburn stood face-to-face with Grant.

"One of them white boys over at Catawba Point. Don't know who. They don't usually hold with laying down with black girls."

Grant looked him in the eye.

"But Nona was an equal-opportunity trick?"

Washburn didn't back off.

"She did what she had to do. Only handout you get in this world is a pension and a folded flag."

Grant looked at the ground. He'd been to too many funerals.

"You were there? With his mother?"

Washburn paused for a moment, then gave the faintest of nods.

"When he died. And when they buried him."

He nodded at the men sitting around him.

"It was us folded the flag."

He braced his shoulders.

"Us and his younger brother."

Grant sensed a change in the atmosphere. Ugly was coming. He'd made the fatal mistake of being lulled into a false sense of security. Washburn put a hard edge in his voice.

"You might not have broken his neck."

He started to move forward, balling his hands into fists again.

"But this is for throwing him off the balcony."

The punch came out of the sun and caught Grant by surprise. It was short and sharp and went straight for the chin. Grant saw it too late and only managed to turn his head to one side. The blow brought stars to his eyes. His head snapped sideways and all the pain he'd forgotten from the accident came rushing back in one massive attack. The second blow was a gut punch that made Grant throw up on his shoes, but he didn't go down. In a situation like this, you needed to stay on your feet because once you were on the ground you were dead meat.

Grant's head spun in the bright afternoon sun. He tried to bring his arms up to protect himself but Washburn stepped back instead.

"Let's call it a draw. Honors even."

The sound of guns being cocked spun everyone around, the six men on the ground as well as Grant and Washburn. Shadows broke the skyline atop the ridge, and a dozen men pointed guns down the embankment.

"Well look at this. Looks like the cavalry came just in time."

THIRTY-THREE

Two things went through Grant's mind in quick succession. The first was Bruno Morris and the Blind-Eye cop warning him not to get caught between the rival gangs. The second was, I'd rather be lucky than good. Because the pimply-arsed white guy was part of the white supremacists from Catawba Point, and Grant was guessing that's exactly who was standing atop the ridge. Being saved from the nasty black men put him in a good position to find out who the guy with the laptop was. Grant straightened up and rubbed his jaw.

"Glad you boys happened to be passing."

He jerked a thumb toward Washburn but gave the black ex-soldier a barely noticeable shake of the head.

"Things were getting out of hand."

The leader came down the banking in slow, lazy strides. The dry red earth crumbled into narrow landslides that followed him down. The rest of his men kept their guns trained on the black men at the bottom of the slope.

"You got to be careful what neighborhoods you hang around in. There's rough elements in this neck of the woods."

Grant looked at the woods that bordered the northern edge of the Wilderness Estates. The treeline started at the cul-de-sac turn-around at the end of Angel Way Court and continued over the embankment. No doubt where the white supremacists had snuck up on them from.

"I'll try and remember that."

He waved a hand around the empty streets.

"Who'd have thought you could run into so many fellas in the middle of nowhere?"

The leader stopped at the bottom of the embankment.

"Middle of nowhere's where their kind belong."

He gave Washburn a hard stare.

"I see Leroy got no further with this than his returning veterans bullshit."

Washburn glanced at Grant then back to the leader. Grant could see he was seething inside but held it in check. You had to choose your battles. There was no point starting a fight you couldn't win. Grant considered him with growing respect that made it harder to say what he had to say.

"Yeah. This place is full of nothing and dog shit. Guess you need more than a couple of brain cells and pimp money to become a property tycoon."

The leader smiled.

"You got the coon part right anyway."

Grant laughed, that was hard too, but didn't speak. The leader filled the void.

"You got a close-up of that when you threw him off the balcony."

Grant walked toward the leader, dusting off his clothes.

"Seems to be a story going round about that. It's not strictly true."

The leader looked at Grant.

"We ain't the cops', boy. Don't need to make excuses to us."

He jerked a thumb toward the entrance on Amos Smith Road.

"Not sure you should be driving a black man's wheels though."

Grant stopped opposite the white supremacist.

"Funny. Back when I was a cop in Bradford, this mainly black town in Yorkshire, they were always driving BMWs."

The leader frowned.

"Them German cars?"

Grant smiled.

"Black Man's Wheels."

The leader laughed. The men atop the ridge laughed with him. Grant thought he'd wandered into a scene from *A Fistful of Dollars* except these weren't badly dubbed Italians. The sun had moved all the way west and was dipping toward the horizon. It was still hot and steamy. The situation was hot too. Grant had to decide whether to play along with these guys or head back to the motel. Part of that process was considering which faction had petrol-bombed his room and put Nona in the hospital and who was driving the panel van that tried to get her out.

Grant looked at Washburn, then at the white supremacist. His money was on the white supremacist or part of his group. That said, the next thing to consider was the best way to prove that. That one was easy.

"But I take your point."

He tossed the pickup keys at Washburn, then turned back toward the leader.

"Don't suppose you could drop me back at the Sleepy Nook?"

The leader made a circling motion with one finger around his head, and the men atop the ridge came down the slope. The landslides raised dust behind them. They crossed the flat base foundations ignoring the hatch and gathered on the cracked tarmac of Angel Way Court. The leader guided Grant toward his men.

"We can do better than that."

He clicked his fingers twice and the men headed toward the woods at the end of the cul-de-sac. He fell in behind them, keeping Grant at his side.

"Got a barbecue planned. Why don't you join us?"

THIRTY-FOUR

It wasn't a long drive. The journey took in some familiar sights and a couple he'd only heard about. Catawba Point was directly south of Notebook Trail but driving directly south wasn't an option. Grant traveled in the second car of a three-vehicle convoy. A pickup, an SUV, and a big square American car. Grant sat in the backseat of the big American car and watched the world go by. Using the map in his head and the angle of the sun, he managed to maintain his sense of direction. Passing the airport helped. The rest was common sense and having a general overview.

The convoy drove south on the boundary road that paralleled Charlotte Douglas Airport's westernmost runway then crossed a bridge over the I-485 heading west. The first half a mile of Walkers Ferry Road was dotted with houses and grassy knolls but then the houses dried up and the woods closed in. Grant caught a glimpse of Danga Lake through the trees, but the southern tributary of Little Paw Creek was all but invisible. The road crested a gentle ridge then curved south without any turn offs until they passed a broad, flat clearing and the reason they had the best phone signal in Charlotte.

North Carolina's most powerful cell phone tower was tall and solid and built around a central rotunda of brick and concrete. Not massive but big enough to need a door for access to the inner core. The tower grew narrower the higher it went and had all sorts of fancy antennas and satellite dishes and things Grant knew nothing about. Maybe Evelyn Cover could have explained, but she wasn't here. The road continued down the slope, and a sign indicated that Walkers Ferry was straight ahead. The convoy didn't go straight ahead; it took a sharp right up an unmarked road and was immediately smothered by trees that blocked out the sky.

Several twists and turns later the convoy came out of the woods. The sun was low and straight in their eyes but it couldn't hide the beauty of Catawba Point, the other place Grant had only heard about.

"We ain't fired up the barbecues yet, but you won't be disappointed."

John Carter came over from the SUV once the convoy pulled in at the overlook. The leader had introduced himself before setting off from Notebook Trail, and Grant got the impression that stopping on the edge of the woods was purely to let Grant see the difference between the abandoned housing development of Notebook Trail and the most certainly not abandoned complex before him. Grant played along.

"It's not a disappointment so far."

Carter nodded his appreciation.

"Life's not all black and white. But this here's what you can achieve when you're organized and white."

He waved a hand around the clearing.

"I'd say this proves we're organized."

Grant nodded.

"And there's no arguing you're white."

Carter smiled.

"I knew you were a kindred spirit. Although I don't advocate throwing black fellas off the balcony. We're more of a peace-loving movement."

Grant looked at Carter.

"That why you took the high ground with twelve armed men and the sun at your back?"

Carter shrugged.

"We didn't shoot nobody."

Grant smiled.

"I didn't throw nobody off the balcony neither."

Carter laughed. The badly dubbed Italians didn't join in this time. He slapped Grant on the back and moved back to the SUV.

"Of course you didn't. Come on. Let me show you around."

Catawba Point was two acres of grassland surrounded by dense woods and nudging up against a backwater inlet of the Catawba River that went nowhere. The dying sun sprinkled jewels over the waters and threw long shadows across the rolling lawns. The setting was idyllic, the atmosphere calm and peaceful and borderline loving. No, not borderline. Between the women washing clothes by the river and the men doing chores around the outbuildings, this was an Amish community without the funny hats and beards. Everybody moved with slow, deliberate steps and nobody had a harsh word to say about anything. Except black fellas.

The main house was a two-story cabin with stripped wood panels and a green-tiled roof. Two dormer bedrooms either side of a central extension broke the angle of the roof facing the river. A wide raised porch overlooked a wooden jetty that jutted out into the bejeweled waters. There was a cluster of smaller houses to the south beneath an occasional stand of trees for shade. A barn and storage shed took pride of place next to a gravel turnaround that formed the hub of the complex. Several bungalows fanned out to the north near the treeline. Washing hung limp in the dry evening air. A Stars & Stripes tried to find some breeze at the top of a flagpole beside the main house, but the air was as still and lifeless as the compound seemed full of life. If these were white supremacists, they were the most domesticated white supremacists Grant had ever seen.

Apart from the guns.

"You look like you could do with freshening up. I apologize."

Carter drew the tour to a close.

"Let's find you a room so you can get a shower and change your clothes."

He led Grant up the stairs onto the porch and threw a friendly wave at a woman coming up from the river. The woman beamed a smile, then lowered her head when she saw Grant watching. Carter stood at the railing and took a deep, satisfied breath. This was a man at ease with his surroundings and not embarrassed to show it.

"You just came to heaven for dinner."

Grant could find no argument against that. He nodded and followed Carter into the house. There were more women preparing food in the kitchen. They all stopped and smiled at Grant. The welcome was complete. Carter led Grant up a wide central staircase that branched off onto balconies at either side. Carter took the left balcony and spoke over his shoulder.

"Guest rooms have their own bathrooms."

He gave Grant a quick once over. "I'm guessing you're extra-large. I'll have Millie bring you some clothes." He then opened a door off the corridor.

"You'll hear the bell when dinner's ready."

The bedroom was ablaze with evening sunlight. There was a king-size bed, a chest of drawers, and a heavy wooden wardrobe. A narrow door to the right led to the bathroom and toilet. Lace curtains diffused the light through the open windows. The room smelled of freshly cut grass and lilac. Carter ushered Grant in but stood in the doorway.

"Big Dog don't get in 'til the morning. He's looking forward to meeting you."

Grant looked at Carter.

"I thought you were in charge."

Carter raised his eyebrows.

"Me? Hell no. I'm just a fisherman to the carpenter."

Grant slipped out of the windcheater and dropped it on the bed.

"A fisherman with a .45 automatic."

Carter smiled and proved he knew his movies as well as his tactics.

"Well, barramundi is a bloody big fish."

The Australian accent was a bit off but the smile was pure *Crocodile Dundee*. He nodded and stepped outside. The door closed with a thud, leaving Grant to soak up an atmosphere that was as surreal as it was peaceful, but he couldn't shake the feeling that he was a captive in a mink-lined prison.

THIRTY-FIVE

The shower was better than a prison shower and safer than the one Leroy had supposedly slipped in. There was nobody looking to snap Grant's neck, and he didn't have to worry about bending over for the soap. The No Entry tattoo at the base of Grant's spine glistened as he rinsed the soap off and washed his hair. The woman who had brought Grant a change of clothes also left a disposable razor and a folding toothbrush. It felt like he'd gone back in time. New clothes and throwaway toiletries and a mirror that didn't steam up because of the ambient temperature.

By the time he toweled down in the bedroom, he felt bright and fresh and clean all over despite not having slept since the night before last. The sun had dipped below the horizon and the fiery glow turned the lace curtains red. The smell of barbecue coals being stoked drifted through the window. Grant drew back the curtain and looked out.

The porch was a hive of activity, the extended wooden deck busy with women putting salad and vegetables on collapsible serving tables. The barbecue pit was down the slope on the right, a leveled patch of grass shielded from the river by a stand of trees and an uneven rockery wall. There were three heavy-duty barbecues, the kind that American men liked to dominate because it was the only time they did the cooking. Some men in Yorkshire as well. Meat sizzled. Flames spat. The smells were mouth-watering.

Grant leaned out of the window and craned his neck to look round the side of the house. He could just make out the first couple of picnic tables and the lanterns strung between the trees and the porch. Colored lights danced in the evening breeze, a gentle offshore wind that was as warm and dry as the rest of Charlotte. There were no parked cars because they were around the front. He'd seen them earlier, along with cars parked at each of the bungalows and the other houses to the south. No red panel van, not that he'd expected it to be here, but he'd bet a pound to a pinch of shit that the driver came from Catawba Point.

He closed the window and unwrapped the towel from around his waist. The fresh clothes were laid on the bed: a pair of desert combat trousers and a khaki T-shirt. Unlike Leroy's 101st Airborne patch, Grant doubted these had seen combat. The thing about white supremacists is they nearly always inhabited a world of wannabe hunters and failed soldiers. Grant considered putting his own clothes back on but didn't think that was the best way to get on Carter's good side. Reusing his socks but going commando, he pulled on the combat pants and was about to unfold the T-shirt when his phone started vibrating. He looked at the caller ID and frowned. This was either good news or bad. He pressed answer.

"You just can't keep out of trouble, can you?"

Evelyn's voice was like a breath of fresh air. Grant smiled even though she couldn't see him.

"I try. Why, what's happened now?"

Evelyn laughed down the phone.

"Apart from stealing an ambulance and running over a burns victim?"

Grant sat on the edge of the bed and wished Evelyn was with him.

"I didn't run her over."

"You hospitalized her."

"She was already hospitalized."

The bed was clean and inviting and not just for sleep. It felt sad to be talking with a sexy woman who was half a city away and unlikely to be available before he flew back to England. Evelyn must have been thinking the same thing.

"You going to manage dinner again before you fly away home?"

Grant thought about Yates telling him he wasn't going to make his flight so at least that gave him some hope, but tonight wasn't the night.

"Absolutely."

"You free tonight?"

Grant let out a sigh.

"I'd love to. But something came up. Looks like I'm going to be busy."

"Looks like?"

"Am. Delicate situation."

"Delicate how?"

Grant looked out the window where a bunch of white supremacists were preparing to feast him while keeping their guns under the table.

"Delicate like trying not to piss off the guys who petrol-bombed my room and tried to kidnap Nona from the hospital."

Evelyn couldn't hide her concern.

"They've got you?"

"They invited me to a barbecue."

Evelyn went quiet for a moment then tried to lighten the tone.

"Make sure you're not the main course."

Grant shifted on the bed.

"Oh, I'm pretty sure I am the main course. For them to see what I know and what I plan to do about it."

"What do you know?"

"Not much. Lots of suspicions."

Grant took the phone away from his ear and looked at it before raising it and talking again.

"Can you track my phone?"

Evelyn chuckled.

"You think I'm the CIA again?"

Grant lowered his voice.

"You're my IT backup."

Evelyn paused while she considered that, then spoke into Grant's ear.

"If we activate Find My Phone."

Grant shrugged.

"How do we do that?"

Evelyn explained in words of one syllable but even then it was complete gobbledegook. It took Grant five minutes to follow her instructions before she pronounced herself satisfied.

"I've got you. Over by the river?"

Grant nodded.

"Catawba Point. It's like a holiday camp for white supremacists."

"They must love balcony-throwers like you then."

"I think that helped."

Grant leaned back on one hand and sighed.

"You sound like you're right next to me."

"I told you it was a great signal over there. I'll bet the steaks are good too."

Grant looked at the window again.

"Rather be at The Cowbell. I've gone from cargo pants to combat trousers."

He thought about the burger restaurant and the motel and the charger he'd given to Evelyn. Loose and easy linkage that led to his next question.

"Did you manage to trace the laptop owner?"

There was the sound of rustling paper before Evelyn answered.

"Fake name. Unless one of our founding presidents got reincarnated and bought a computer."

The smell of cooked meat was strong even through the closed window. The dying light of day changed to the colored lights from the lanterns on the lace curtains. A sharp ringing noise sounded outside, the metal striker rattling around the heavy triangle hanging over the barbecue pit. Carter had been right, there was no mistaking the dinner bell. Grant stood up and straightened his back. He was about to say goodbye when another thought struck him.

"Do they have a Find My Laptop thingy we can hack?"

Evelyn rustled papers as she put them away.

"Won't need to. You're probably going to be sitting right next to him."

The dinner bell stopped ringing. Evelyn put a full stop to the conversation.

"The president didn't hide his registered address. It's shown as Paschall Road. At Catawba Point."

THIRTY-SIX

In Grant's experience, the best way to keep a secret was to not talk with anybody about anything because if you do, sooner or later you're going to let something slip. The more people that know the secret, the more chances there were of somebody slipping up. Half the people at the Catawba Point barbecue knew what they were trying to hide, so it was no surprise that hints were given, no matter how much they tried to keep it to themselves.

"Glad you could make it. I was about to send out a search party."

Carter stood on the rear deck directing people to the salad trays before sending them over to the barbecue pit to collect their choice of steak, chicken, or sausage.

"You get lost coming out the bathroom?"

Grant came through the patio doors and looked at the deputy leader.

"Have to be careful in there. Don't want to slip in the shower."

Carter barked a laugh.

"Yeah. You're pretty slick with showers, ain't you?"

Grant looked at Carter to see if he was testing him.

"That wasn't me."

Carter kept a steady eye on Grant.

"And it wasn't you threw him off the balcony either, huh?"

There was a moment of locked eyes and stern expressions, then the moment passed. Carter gave Grant his best Crocodile Dundee smile and waved him toward the stack of plates.

"Help yourself to salad or vegetables."

He pointed toward the pit where the barbecues were spitting fire.

"The boys have plenty of meat over there."

He handed Grant a plate and a napkin.

"Beer's in the cooler if that's your poison."

Grant nodded his thanks and took the plate to the nearest fold-out table. Using a pair of salad tongs, he put lettuce and tomatoes and peppers on his plate. He squeezed honey and mustard dressing over the salad from a plastic bottle then went down the porch stairs.

The meat was enticing as it spat and sizzled. Grant was aware of it as he crossed the lawn but what he was wondering was if having a pimply arse meant you had spots on your face.

The picnic tables fell neatly into two categories: men and women who were obviously couples sitting in one group and single men at the other tables. Grant wasn't part of a couple, so he joined the men. Some of the men weren't much more than boys in grownup clothes. Some were a bit more grizzled, like John Carter. Carter split from the woman he was sitting with and came over to Grant's table.

"If there's one thing your black man don't understand, it's a good barbecue."

Grant was halfway through the most succulent steak he'd ever tasted.

"You saying black men can't cook?"

Carter shrugged.

"Oh, they can cook. But they only play at barbecue."

He leaned forward as if sharing a confidence.

"I bet they don't have many barbecues at the White House.

Now we got Obama running the show."

Grant sliced a piece of chicken.

"They had barbecues before?"

Carter slapped the table.

"Hell yes. All the time. Over where Marine One lands."

Grant spoke between chews.

"The helicopter on the White House lawn?"

Carter nodded.

"To the side near the trees. You think Obama has his friends round for barbecue steaks? Shit. I doubt he knows his ranch dressing from Paul Newman's Own."

Grant took a drink of iced Coca Cola.

"Notebook Trail certainly didn't have a barbecue pit."

Carter stabbed a slice of sausage.

"You see, that's what I'm talking about. Leroy couldn't find his ass with both hands, never mind run a family barbecue. That place was a fool's errand."

Grant smiled.

"Nowhere for Marine One to land either."

Carter chewed his sausage.

"Wouldn't surprise me if Obama wasn't thick as thieves with all them black ex-military. All that Tuskegee Airmen shit."

He prodded a finger at the table.

"You start loading the military with blacks and you giving them a leg up they won't stop taking until they humping your momma."

Grant went back to slicing steak.

"I wouldn't like that."

Carter was getting the bit between his teeth.

"Damn right. Weren't no white girl Leroy was pimping out of his room. And it weren't no white ass you threw off the balcony. Tuskegee Airmen that, Leroy."

Grant paused with a fork of steak halfway to his mouth.

"He sure could fly though."

Carter laughed at the first admission from Grant.

"No wonder he torched your room. Damn fool. Right in the flight path, you know? Idiot."

The other diners at the table paused and looked at Carter, then quickly got back to eating. Nobody dared speak. Carter patted Grant's arm.

"You're due out tomorrow, ain't you?"

Grant nodded. This wasn't the time to mention being delayed. The other men at the table paused again, warning looks passing between them. Carter didn't seem to notice.

"You might want to hold off for a few days."

He didn't wink, but the look on his face came close to it.

"Fire in the flight path puts everyone on high alert."

A big guy at the next table stood up abruptly and knocked his beer across the gap. He came over and picked the glass up and stared at Carter.

"Sorry, boss. Need to be more careful."

Carter looked dazed for a moment, then blinked his eyes as if clearing his head. The other diners watched the deputy leader with worried eyes. Carter looked up at the big guy with the bad case of acne scars.

"No problem. Let's keep it tight."

Both men nodded. The big guy turned away. He didn't look like a computer nerd, but Grant wondered if he had acne scars on his backside.

THIRTY-SEVEN

The barbecue settled into an uneasy mix of small talk and silence. At least at Grant's table. There was mention of fishing and hunting and keeping the bloodline pure. Grant took that to mean not sleeping with black ladies, a stance that the guy with the pimply arse he'd seen in Nona's room didn't seem to share. There was no more talk about flight paths and fires or delaying Grant's flight home. In the absence of further disclosure, Carter's slip took on more significance.

"So, you're a cop, huh?"

A skinny blond kid not much out of his teens spoke from the far corner of the picnic table. Opposite side to Grant. He had the tanned, clean good looks of a sports star but was too slight for football—not soccer, but the American kind with all the shoulder pads and helmets. Grant put him as a baseball guy.

"Up in Boston. Yeah."

The kid slid along the bench seat until he was opposite Grant.

"I bet you seen some action then, haven't you?"

Grant pushed bits of food around his plate.

"I prefer to talk things out. Saves a lot of trouble."

The blue eyes and blond hair wouldn't have gone amiss in the Hitler youth.

"Some folks ain't big on talking things out."

He leaned forward over his plate.

"Now, you take your average black man. Ain't no talking him down. Otherwise, you wouldn't have had to throw him off the balcony."

Grant laid his knife and fork across his plate. He'd had enough.

"Has that story been printed in a local comic book? Because I don't remember that many people being around at the time."

The kid held his hands up.

"Just saying, is all. Thing of legend. What with all that Resurrection Man stuff as well. You're a celebrity around here."

Grant took a deep breath, then blew out his cheeks.

"Yeah well, it's kinda wearing thin. The celebrity thing."

He flattened one hand on the table then motioned like a plane taking off.

"I'm just passing through."

The kid stuck a hand out for Grant to shake.

"Glad I got a chance to meet you. We need more like you."

Grant shook it and waved his other hand to indicate everything around him.

"Doesn't seem like you're short of manpower."

The kid followed Grant's gesture.

"True. But passive don't get as much attention."

Grant leaned forward and lowered his voice.

"Twelve men with guns. That got my attention."

The kid gave Grant an aw-shucks laugh.

"Oh, the guns is just for hunting."

Grant raised an eyebrow.

"Didn't look like hunting guns."

The kid smiled.

"Depends what you hunt."

Grant nodded toward the other houses.

"You live here the whole time?"

The kid sat up straight and puffed his chest out.

"Pretty much. Once you've been inducted. This is a safe community. All white. No trouble. Big Dog keeps it that way."

Grant pushed his plate aside.

"The fella that's coming in tomorrow?"

Pride swelled the kid's chest.

"Cornelius Stout the third. Big Dog. Yes, sir."

"That's quite a mouthful."

"He's quite a handful."

It was the kid's turn to wave his hand around.

"Formed all this so nobody has to handle him."

Grant nodded.

"That's mighty fine of him."

The kid nodded back.

"He's a mighty fine man."

The barbecue flames were dying, and some of the diners had drifted away. The warm air and a full stomach began to work their magic. The lack of sleep began to catch up on him as well. Grant nodded at the kid, then gathered his plate and stood up. He turned to say goodnight to Carter, but he had gone. So had the big guy with the acne scars.

Grant scanned the thinning crowd but couldn't see them. The kid noticed and stood up too. The distraction was complete. Carter had got away. Grant held his plate up and deployed his own distraction.

"I'll just get rid of these and call it a night."

He turned away and went in search of the waste bin, mingling with the crowd while scanning their faces. He looked for height and bulk and the familiar acne scars. It was full dark now, but the colored lanterns lit the scene and a full moon dusted the rest of the clearing. It glinted off the waters out beyond the jetty.

The jetty is where he found them. Two silhouettes stood out against the moon glow. Carter's was the more obvious. The body language was fairly plain as well. A heated discussion and the complete antithesis of the calm the community tried to engender. A motorboat cruised past in the distance, breaking the waters into a million sparkles of moonlight. The silhouettes faced off.

Grant dumped his plate on the nearest table and walked toward a stand of trees near the jetty.

"And you had to bring him here now. Of all times."

Carter balked at the big guy's implications.

"Wouldn't have had to bring him at all if you'd kept your dick in your pants."

The big guy stood tall and thumped his chest twice.

"Without me, this don't work. So my dick will go where it wants."

Carter stepped forward and stuck his chin out.

"There's no crash without Crash. Is that it?"

Crash nodded.

"Damn right."

Carter jerked a thumb toward the riverside community.

"Well, remember this. The crash don't matter if we start laying down with the mud people. Purity above everything."

He let out a sigh and then held his hands out in a placating motion.

"You don't want to be the nail that lost the shoe."

Crash laughed.

"Oh, stop it with the sermonizing. We ain't lost a horse or a battle or the war. We lost a black hooker and her pimp."

Carter stepped in close and stood face-to-face.

"And the element of surprise."

He held a hand up to the sky.

"A fire in the flight path? That's real smart."

Crash backed down. His shoulders sagged.

"I might have overreacted."

Carter stepped forward again, and Crash took a step back.

"Overreacted? And you've got guys chasing around the hospital."

He prodded a finger at Crash's forehead.

"What the fuck were you thinking?"

Crash shrugged.

"Damage control."

Carter shook his head.

"You stick to your keyboard. I'll perform damage control."

Crash nodded and started to turn away. Carter reached out and stopped him.

"Is that everything? There's nothing else you're not telling me, is there?"

Crash stood erect, too eager to answer.

"Hell no. Promise."

They both turned and began to walk back along the jetty. Carter patted Crash on the back as the silhouettes moved out of the moon glow.

"Leave me to square this with Big Dog. Damage limitation is his specialty."

Grant moved back into the trees and waited for the men to walk up the lawn toward the house. When he came out the other side, the world was lit with festive lanterns and moonlight. He skirted the barbecue pit and headed for the porch steps. His mind replayed the conversation and struggled with the implications. Mostly he was thinking about a fire in a motel room not being big enough to trouble Charlotte Douglas Airport. But he thought he knew a place that would.

DAY THREE

THIRTY-EIGHT

Gunshots broke the silence and startled Grant awake. Sunlight blazed outside the lace curtains but didn't shine through the window because the midmorning sun was on the other side of the house. Grant rolled over in bed and forced his eyes open. He'd slept heavy and had to claw himself out of the coma. He checked his watch. It was a little after nine.

The gunshots sounded again, a ragged volley in the distance followed by sporadic returning fire. Not hunters stalking game, gunmen stalking each other. He remembered the kid from last night commenting on the guns Grant had mentioned not looking like hunting guns. "Depends what you hunt." Grant wondered what they were hunting this morning. He swung his legs out of bed and waited for his balance to return. The room was already warm, not that it had cooled down much overnight, and Grant needed to freshen up.

The knock on the door stopped him halfway to the bathroom. Wrapping the towel round his waist, he went to the door. If they were going to shoot him, he doubted they'd do it in his room.

"How d'you like to join the boys on maneuvers?"

Carter stood in the hallway but didn't ask to come in. Grant indicated the towel.

"You mind if I get dressed first?"

Carter looked at the scars on Grant's chest.

"I wish you would. Don't want you scaring 'em with your army past."

Grant kept hold of the towel.

"Nothing to be scared of. I was a typist."

Carter nodded.

"Yeah, I remember that from the news. D'you think anyone believed that?"

Grant shrugged.

"Probably not. But I can type."

"I'm sure you can do lots of things. Be nice for my boys to test themselves against a real-life war hero."

Grant shook his head.

"A hero is a sandwich. I just did my job."

Carter smiled.

"Well get your pants on, chief. See if you can do a job for us."

He waved a hand back along the corridor.

"Millie's rustling up some breakfast. I'll call the boys back in."

He turned and headed for the stairs. Grant closed the door and headed for the shower. He had a feeling it was going to be a long day.

Showered, shaved, and teeth brushed. Grant wished he could go back to the Sleepy Nook Inn and get some fresh clothes of his own, but if the Catawba Point supremacists wanted to play soldiers, the combat pants were probably better suited. He pulled on the khaki T-shirt then fastened his shoes. The shooting had stopped while he was in the shower. That didn't make him feel any better. He was still behind enemy lines with a bunch of gung-ho wannabe soldiers who wanted to rid America of the black menace. He wasn't sure which side of the fence they saw Grant as being on. Especially after the conversation he'd overheard last night. "And you had to bring him here now. Of all times." That didn't bode well for having a pleasant trek in the woods.

Grant wondered about the "now of all times" part and the suggestion that he might want to delay flying home. He also thought about damage limitation being Big Dog's specialty. Cornelius Stout the third. He checked his watch, almost ten o'clock. It didn't look as if Big Dog was due to arrive before the military maneuvers. What would happen after that was anyone's guess. Like he'd thought before, Grant didn't like guessing games. He picked up his phone from the bedside cabinet and hit last-caller redial. Evelyn answered after three rings.

"They didn't barbecue you then."

Grant sighed at the sound of her voice.

"The day's still young."

Shop noises sounded behind Evelyn's voice.

"They planning another one today?"

Grant sat on the edge of the bed.

"They're planning a hunting party. And I think I'm the fox."

"Fox?"

"Oh, yeah. You don't have foxhunts over here, do you? Hare and hounds kind of thing. Jolly toffs in redcoats riding around the countryside. D'ye ken John Peel? All that stuff."

"I have no idea what you just said."

Grant looked at the sunlight outside the window. The lace curtains turned everything white, something that would no doubt please the anti-black stance of the white supremacists returning from the woods.

"When your good-ole American boys go hunting. Whatever it is they hunt. I think I'm standing in for it."

Gravel crunched under tires round the front of the house. A kettle boiled down in the kitchen. Somewhere to the east, a jet plane roared off the runway at Charlotte Douglas Airport. The sound made Grant's decision for him.

"I'm going to call you every two hours."

Evelyn laughed down the phone.

"That's nice of you."

Grant ignored the levity in her voice.

"Keep track of my phone."

He stood up and went to the window. Drawing back the lace curtain, he looked outside. A line of men came out of the trees to the north and walked across the grass toward the barbecue pit. All in combat gear. All carrying guns.

"If I don't call in."

He considered how much to tell her, how much of what he suspected he could expect her to believe. At the end of the day, though, it wasn't Evelyn he needed to convince.

"If I miss once, there's somebody I want you to call."

He stepped back from the window and told her what he wanted her to do.

THIRTY-NINE

The hunting party gathered after breakfast. Breakfast for Grant that is, because they'd already been playing soldiers since dawn. Grant felt like the condemned man being given a hearty meal. He followed the military rulebook and made sure he fueled up because once the battle starts you never know when you're going to eat again. This wasn't the breakfast rush at Hardee's.

"How's this work? You count to ten then shout 'Coming, ready or not'?"

Grant stood on the porch and zipped up his bright yellow wind-cheater. Carter leaned against the railing at the top of the back steps.

"I think we can make it more interesting than that."

He indicated the twelve men who'd been with him yesterday at Notebook Trail.

"We'll stay round back here and give you half an hour head start."

He jerked a thumb toward the river.

"Of course, you can't go west, but everything else is woods. Plenty of cover."

Grant looked at the river.

"I could swim for it."

Carter shook his head.

"That'd be a naval exercise. This here is military maneuvers."

Grant turned to Carter.

"Me being ex-military."

"You being The Resurrection Man."

"You think I'm going to need resurrecting?"

Carter shrugged.

"I think hunting is a dangerous game."

Grant wasn't offered a weapon. He wasn't given a compass or supplies. This was a chance for the white supremacists to have something to hunt that could fight back. They just didn't want the fighting back to include being shot at. The lanterns from last night swayed in a gentle offshore breeze that didn't help cool the day. The Stars & Stripes flapped atop the flagpole. A wisp of dust swirled in the turnaround out front of the barn and storage shed. The men stayed at the bottom of the steps. Carter waved a hand for Grant to set off.

"Coming, ready or not."

Grant turned left at the bottom of the steps and jogged round the side of the house heading south. As soon as he was out of sight he turned north and sprinted toward the bungalows. He glanced over his shoulder to make sure nobody was watching, then un-zipped the windcheater as he approached the nearest bungalow. Without slowing, he snatched a faded green combat jacket off the washing line and turned east into the woods.

Branches snapped and foliage was bent as he crashed through the undergrowth. He wasn't trying to be quiet, just fast. He needed to put as much distance between him and the trackers before Carter finished counting to ten. With twelve against one, this wasn't about finding a good place to fight but rather not fighting at all. The best way to do that was to not get caught. In the woods surrounding Catawba Point, that was going to be dif-ficult. Carter's men had been hunting in these woods for years. They knew them like the back of their hands. The only places Grant knew were the entrance road and the cell phone tower. He headed for the cell phone tower.

Ten minutes.

The undergrowth tugged at his legs and low branches whipped his face. He kept one arm up in front of his eyes to protect them but didn't slow down. He crashed through the trees and let them snag his windcheater. The more damage the better. The flimsy material tore easily. A pocket was ripped off. The zip broke. Grant threw the torn pocket aside and used his fingers to make the other tears bigger. He crested a ridge and plunged into a shallow trough. The uneven ground slowed him down but he kept heading east, searching the trees for signs of the entrance road.

Twenty minutes.

He came out of the other side of the trough and veered right. Not a sharp right but enough to intercept the road as it twisted and turned through the woods. He tore another swatch of cloth from the windcheater and tossed it aside. The summer jacket was just a big yellow rag now. He saw the road through the trees and angled toward it. The trees hugged the road. Good.

Thirty minutes.

Coming, ready or not.

Grant burst through the trees onto the narrow road and stopped. He stripped off the remnants of the windcheater and put the combat jacket on, fastening it tight. Twelve angry men would now be tracking from the bungalow and snapped branches. Coming this way. They wanted to play soldiers. Grant turned toward them and nodded. Enough running. If they wanted to play, he'd play.

The first thing Grant did was snap off a few small branches and pull up some more foliage. He scattered them on the road where he'd come out of the trees and set a thinning trail along the tarmac toward the cell phone tower. Not too obvious but hard to miss. He scuffed some of the leaves into the ground to show he'd run over them on his way out of Catawba Point, then carefully retraced his steps until he was past the broken branches.

He walked back ten yards to the first bend in the road, then found space between the trees where he could safely melt into the woods without disturbing the branches. The first rule of camouflage was to break up the human body shape. Once he was far enough into the woods, he pulled up some of the tangled undergrowth that wouldn't show from the road and jammed them into the collar and chest cavity of the combat jacket. He stuffed the folded windcheater inside the zipper so it was hidden; the hunting party would be looking for a man wearing bright yellow, especially since swatches of cloth had been torn off in the woods. He blackened his face with dirt, then lay flat behind a dense patch of undergrowth and trees.

Fifteen minutes later he heard the first sounds of approaching hunters. They weren't being quiet. They weren't observing the golden rule of silent combat; talk by sign language and don't give your position away. The Catawba Point supremacists were working from their country-boy rulebook. Bitch and moan and have a good laugh. This was supposed to be fun.

"Aw, come on. How hard can it be?"

There was the sound of snapping branches and rustling bushes.

"You couldn't hit a barn door at twenty paces."

"Bullshit. I could take the eyebrows off a rabbit at twenty paces."

"Fuck off, man. Until you get that prescription upgraded you couldn't even see a rabbit at twenty paces."

There were more rustling noises and a complete lack of silence protocol. The hunting party was approaching on a broad front, crashing through the undergrowth like a herd of elephants. They might know the woods, but this wasn't shooting at targets or stalking each other. They didn't seem to appreciate the difference between friendly banter and shooting to kill. They hadn't reached that point yet.

"Yeah, well, he ain't no rabbit. I could hit him with my eyes shut."

Somebody laughed. A couple of others joined in.

"That last time? I think you *were* shooting with your eyes shut."

The noises drew closer. Louder. Then they were past Grant way to his left and approaching the road.

"Go fuck yourself."

Somebody made a squealing noise.

"Ah'm gonna make you squeal like a pig."

There was the sound of somebody thumping a shoulder.

"That weren't even funny in the movie."

"Hold up. Here's another piece."

The man up front held up a bright yellow swatch of windcheater, then the men burst out of the woods onto the road and stopped. Grant could see them through a gap in the trees. There was a lot of milling around and looking at the ground. Some looked into the woods either side of the road. A couple followed the diminishing trail toward the cell phone tower. Nobody looked back toward Catawba Point. Why would they? Their prey was trying to get away from the white supremacists, not fall straight back into their hands.

"He must have been a desert soldier, 'cause he sure as shit don't know the woods. Guess he figures to be quicker on the straight."

One of them counted heads.

"What's holding that kid up? He lost again?"

The one bringing up the rear waved a dismissive hand.

"Probably helping JC get ready for Big Dog."

Grant kept his head down in case anybody looked back for the missing kid. He watched from a low angle with foliage sticking up all around him. The group conferred one last time, then the spokesman made an attempt at military leadership by pointing at his eyes then holding a hand out flat along the road.

"Let's pick it up. Don't want to be out here all day."

The hunting party set off toward the cell phone tower and the turn-in from Walkers Ferry Road. The banter didn't stop so much as fade into the distance. Five minutes later, they disappeared around the next bend in the road.

Grant waited until he was sure they weren't going to double back before pushing himself up into a crouch. The woods fell into an uneasy silence. He listened for a few minutes, letting the silence build into the natural rhythms of a forest. Not silence at all but birds and wildlife and the constant movement of trees and branches and wind. He let the hunting party build a good solid lead, then stood up slowly.

All this hunting and stalking was okay for playing at soldiers, but the main thing about combat is doing the unpredictable. Grant's instructors had delighted in telling him that even the best military plans fell apart as soon as the first shot was fired. The hunting party was tracking a man through the woods. That was fine if you were out in the wilds. Catawba Point was maybe two miles from an international airport and just a few miles from Downtown Charlotte. Grant didn't need to trek through the woods. He was going to steal a car.

FORTY

Grand theft auto is one thing, but you have to get to the auto before you can steal it. Grant was half a mile from the Catawba Point commune along the winding entrance road. Perhaps a bit less as the crow flies. Taking a straight line would mean hacking through the woods again. He'd had enough of hacking his way through the woods. He was going to take the easy way. Along the road.

He flexed his knees and stretched his back to get the stiffness out after being laid in the undergrowth for so long. The trees around him were thick and heavily leafed. He stood amid the dense foliage and pulled the camouflage out of his combat jacket. The branches irritated his neck, and he rubbed the itch until it eased. He hunched his shoulders and twisted his head one way, then the other. The bones in his neck grated and cracked. The loud crack behind him wasn't his neck.

The kid from the barbecue last night had been quieter than the others until he stood on the dry twig. The wood snapped like a gunshot in the quiet, spinning Grant round in a flash and bringing the kid up short. He jerked his head up from watching the ground just in time to see Grant's elbow slam across his jaw. The gun he was holding loosely at his side flew upwards and out and went sailing through the air. It dropped with a rustle of bushes into dense undergrowth beyond the trees.

Grant stepped behind him and clamped his neck in a headlock. The kid went red in the face as Grant applied pressure to the illegal chokehold. Five seconds later, his legs went limp and Grant lowered him to the ground. He checked the kid's pockets for car keys but came up empty. That would have been too easy. Using the fingers of one hand, he pressed them into the kid's throat to feel his pulse. It was strong and healthy, his breathing coming in ragged gasps. Down but not completely out.

The woods fell back into their own version of silence. Constant creaking and swaying sprinkled with birdsong and woodland creatures. Grant tore a strip off the already ragged windcheater and balled it in the kid's mouth. He tied another strip around his head to keep it in place, making sure he didn't block his nose. He wanted to keep him quiet, not suffocate him. He yanked the kid's jacket down off his shoulders to clamp his arms and used his belt to tie his legs. Nothing the kid wouldn't be able to get out of eventually but enough to buy Grant some time. He didn't waste any looking for the gun in the undergrowth, setting off toward the commune at a jog instead.

Two bends later he came out at the overlook and stopped.

"Oh, shit."

All the cars had gone.

Grant scanned the two acres of grassland and the clusters of buildings. There were no cars parked out front of the bungalows to the north or the houses to the south. There was nothing parked behind the main house or in the dust and gravel turnaround where Grant had heard wheels crunching this morning. The road he'd just come along was the only way in or out, and nobody had driven past while he'd charged through the woods. The convoy he'd arrived in had to be here somewhere.

He checked again, paying as much attention to movement as

looking for the cars. This would all be for naught if John Carter saw him crossing the grass and shot him where he stood. There was no movement. Whatever activity was going on preparing for the arrival of Big Dog must have been at the back of the main house. That made sense. You don't welcome your supreme leader with a bungalow and a washing line.

None of the houses had carports or garages. There were no driveways round the back of the buildings. That only left the barn and the storage shed at the turnaround. The storage shed wasn't big enough. Grant set off down the slope to the barn, keeping his eyes peeled for anyone looking out of the windows from the main house or the satellite buildings.

He stopped at the side of the barn, out of sight from the other buildings, and listened. Grant never underestimated the value of sound. It was often the first thing you noticed before seeing anything. There was no sound inside the barn.

Stepping round the front, he went to the main doors. They weren't locked. This was an enclosed community; they didn't need to lock their doors. He opened the left-hand door a few inches and looked inside. He nodded his satisfaction. This wasn't a barn. It was the motor pool.

Grant stepped inside and closed the door. The floor space held five vehicles including the pickup and the SUV from his arrival convoy. The big American car he'd ridden in was parked against the far wall. Two of the cars had their hoods up for servicing. There was a workbench along one side and shelves containing tools and oil and cleaning products. A glass-fronted office took up one corner next to the big car, but Grant doubted the repair shop needed to keep records like the Citgo near the Sleepy Nook Inn. Before Brubaker turned the repair bays into a meeting hall.

The cars were parked two abreast and three deep. The office and the big car took up the third tier. The front row held a rusty foreign car and the pickup. Grant chose the pickup. He was getting used to borrowing people's flatbacks. He wondered if this one had a Satnav.

What it didn't have was keys in the ignition. Grant tried behind the sun visor and in the glove box. No keys. Nothing. He looked around for a screwdriver and found one on the workbench. The steering column was textured plastic with the ignition barrel jutting out of one side. He ran his fingers around the back and gave the cover a gentle pull. There was no give. The column was solid. He jammed the screwdriver in behind the cover and tried again. Still solid but there was a little movement. He gripped the handle tight then paused.

Why bother with an office if you aren't going to use it? Maybe for servicing records and maintenance? Vehicle details and registration? And car keys.

Grant took the screwdriver out from behind the steering column and crossed to the office. He opened the door and looked around the narrow space. There was a desk and a cupboard and some inspirational sayings on the back wall. The thing that inspired Grant was the key rack above the desk. The Catawba Point militia were as organized as they were insular. The key hooks were arranged in the same order as the parking spaces. There was even a floor plan with a little square denoting the office. He didn't have to check the make of the pickup to find the keys that matched. All he had to do was find the right space and, bingo.

Grant smiled and took the keys. He checked that the pickup would start, then left the engine running and walked to the front doors. He opened them a few inches to look outside. This wasn't the snowplow bus in *Where Eagles Dare*. He wasn't going to crash through the doors and skid across the turnaround. Once he was satisfied there was nobody waiting to ambush him, he opened both doors wide and committed grand theft auto.

FORTY-ONE

Once he was out of the barn, there was no avoiding putting his foot down and beating a hasty retreat. The wheels spat gravel and raised a cloud of dust as the pickup skidded left on the turn-around and sped up the hill past the overlook onto the entrance road. The trees swallowed him immediately, blocking out the powder blue sky and the sunlight.

Everything was green. The woods and the undergrowth and even the light were all tinged with green. The tarmac fought to add a hint of grey but even that was contaminated by everything around it. The bright yellow windcheater was a thing of the past. The faded combat jacket still had snatches of foliage he hadn't fully cleared. Grant eased his foot off the gas after the first bend. He didn't want the hunting party to hear the urgency in the motor approaching when he caught up with them.

A crow squawked and flew across the road.

The twists and turns of the road forced Grant to slow even more until he was driving at a pedestrian pace more in keeping with a funeral procession than a getaway. He passed the trees where the kid was tied up. There was no sign of movement. Grant looked through the side window and caught a glimpse of the bound figure in the undergrowth. Then he drove through the false trail he'd set after coming out of the woods. Everything up ahead was now a threat. There were no friendlies from here on out.

A deer wandered out of the trees twenty yards in front of him and stopped at the sound of the pickup. Grant slowed to a crawl. The deer looked at him. Grant looked at the deer. There was a moment of clarity between two animals that were constantly under siege. There was deadwood along the side of the road, storm damage pulled aside long ago to the clear the way. Grant stopped the pickup. The deer stared at him a few seconds longer, then ambled off into the woods. Grant watched it go but didn't slip the pickup into gear. He looked at the space where the deer had stood and let out a sigh. He nodded once, then set off again. A bit faster this time but still not at breakneck speed.

Grant kept his eyes peeled for movement up ahead. The ragged platoon of hunters couldn't be far away now. He moved through the gears until the pickup was hitting forty. Too fast for the winding road but not fast enough for Grant's liking. The hunting party might think they were tracking a man in a yellow windcheater, but they weren't blind. They'd see it was Grant driving as soon as they looked through the windshield. He put his foot down.

Forty-five.

A better pace but not getaway speed. The bend rushing toward him was more like a moderate curve in the road. He added weight to his foot.

Fifty-five.

Sixty.

Anytime now he was going to run into the hunting party, and they were going to realize they'd been taken for fools. The sweeping bend came on fast. Grant used soft hands to ease over to the outside of the curve so he could cut the corner and maintain his speed. Standard police driver training technique. Never go faster into a bend than you could safely see ahead. Grant took the bend too fast. And saw that the hunting party weren't fools after all.

The splintered piece of deadwood was a wide, straight tree trunk devoid of branches and foliage. It wasn't lying at the side of the road; it had been pulled across the tarmac to block any traffic coming out of Catawba Point. The hunters were evenly spaced either end of the tree on the far side. Either end in case Grant decided to smash through the trunk and splinter them all to death.

Grant stamped on the brakes. The pickup skidded but didn't slow. It screeched sideways and broadsided the tree with a shuddering crunch. The side window shattered. The airbag deployed and smacked Grant in the chin, his second airbag in two days. The radiator burst and steam hissed from the crumpled hood. Dust and splinters danced in the stagnant air.

Half a dozen figures emerged through the dust. The rest stayed back to cover their colleagues. They fanned out so the first six weren't in the firing line. Good tactics. Right up there with taking the high ground at Notebook Trail with the sun at their backs. Carter had taught them well.

Grant patted the airbag down and slid across the bench seat to the passenger side. His ears were ringing with the impact. His jaw ached. He shook his head clear and got out. He swayed slightly until he regained his balance then stood tall, hands in the air.

"Looks like you got me."

The spokesman stepped forward pointing a bulky weapon that looked to be somewhere between a machine gun and a revolver. He kept his arms tucked in for stability. Gun extended.

"Stealing a truck. Smart. But not exactly playing fair."

Grant shrugged.

"Oh, I didn't know there were rules. I thought Carter wanted you to get some real-world experience."

He emphasized his hands being up in the air.

"Well. You caught me."

The spokesman shook his head.

"Thing about hunting. You ain't caught until you're hung and dried."

Grant was about to ask what that was supposed to mean when the spokesman raised the gun and shot him in the chest.

FORTY-TWO

They returned Grant to Catawba Point lying flat on his back in the load bed of the pickup. The bodywork was damaged and the radiator leaked, but the pickup worked just well enough to make the trip. Grant felt about the same, damaged and leaky and banged up once too many times since he'd come to Charlotte, North Carolina. The pain in his chest eased but it was still pain. Grant didn't like pain. He didn't like being shot point-blank in the chest either.

"Paintball?"

"It was a training exercise. D'you think we'd shoot you for real?"

Grant shrugged and took a drink of iced tea on the rear deck of the main house.

"For a minute there, I thought someone was going to play 'Dueling Banjos.'"

Carter laughed, leaning against the railing like nothing had happened.

"Wrong woods. But I see your point."

He took some of the jovial out of his voice.

"Although you were the one doing the hog tying."

Grant's tone reflected the change of mood.

"Sorry about that. Things seemed to be getting a bit serious out there."

Carter looked at Grant, with the splash of red paint on his chest.

"They certainly did."

If there was hidden meaning, he quickly diffused it. The Crocodile Dundee smile returned, full wattage.

"My fault. I wanted the boys to taste real combat before they went to war."

Grant leaned back in his chair.

"There's a war?"

Carter's smile disappeared.

"This is America. We're always at war."

He folded his arms across his chest.

"Rich against poor. North against South."

Grant rattled the ice in his iced tea.

"I thought they'd sorted that one out."

Carter ignored the remark.

"Black against white."

He tilted his head at an angle and scrutinized Grant.

"Which kind of begs the question."

All the humor drained out of his voice.

"Why exactly are you here? Really?"

Grant considered telling Carter about the innocent girl fighting for her life and the black fella getting his neck snapped in the shower. He thought about telling the white supremacist that he didn't like bullies or loudmouths or people of low moral fiber. But this wasn't the time for that. Grant was surrounded by people of low moral fiber. There was no point antagonizing them any more than he already had. No, this was a time for tact and diplomacy. Tact and diplomacy weren't Grant's strong suit. He took a sip of iced tea to give himself time. When he put the glass on the table, he sat up straight.

"You brought me here. Remember?"

Carter wagged a finger.

"You know what I mean."

Grant let out a sigh and nodded. He knew exactly what Carter meant and didn't want to tell him. Whenever that situation arose, the best way to deal with it was to stick to the facts and avoid adding color or inflection.

"A bunch of black fellas was about to kick the shit out of me."

He held his hands up toward Carter.

"A bigger bunch of white guys stopped them."

He waved to indicate his surroundings.

"Icing on the cake is being welcomed into a community that I didn't think still existed. Where white is right and you can still call a spade a spade."

Carter kept steady eyes on Grant.

"And that's how you feel?"

Grant shuffled sideways in his seat and leaned on the table.

"Back in Bradford, where I was a cop. Textiles. Milltown kind of place. Used to be hardworking white folk keeping the industry going. Lot of colored types brought in."

He shrugged at Carter.

"You know how that works. Anyway. Textile trade dried up. Lot of displaced immigrants. Government handouts. Immigrants started saving to bring their families over. They saved their handouts to bring even more over. All getting benefits from the state. Only winners were black fellas and furniture manufacturers."

He held his hands up in feigned surprise.

"I went in a house once, had four settees and three armchairs in the living room. The beds upstairs? Nose to tail. No floor space whatsoever. More people than a hotel."

He let out a heartfelt sigh.

"It got to where you couldn't mention color, lest you got branded a racist and lost your job. We got criticized because midnight stop-and-searches were stopping too many blacks and not enough whites."

He snorted a laugh.

"It was Bradford. You couldn't find a white face to stop after midnight."

Grant hoped he wasn't laying it on too thick. Looking at Carter's face, he didn't think he was. Sympathy oozed out of the white supremacist's pores. Grant sighed one last time.

"This here. A little bit of heaven."

Carter nodded.

"I appreciate that. And I know just where you're coming from. Blacks is ruining this great country of ours. Dragging everyone down to their level."

He jabbed a hand to one side.

"Damn right."

Then he indicated Grant.

"At least you don't have a black president."

Grant tried to lighten the mood.

"We had a woman Prime Minister once."

Carter was on a roll.

"Government needs teaching a lesson. We need to bring 'em crashing down. They'll pay attention then."

A shiver ran down Grant's spine. He'd been due to fly out this evening. Anything coming crashing down would have had serious implications for him. It certainly would for a lot of other people who didn't deserve to be caught in the black versus white crossfire. He glanced at his watch. It was almost time to call Evelyn, or she'd be setting Plan B in motion. Sitting here listening to Carter, Grant thought maybe he should let her. Carter puffed out his cheeks and shook his head clear.

"Sorry. Sometimes I get carried away."

Grant shrugged but didn't speak. Carter's smile turned sheepish.

"As you can imagine, it's a subject close to this community's heart."

Grant tapped his upper arm.

"Nothing wrong with wearing your heart on your sleeve."

He shoved his chair back and stood up.

"Nothing wrong with standing up to be counted either."

He jerked a thumb toward the house.

"But I need to take a leak."

Carter pushed off from the railing and nodded. He heard something and turned toward the river. Grant heard it too, engines coming along the backwater from the main channel. He looked beyond the jetty and saw three powerboats knifing through the water toward Catawba Point. Carter turned back to Grant.

"Make sure you wash your hands. Big Dog is in the building."

FORTY-THREE

Grant told Evelyn to hold off on making the call. From his room after flushing the toilet. Plan B would have to wait. She had lots of questions, but he didn't have time to elaborate. He did give a list of names though, just in case things went south. John Carter, Crash Davis, and Cornelius Stout the third. After ending the call, he washed his hands just so he could say he did. The last name on that list was the one he'd be shaking hands with.

"So, this is the man who's been causing us so many problems."

"I like to think it was the fella petrol-bombed my room caused the problem."

"The petrol-bomber being the guy you threw off the balcony."

"That's one theory. Yes."

Big Dog sat at a picnic table near the barbecue pit and made it look like he was holding court from his throne. The king of all he surveyed. What he surveyed now was a Yorkshire cop looking somewhat the worse for wear in combat clothes and a blood-stained jacket. The blood being red pigment from getting shot in the chest with a paintball. Grant could understand why everyone called him Big Dog. He was Stout by name and stout by nature, a big man with the haggard visage of a fighting dog that had seen off all the competition. The competition round these parts was a contingent of black ex-paratroopers setting up a rival commune at Notebook Trail.

Stout sat up straight and became even bigger.

"So it's really all down to you throwing Leroy into the hydrangeas."

"Is that what they were?"

Stout was unmoving, like a rock.

"Creative license."

Grant twirled a hand in the air.

"You could argue it's all down to Crash Davis sleeping with the little black hooker Leroy was pimping. And the three of them making so much noise they woke me up."

Stout glanced at Carter, who had regressed to being a timid acolyte in the presence of his master. There was nobody else at the table. This was a high-powered powwow where the only power was Jabba The Rock. Carter cringed under Stout's glare. Stout turned his attention back to Grant.

"I don't argue. I just say what is."

Grant held his hands up in surrender.

"So, it's all my fault then?"

Stout waved for Grant to put his hands down.

"There's no fault. Only circumstance."

He rested both hands on the table and stared at the Yorkshire cop.

"And bad timing."

Grant stared back at him.

"Don't forget, being in the wrong place at the wrong time."

Stout kept his expression deadpan.

"That too."

Grant let out an exaggerated sigh.

"Both those things. The timing and the place parts. Story of my week."

He put his hands down on the bench either side of him and leaned back as best he could, the bench seat of the picnic table not having a back to lean on.

"Three days ago it was simple. New York to the old homeland. Timing sucked. Storm coming up the eastern seaboard canceled my flight and sent me here. Timing didn't stop messing with me there. Bunch of little old ladies at a knitting circle conference took all the hotel rooms. Dumped me out in the sticks, up two flights of stairs and a balcony."

He cocked his head to one side and lowered his voice.

"You already know about the balcony."

He sighed again.

"Then I hit bad timing central. Smacked on the head at Nona's place. Same again at the shopping mall, with a plant pot this time. Crashed an ambulance at the hospital and got jumped at Notebook Trail."

He nodded, his head still cocked to one side.

"You know about that part too, right?"

He tapped the red stain on his chest.

"Then to cap it all, your boys go all Deliverance on me. Stalking and trapping through the woods. Until one of 'em shoots me in the chest to make a point."

Stout didn't move. His lips barely formed the words.

"I understand you stole a truck."

Grant shrugged.

"I was going to give it back."

Stout blinked.

"But you didn't."

Grant indicated John Carter.

"He wanted them to get some real-world practice."

Stout's eyes flicked to Carter then back at Grant.

"Paintballing ain't real world."

Grant frowned.

"Tree across the road felt pretty real to me."

Stout almost smiled.

"Wrong place at the wrong time again, huh?"

Grant nodded.

"Taken all together. My timing's been real bad."

He glanced skywards.

"Supposed to be flying home today. Look how that worked out."

Stout looked for hidden meaning on Grant's face. It was Grant's turn to remain deadpan. He stared back at the king of Catawba Point.

"I hear they don't like fires in the flight path."

If there was any reaction, Stout kept it hidden behind granite features. He didn't blink or frown or take a deep breath. There might have been the faintest of smiles playing at the edges of his mouth. Carter took a step back, but that was the only indication that Grant had scored a hit. Silence descended on the table that had become a throne. The quiet emphasized the sounds of nature. Water rippled against the shore. Trees swished in the breeze. Birds chirruped in the trees that sheltered the trio. Stout leaned forward and broke the silence.

"Every cloud has a silver lining."

Grant wanted to ask about the cloud but had a fair idea what that was. The only question was whether he would be allowed to get out of here and tell anyone about it. Stout concentrated on the silver lining.

"After all. You wouldn't have had dinner with Evelyn Cover."

Grant blinked. The silver lining suddenly felt like it became a cloud. The fact that Stout knew her name was bad enough. It suggested he knew a lot more and wasn't afraid to use it. The unspoken threat hung over the table. Grant had no answer to it right now but, given the chance, he'd like to make Big Dog take a squat. He kept his tone light.

"Always look on the bright side."

Stout nodded.

"I always do."

Grant didn't.

"At the same time as saying what is?"

Stout leveled cold eyes on Grant.

"All the time."

Engines started up round the front of the main house. Gravel crunched as a convoy formed on the turnaround. Stout stood up and puffed his chest out. It was a big chest on a mountain of a man. Grant stood too. He was the same height as Stout but nowhere near as wide and solid. They both looked toward the noise. Stout nodded at Carter, and the acolyte set off at a fast walk. Stout turned back to Grant.

"Looks like maneuvers are over."

Three vehicles lined up outside the barn: the SUV and two cars. Not the rusty foreign job and not the damaged pickup. The men from the hunting party stood beside their transport. The guns they were holding this time weren't paintballs. This was a live-fire exercise, whatever it was. Grant had a feeling he knew exactly what it was and where they were headed. Stout glanced at the convoy then back at Grant.

"Why don't I drop you off?"

Grant looked at the gift horse and waited for the punchline. Stout didn't move toward the turnaround, turning instead to the flotilla of powerboats at the jetty.

"Not literally, of course."

FORTY-FOUR

The half a dozen men who escorted Grant to the boats looked more seasoned and capable than the hunting party earlier. They could have been Big Dog's honor guard but were more likely just the longest serving members of the Catawba Point Irregulars. Even white supremacists had a pecking order. Being at the top of the food chain meant you rode in the middle boat. Being a guest of Cornelius Stout the third meant you rode with Big Dog. Grant climbed aboard.

The good thing about taking all three boats was that the armed guards were split into two per boat. The bad thing was that Grant couldn't reach four of them because they were outriders to the main boat. The boat rocked as Stout sat on the cushioned bench seat in the stern. He waved for Grant to join him. The boat rocked some more as Grant balanced the load. The outboard motors drowned the sound of the departing convoy as the flotilla pulled away from the jetty. Stout shouted above the noise.

"This is the nearest thing to a cool breeze you'll get in North Carolina."

Grant closed his eyes and held his head up high. The wind was refreshing but hardly cooling. He took a deep breath then looked at Stout.

"You could always run a fan through an ice bucket."

Stout gave a deep and throaty laugh.

"Caravelle don't do air conditioning."

The boats settled in the water as they picked up speed, not in the V formation they'd used when they arrived but line astern. Spray was forced outwards the faster they went. The air was damp with it, but even that didn't cool Grant down. It took all Grant's energy to keep his cool as he wondered where Stout planned to drop him and how. Afternoon sun formed a rainbow around the flotilla. Grant focused on the best way to jump ship without getting shot. He edged toward the starboard quarter and rested his arms across the back of the seat.

"You always travel by boat?"

Stout was more relaxed.

"Depends where I'm going."

He waved at the scenery.

"We've got lots of waterways."

Grant jerked a thumb back the way they'd come.

"You've got lots of roads as well."

The boats began to follow a gentle zigzag course, left then right then left again. The lead boat went left. Stout's went right. The last boat went left. They changed course one at a time and carved the water into an intertwining pattern like a DNA chain. The Caravelle bounced as it crested the wake of the lead boat. The curves grew longer, the zigzags wider. Stout settled back in his seat.

"Soulless tarmac."

He turned his gaze on Grant.

"Rivers have hidden depths."

Then he gave a smile that didn't touch his eyes.

"You haven't got hidden depths, have you?"

Grant's smile was more genuine. He'd learned to fake it over the years, working on the theory that bad guys were less likely to hit a man who was smiling at them. It didn't always work.

"We all go more than skin deep."

He nodded back over the stern.

"I'll bet you've got more going for you than roads and rivers."

229

Stout's eyes still didn't soften. He let out a sigh that was swallowed by the wind.

"It's a heavy burden, I'll grant you that. Responsibility. Balancing the needs of the many with the wants of the few. The minority."

Stout didn't mention who he considered to be the minority. Grant shrugged.

"Are black fellas still the minority?"

The flotilla fell back in line following a unified course. The wakes merged as the boats came out of the backwater and turned north heading upriver. The houses on the eastern shore were big and sumptuous. They all had private jetties, many with sturdy boathouses to protect their cruisers. Grant doubted there were many black homeowners, and he was damn sure there weren't any training camps behind the white painted mansions. Stout kept his eyes on Grant.

"You just put your finger on the problem right there."

He jabbed a finger on the seat to make the point.

"It's like you were telling Carter about your Bradford furniture."

He leaned toward Grant as if that made it more conspiratorial.

"Your white folks have two kids, then bring them kids up right. They grow up and have two kids of their own and so on and so forth."

He slapped the seat between them.

"Your blacks, they pop out five or six and dump them on the world. Those five or six have five or six more. You do the math."

He held one hand out at waist level.

"We maintain."

Then he held the other hand above his head.

"They expand. How long you think before we're the minority?"

The flotilla swept up the Catawba, knifing through the waters with a vicious three-boat wake. Up ahead, the railroad trestle crossed the river at the Greenway Circle Trailer Park. Stout waved a hand toward Notebook Trail through the trees to the east.

"Buying all the land."

He pointed at the road running parallel to the river.

"Taking over the goddamn roads."

Stout turned back to face Grant. He didn't need to calm down because he'd barely raised his voice. He added flint into his stare.

"Which brings us back to you and the road question."

He leaned toward the Yorkshire cop.

"You ever see an alligator crossing the road?"

Grant couldn't help glancing over the side before looking back into the cold, dead eyes. He wasn't sure if Stout was joking. Big Dog didn't seem like the joking type.

"Not crocodiles, huh?"

Stout shook his head.

"They're more down Florida. Up here, you fall in you're gator bait."

The boats aimed for the middle trestle. They didn't slow down. A freight train rattled across the bridge, the length of it staggering in the afternoon sun. It was so long, Grant couldn't see the engine or the caboose as it trundled forward. He craned his neck as the flotilla approached the bridge. The train kept coming. The rattling grew louder. The lead boat flashed through the trestle. The train shook the bridge. Dust fell from the spars and railroad sleepers.

Grant looked at the armed men driving Big Dog's boat. One was busy steering for the center span. The other sat in the co-pilot's seat. Neither had a hand on their guns. The first boat was already through the other side and out of the equation. The trail boat had eased off to give Big Dog's crew time to line up on the gap. The train noise echoed all around as the boat went under the bridge. Six armed men were reduced to two. Grant didn't need to do the math to know these were the best odds he was going to get.

The backwash of the first boat's passage buffeted the Caravelle. The noise overhead was deafening. Even so, Stout managed to make it sound like he was whispering, the booming voice was so relaxed.

"What you're thinking. That's a bad idea."

Their eyes locked.

"Gators love hanging about under bridges."

The boat shot through the gap.

"And it's hard to swim without your legs."

Grant checked the water but couldn't see any reptiles. He still wasn't sure if Stout was joking. By the time Grant decided Stout was exaggerating, it was too late. Big Dog's boat was out the far side, and the third boat followed. They were back to being a three-boat flotilla, and Grant still hadn't seen any alligators. The bridge fell away behind them and the wake sloshed the trestles. The train finally made it to the other side and disappeared along with Grant's chances of escape. Greenway Circle Trailer Park slid by on the left, and Notebook Trail hugged the railroad cutting on the right. The three Caravelles throttled back to a more leisurely pace now the danger was over.

Grant focused on the river ahead.

Stout focused on Grant.

"So, you like our setup here?"

Grant took one final look ahead, then turned to Stout.

"Minus the alligators."

Stout waved a dismissive hand.

"Oh, we've got more dangerous wildlife than gators."

He concentrated on Grant.

"You threw one of 'em off the balcony."

Grant sighed.

"Everybody keeps mentioning that."

Stout settled back in his seat.

"In my experience, if enough people talk about something, it's because that something actually happened."

Grant kept half an eye on the boat crew while scanning upriver.

"If enough people say the sky is pink, it doesn't make the sky pink."

"You saying you didn't throw Leroy over the balcony?"

"I'm saying, just because everyone says I did, doesn't make it so."

Stout frowned.

"That's a shame. Because you throwing his black ass over the side is the only reason we're talking. You being a white cop with an attitude."

Grant shrugged.

"My attitude is: I'm not defending Leroy. But I can't abide a man who puts an innocent girl in the hospital."

Stout nodded.

"A man of principle. I like that."

The riverbank was sliding by more slowly now, the next bridge approaching at a crawl. The Andrew Jackson Highway heading into Belmont. Grant scanned the bridge supports for alligators, then turned back to Stout.

"You've got principles too. And you stand up for them. I can appreciate that."

Stout swiveled in his seat to face Grant.

"A man's got to stand up for what he believes in."

He focused on Grant's eyes.

"What do you believe in?"

Grant returned Stout's gaze.

"I believe if certain things go unchecked, there will be blood."

Stout slitted his eyes.

"There's nothing wrong with blood."

He leaned forward.

"As long as the right blood gets spilled."

Grant let out a sigh.

"I've spilled blood. Not always happy about it."

Stout frowned.

"Happy is just a state of mind. Some things have to be done. For the greater good. Not everyone understands that."

Grant looked Stout in the eye.

"Oh, I think I understand."

The highway bridge drew closer. The boats aimed for the center span again. Grant checked for traffic crossing the bridge. Stout clicked his fingers, and the co-pilot swung his seat toward Grant, one hand resting on the butt of his gun. Stout let out a long, deep sigh.

"Not everyone agrees. The police give us a grudging respect. Doesn't stop them trying to find out more. Even tried to get somebody on the inside a couple of times."

Grant threw one last glance at the bridge, then nodded at Stout.

"Like in that spaghetti western? Eastwood joining both gangs and playing them off against each other?"

Stout shook his head.

"More like DiCaprio's undercover cop infiltrating Jack Nicholson's gang."

The co-pilot drew his gun and rested it on his leg. The bridge grew large as the boats steered for the center span, close enough to see a car parked on the bridge with somebody standing beside it. Stout looked at Grant and frowned.

"You're not DiCaprio are you?"

Grant looked at the gun, then back at Stout.

"I'm not undercover."

He nodded toward the figure filming from the bridge.

"I'm under surveillance."

He waved at Stout and stood up.

"Smile, you're on Candid Camera."

FORTY-FIVE

Evelyn Cover kept filming Grant until the big guy in the boat dropped him off at Jackson's Landing. She waited until the power-boat pulled away from the dusty sand spit just below the bridge, then turned off the camera on her phone. As soon as she saw that Grant was safe, she jumped in her car then cut across the median strip at T&T Auto Repair and drove down the dirt track. Grant waved for her to pull over near the concrete slipway. He wasn't smiling.

"You drive. I need to make a call."

Grant got in the passenger side. Evelyn gave him a deadpan look.

"You're welcome."

Grant took out the phone she'd been tracking and paused. He gave her a sad little smile that was the only apology she was going to get.

"It's bad."

She nodded and turned the car around, then waited for directions. Grant checked the contacts in his phone then called Daniel Yates' private number. The detective sounded like he was eating when he answered. Grant didn't wait for him to swallow.

"Spit it out and listen."

Grant's tone told the detective he was serious. Yates gulped down the last of his mouthful and was serious in return.

"Go."

Grant indicated for Evelyn to drive to the top of the track, then spoke in short sharp sentences.

"You need SWAT. You need air traffic control. And you need them now."

Yates was just as sharp in response.

"One thing at a time. Why SWAT?"

Grant rubbed the red stain on his chest.

"Because there's a dozen of them. They're armed. And they're gonna know we're coming."

Yates sounded exasperated.

"How do they know that? Even I don't know we're coming."

Grant took a deep breath then puffed his cheeks out.

"Because I just let slip I know what they're doing."

"Who are they?"

"The white supremacists."

"Catawba Point?"

Grant nodded.

"Yes. But not there."

Yates changed tack.

"Why air traffic control?"

Evelyn stopped at the top of the track behind T&T Auto Repair. Dust swirled around the car. Grant didn't give her further directions. He spoke to Yates instead.

"You're going to have to close all airspace north of the airport."

Yates let out a sigh down the phone.

"The flight path over the motel?"

Then his voice got real serious real quick.

"They're gonna torch the Sleepy Nook?"

Evelyn's face went drip white. Grant shook his head.

"Bigger."

He looked at Evelyn as if his expression could get through to Yates.

"They're going to blow the refineries. The ones straight north past Paw Creek."

FORTY-SIX

Grant was under no illusions. He knew how big a task he'd just handed Yates. They don't close the airspace above a major airport without lots of evidence or a credible threat. Grant couldn't provide either of them. He only knew what his nose told him and what Carter had let slip, but none of that was likely to sway the authorities at Charlotte Douglas International.

So that left Charlotte-Mecklenburg Police and whatever SWAT teams they could deploy at short notice. Grant knew that getting authorization for a major assault would also take time, but the convoy had already set off from Catawba Point. Time was one thing Grant didn't have. He twirled a finger in the air at Evelyn then pointed at the highway.

"Citgo. Quick as you can."

Evelyn didn't complain about his abrupt tone.

"Right."

She put her foot down and screeched out of T&T Auto Repair onto the Andrew Jackson Highway, laying down rubber as she took the bridge at speed. The river fell away behind them. Grant checked his watch. He was cutting it fine. The convoy would be traveling at normal speed to avoid being stopped by the police. Evelyn was driving flat out. Grant threw her a sideways glance. He wouldn't tell her the next part until she was safely with Brubaker.

238

* * *

"What you want to leave her with me for?"

Grant fixed the old man with a knowing stare.

"Because the last girl I tried to help ended up in hospital."

Evelyn just fixed Grant with a stare.

"And you're trying to help me, how?"

Grant gave her a look like he was explaining to a child.

"By not having you stand next to me when the petrol goes boom."

Evelyn nodded out the window at the petrol pumps.

"Leaving me at a gas station full of petrol."

Grant twirled a hand to include the filling station.

"This isn't the petrol they're going to blow up."

Brubaker lifted the flap and came out from behind the cash register.

"That's good to hear."

He leaned against the counter.

"But you could have dropped her at Hardee's or the Sleepy Nook."

Then indicated the shelves of the Little Rock Food Mart.

"Why d'you really want to leave her here?"

This was the part Grant hadn't wanted to tell her. He glanced at Evelyn, then turned to Brubaker.

"Because they don't keep a gun behind the counter in case they get robbed."

That straightened Evelyn up.

"What do you need a gun for?"

Grant let out a sigh.

"I already got shot with a paintball."

A dull roar sounded in the distance and grew quickly as the plane came in to land. It throttled back and applied half flaps as it followed a line south over the refineries and the motel. The noise reached a crescendo and rattled the fittings of the two-pump Citgo as the landing gear was lowered for the north-south runway.

Grant glanced skywards. Yates hadn't managed to close the airspace. He hoped the detective had more luck with the SWAT teams. Evelyn seemed to read his mind.

"They're sending in the SWAT team. Aren't they?"

Brubaker looked at the attractive woman in the business suit, then at Grant. He went back through the hatch and stood beside the cash register. Tires screeched as the airliner touched down. The engines reversed and the brakes came on. The noise receded but only served to emphasize the weight of the problem. The number of lives at risk if this wasn't stopped. Grant ignored the old man and looked at Evelyn. He lightened his tone but knew there was no way to make this sound good.

"They should be on their way by now."

Evelyn's bottom lip quivered.

"Then why do you need to go?"

Grant took a deep breath and let it out slowly.

"Because somebody has to."

She shook her head.

"But you don't. That's what the police are for."

Brubaker brought a grubby, black revolver out from under the counter and held it out for Grant. Grant nodded his thanks then looked on Evelyn.

"I am the police."

She was still shaking her head.

"Not around here. You said so before."

He took the gun from Brubaker and flexed his shoulders.

"I am today."

FORTY-SEVEN

Evening turned to dusk as Grant drove north through neighborhoods he didn't know existed. Pawtuckett, White Oak Park, and Paw Creek. Calling them neighborhoods was an exaggeration. They were just a handful of streets loosely tied together behind trees that hid them from the road. Three miles north of the Sleepy Nook Inn and four miles north of Charlotte Douglas International. Right in the glide path for incoming flights. Grant had looked out of his window during landing and felt like he could reach out and touch the glowing red lights that warned low-flying aircraft. Every aircraft coming over the refineries was low-flying. That's what made the refineries such a good target.

Refineries. Plural. It was the plural part that made them even better targets, because the Catawba Point Irregulars only had to blow up one of them to take out all three, and Grant didn't know which one. It could be the one owned by Citgo Petroleum up the middle, BP to the right, or the Marathon Petroleum Corporation on the left.

The reason Grant couldn't tell which one they were going to attack was that the attackers hadn't arrived yet. Neither had the SWAT team nor the Charlotte-Mecklenburg Police. Grant was the first one there. And he was all alone.

* * *

First things first, a quick check of the perimeters for the vehicles that had left Catawba Point in convoy. It was an easy check because the refineries had closed for the day and the staff parking lots were empty. Red lights blinked atop the metal towers. Huge gas storage tanks stood out in the gloom. There was no movement among the stanchions and walkways. The place was still and dark and silent as the grave.

Next thing was to familiarize himself with the battlefield. One of the main rules of combat. If you can get there before the fight, choose your battleground. Grant didn't have a lot of choice in the matter; the target would be whichever refinery the white supremacists decided to attack. The only positive was that the approach road came right up the middle before splitting to go east or west. The Freedom Drive Truckstop stood in the middle of the intersection. The truck stop was a small daytime diner for truckers hauling tankers to and from the refineries. It was closed and dark and offered perfect sightlines to all three petroleum companies.

Grant gave one last look along Freedom Drive, then parked Evelyn's car behind the truck stop. He clambered up a dumpster onto the low flat roof and crouched behind the chimney. The dying sun painted the sky a brilliant red. There were no clouds to make this a perfect western sunset, but the treetops dripped blood as the red faded to black and the stars twinkled overhead. Best time to attack. Just as it was getting dark. Enough light to see by but plenty of shadows to hide in. Grant felt like a frontier pioneer circling the wagons until the cavalry arrived. It looked like the cavalry were going to be late.

Grant settled behind the chimney as the convoy came into view.

Headlights speared out of the darkness and lit everything before them. Just one set at first, then the lights bifurcated turning into three pairs of full-beam searchlights as the convoy drew closer. They glinted off the chain-link fence that bordered the road and picked out the gravel on the parking lot in front of the diner. The vehicles crested a gentle ridge before Freedom Drive reached the intersection, the angle shining the headlights straight into Grant's eyes. The convoy slowed on approach, meaning Grant was blinded for longer. He could see the shape of the vehicles but nothing else. Soon they would reach the truckstop and make the turn. The only bottleneck was the narrow stretch coming over the ridge; after that, they could go any direction they wanted.

Grant knelt beside the chimney and used one knee to rest his gun arm. He leaned against the masonry for added stability and aimed at what little he could see. The tires beneath the leading headlights. The car was coming straight ahead so tracking the movement was easy. He aimed low to compensate for the recoil, then let the wheel come toward him.

He fired.

The muzzle flash lit him up.

He fired again.

The front tire burst and the first car slewed across the road. The second car slammed into the back of it, but the third managed to stop in time. Doors flew open and there was an immediate return of fire. The masonry exploded with bullet hits, but Grant was already down off the dumpster and running for the opposite corner of the diner.

Grant peered round the side of the building. The first two sets of headlights were skewed at opposing angles. The third set of headlights silhouetted the lead vehicles and lit the front of the diner. Grant saw activity behind the silhouettes, but there was no more gunfire. The sky had darkened from blood red to maroon and was rapidly turning into night. The trees either side of the road were just darker shapes against the greater dark. He checked the narrow stretch of road. It was completely blocked by the collision. The third car couldn't get past because of the boundary fence. Bottleneck complete. Delaying action successful. Now all he had to do was wait for the cavalry to arrive.

Three shots in quick succession slammed into the corner of the diner. It didn't look like the white supremacists were going to wait. Grant was going to have to hold them off a while longer. He wanted to take out the headlights that were covering him, but the revolver only had four more rounds. He was an okay shot, but it had taken him two to hit the tire. Shooting out the lights wasn't as easy as it looked in the movies. Not with a handgun.

He took his phone out and ducked behind the dumpster. He was about to call Yates and see how long he was going to be when he heard a crash and screech of metal. He looked round the other side of the diner. The last car was scraping past the collision and tearing the wire fence. He put the phone down and used the building to keep his gun arm straight.

He fired.

The muzzle flash pinpointed his position.

He fired again.

Two misses.

The car ripped through the fence and scraped around the collision. Grant only had two shots left and nowhere to hide. The delaying action was over. It was time for an all-out assault. The only way for that to work was to close the distance. Quickest way to do that was to use Evelyn's car. He scampered across the gravel and climbed in.

"Shit."

He'd got in the wrong door. The steering wheel was on the other side. He clambered across the center console and took the phone out again. He hit last-number redial as he started the car. Yates wasn't eating when he answered this time.

"Bad time, amigo."

Grant wasn't interested in excuses.

"No shit. Where the fuck are you?"

Grant could hear raised voices down the phone. A lot of frantic activity and barked instructions. Yates sounded out of breath.

"We just took some hits on the approach."

Grant turned the engine off.

"Approach? You're here already?"

The chain-link fence twanged as it finally snapped. Grant

could hear it beyond the diner and down the phone. Yates had to shout above the noise.

"Yes and no. They left somebody guarding the main road."

Grant slumped in the driver's seat and let out a sigh.

"Double shit."

FORTY-EIGHT

The SWAT guys weren't gentle, even after Grant told Yates he was coming out with his hands up. Out to his side more accurately, like Jesus on the cross, dangling the gun by the trigger guard so nobody would shoot him. Nobody shot him, but they did wrestle him to the ground and give him a vigorous full-body pat-down. Grant considered himself lucky they didn't do a cavity search. Being shot at can provoke extreme reactions. He understood that but was only going to take so much.

"Can I get up now?"

Yates helped him to his feet.

"Explain."

Grant nodded. It was a reasonable request. He kept it simple.

"I thought you were them. Wanted to slow them down until you arrived."

Yates handed Grant his gun back.

"Except *them* haven't arrived. And it doesn't look like they will."

Grant couldn't argue with that. He looked at the carnage blocking the road. The police vehicles didn't have their blue lights flashing, but they were as big and obvious as a train wreck. There were procedures to be followed before Yates' observations could be confirmed, but Grant nodded anyway.

"Seems that way, doesn't it?"

* * *

The procedures were followed to the letter: a more complete search of the refineries to confirm that the Catawba Point Irregulars hadn't already arrived and were hiding among the gas tanks and pipelines. More importantly to make sure they hadn't arrived earlier and placed explosives to do their job for them. They hadn't. The site was declared clear of white supremacists in thirty minutes. The search for explosives took a little longer, but Yates was satisfied enough to relax.

"Looks like you got it wrong."

Grant leaned against Evelyn's car.

"Only in the particulars. They're doing something. And they're doing it now."

Yates came and leaned next to Grant. He folded his arms.

"Run it by me. What you know."

Grant looked at Yates and gave the faintest of nods. It was good to see that the detective hadn't dismissed the threat entirely. He'd no doubt had to make judgment calls himself and if there's one thing that's true across emergency services and military action it's that your judgment is only as good as your information.

"Okay. Here's what I've got."

He told Yates about the picnic at Catawba Point and John Carter's veiled suggestion that Grant delay his flight. He mentioned the comments about fires in the flight path and Crash Davis' involvement with bringing things crashing down. He ended with Cornelius Stout's assertion that some things have to be done for the greater good. All that was tied in with the fire at the motel being a bad idea in case it gave the authorities a heads-up and the best place for a fire in the flight path being the refineries. By the time he'd finished, the SWAT team confirmed there were no explosives. The SWAT commander ordered his men back to the vehicles then stood in front of Yates.

"Next time you call one of these things, get your facts straight."

Yates pushed off from the car.

"Next time I call an operation, make sure you get here on time. Instead of an off-duty cop holding the line on his own."

The commander didn't answer. He stalked off to the convoy to get his vehicles roadworthy. Grant nodded his thanks but didn't speak. Yates turned toward him.

"But he's right. Thin. Only reason I okayed this is because if you were right and we didn't act, there'd be a shitstorm that would rock the world."

Grant stood straight.

"I know. Thanks."

Yates locked eyes with him.

"I'm going to be writing reports for a week."

He shrugged.

"Bottom line. If they set off when you said, they'd have been here long before you. And we'd be picking body parts off the motel lawn."

Grant didn't back down.

"You still could be."

Yates shook his head.

"They're going to need more than a bottle of petrol in your room."

He turned to join the convoy and spoke over his shoulder.

"Don't call us; we'll call you."

Grant walked around the car and looked across the roof at the detective's back. He drummed his fingers on the roof. Yates was right on so many levels, but the white supremacists only had to be right on one. Petrol-bombing Grant's room had been a mistake. It drew his attention to something they didn't want him to know about. A fire in the flight path. But why was that so important? Why was the timing so critical?

Grant stopped drumming.

The fire in the flight path was obviously important, but what if that wasn't the main thing they wanted to hide? A pint of petrol in a bottle wasn't as important as where that petrol had come from. The Citgo gas station just across the I-85. Somewhere else that stored a lot of petrol. Somewhere else in the flight path of Charlotte Douglas International. And only a mile from the end of the north-south runway.

FORTY-NINE

Grant was oh-for-two on exploding petrol storage when he reached the Citgo filling station. The Catawba Point Irregulars had been there though; he could sense that as soon as he pulled onto the forecourt. Whether they were still inside remained to be seen.

He parked next to the air and water bay and scrambled out of the passenger door, keeping the car between him and the main building. The lights were on inside the store but there was no sign of movement. There was no sign of Evelyn or Brubaker either. Grant knelt behind the hood, using the engine block for protection if anyone decided to take a shot at him. Bullets puncture bodywork like passing through tissue paper. A car engine will stop most ordnance. He kept low and scanned the building. The angle gave him a view of two sides. The far corner and the repair bays were out of sight.

He leveled Brubaker's gun across the hood. Two bullets left. He wished he'd borrowed a second gun from Yates, but the detective was all out of favors for the cop he'd cut too much slack for already. This was a one-man show from now on. If it came down to shooting, he'd better make every shot count.

Somebody had already done some shooting. Twice. Light from the forecourt reflected off the front window and highlighted the network of cracks around the bullet holes. Chest-height just above the cash register. Boxes of Frosted Flakes had been knocked off the display shelf. Right where Evelyn had been standing when he left. A fluorescent light flickered inside the store. Grant was halfway across the forecourt before it came back on.

"Well, you were right about this not being the petrol they wanted to blow up."

Brubaker was on the floor behind the counter, blood congealing on a cut down the side of his face. One eye was swollen but not quite shut. There was no sign of Evelyn. Grant fetched a bag of frozen peas from the refrigerator and knelt beside the old man. The cold compress stung as Grant held it against the swelling. Brubaker didn't complain. Grant helped the old man sit up and let him take over holding the frozen peas.

"I was wrong about the other place as well."

Brubaker pointed at the gun in Grant's hand.

"You hit anything?"

Grant let out a sigh.

"Let's just say I'm not in the Charlotte PD's good books."

"You shot at the police?"

"I didn't know they were the police."

"Not much of a detective then, are you?"

Grant put the gun on the counter and got serious.

"Evelyn?"

Brubaker leaned his back against the wall and shifted the peas in his hand.

"They took her."

"How many?"

"Three."

Grant frowned.

"That all?"

He glanced through the cracked window.

"The rest of them wait outside?"

Brubaker shook his head and wished he hadn't.

"There was no rest of them. Three's all there was."

Grant stepped back from the counter and looked down at the old man.

"How'd it go down?"

Brubaker pointed at the bullet holes in the window.

"That got our attention."

He waved toward the back of the store.

"Other two came in the back."

He lifted the peas off the swelling.

"Did this. Grabbed her. Threatened me if she didn't talk."

Grant raised his eyebrows.

"Talk?"

Brubaker shrugged.

"Big guy. Some kind of computer geek. Asked lots of technical stuff."

"What kind of stuff?"

"Kind of stuff I don't have a clue about."

Grant thought about Crash Davis and the laptop in his motel room. He wondered what Nona could have known for Crash to petrol-bomb her then try and snatch her from the hospital. His first thought was it must have been something to do with blowing up the refineries, but he'd already proved that wasn't the case. But computer stuff? What the hell was that about?

Brubaker shifted his position on the floor.

"Seemed to think you'd given her Nona's USB stick. Wanted to know if she'd seen what was on it."

Now Grant was really confused.

"USB stick?"

Brubaker formed a circle with his thumb and forefinger.

"At the meetings. After ninety days. Inspirational messages."

Realization dawned on Grant's face.

"The ninety-day chip?"

FIFTY

Grant fished the oversized poker chip out of his pocket. He looked at the embossed letters round the edge—A.E.L.T.C, Brubaker's little joke—and the big red ninety on one side. It was just a big plastic disc, not a USB stick. He turned it over in his fingers, looking at the zigzag crack that denoted something broken made whole again. It was still just a big plastic disc.

Brubaker clicked his fingers to get Grant's attention.

"The join."

Grant looked blank. Brubaker made a zigzag in the air with one finger. Grant looked at the zigzag crack again and nodded. Gripping both sides of the crack, he pulled. The disc came apart, one half revealing a USB connecter. It looked so small to have caused this much trouble. He held it up to Brubaker.

"You got a computer handy?"

Grant was even worse with computers than he was with mobile phones. He wished Evelyn were here to show him what to do. That thought spurred him on. Finding where they'd taken her and getting her back was his new priority. Learning what Nona Hartley had been hiding might go a long way toward doing that.

Brubaker opened the meeting hall door and turned the lights on. The three rows of wooden pews and the lectern were still there, as was the refreshment table. The noticeboard on the wall still had A.E.L.T.C. across the top with the inspirational message below.

Add
Everything
Lots
To
Close

What Grant hadn't noticed was the laptop on a desk near the false wall that separated the meeting hall from the living quarters. Brubaker pulled up a chair so they could both sit down and opened the laptop. It powered up automatically. He waited for it to cycle through the welcome screen then pushed the USB drive into a socket on the side. The laptop detected the external drive and opened a separate screen. Brubaker moved to one side to let Grant take over. Grant held his hands up and shrugged.

"Don't look at me. I arrest people, not pixels."

Brubaker dumped the frozen peas in a waste bin next to the desk.

"Not a lot of help if you don't know where the people are."

There was no answer to that because it was true. Grant's shoulders sagged.

"I know."

He indicated the laptop screen.

"But one of those people didn't want anybody knowing about this."

He looked at Brubaker.

"Whatever's on it."

He raised his eyebrows.

"Good indication what he's been up to."

Brubaker sat in front of the laptop and tapped the keyboard. He wasn't a fast typist, but he seemed to know what he was doing. He slid a finger across the trackpad to move the cursor and tapped some more keys. A menu came up on the screen. The old man pointed at the list.

"Videos recorded at the ninety-day ceremony."

He scrolled down the list.

"And the inspirational message if she ever needed support."

Grant didn't understand the jumbled letters and numbers denoting file type and location. There was an occasional word he could make out, but they were mixed in with computer code and tech-speak. It was all double Dutch to him.

"That's all?"

Brubaker scrolled down to the bottom and stopped.

"She added a video file."

He scrutinized the line of code.

"Three days ago."

Grant leaned forward.

"The day I saw her in the stairwell."

Brubaker clicked the file and another window opened.

"The day you threw Leroy off the balcony."

The new window had a still image of the motel room with a circle in the middle with the universal video symbol for play. Grant examined the room in the photo. It was the same décor as his room. The curtains were closed, but it was clearly dark outside. The bedside lamps were on. He felt a little awkward about what Nona might have recorded, but it was the only way to find out what Crash Davis wanted to hide. Grant let out a sigh and nodded at the screen.

"Let's see what she was up to."

Brubaker didn't speak. He pressed play and the image began to move.

"Come over here, baby."

Crash Davis positioned his laptop on the bedside cabinet, then angled the screen so the camera faced the middle of the room. Nona Hartley came into view, standing between the beds: two queen-size beds with duvets and throw covers. She was wearing the same figure-hugging leggings and crop top that Grant remembered from the shopping mall. Her posture suggested she wasn't shy about letting Davis see the body inside the fabric.

The camera shook then settled down once Davis got the angle right.

"Let me see that little black body of yours."

Nona put her clutch bag on the bedside cabinet and stood in front of the camera.

"Sho thing, honey."

The accent was thicker than Grant remembered. Maybe it was part of the act. She performed some slinky little twirling movements and pulled the crop top up until it reached the bottom of her small, firm breasts. She swayed some more, then pulled the fabric up, an inch at a time.

One inch.

The symmetrical curves of the underside of her breasts were revealed.

Two inches.

The curves became orbs as the swellings stopped short of her nipples.

Three inches.

Crinkly dark aureole as hard as bullets pointed at the camera.

Four inches and more.

Her breasts jiggled slightly as they were released from the crop top. Nona pulled it over her head and tossed it aside. She did some more swaying and hooked her fingers into the waistband of her leggings. Same as she had done in Grant's bathroom before he stopped her. Davis didn't stop her. He let her slide the leggings down, revealing a smooth, flat stomach and muscles that had nothing to do with the gym. Nona had hard-life musculature and strong abs. She swayed her hips as she slid the leggings to the top of her thighs then stopped. She turned around and wiggled her backside at the camera, then bent over and pulled them all the way down. Brubaker turned away. Grant felt guilty watching but didn't want to miss the clue when it was revealed. What was revealed now prompted Davis to speak.

"What you're gonna get tonight you'll remember the rest of your life."

Nona stepped out of the leggings and turned to face Davis. She planted her feet a full step apart to show her love mound at its best. Young and smooth and hairless.

"You too."

She moved forward, and a hand reached out to touch her. Davis stroked where all men wanted to stroke but couldn't keep his plans to himself.

"I can hack your bank and fill your account."

He slid one hand down her stomach and touched soft velvet.

"I once planted a news story with NBC they didn't know was bogus until there was a stampede for snow shovels in Charlotte."

He sniggered at his own joke while working his fingers.

"We ain't had summer snow since the ice age."

He sounded more excited talking about his computer skills than he was stroking the beautiful black girl. When he spoke, it was in short bursts with added punctuation as if he were out of breath. His hands moved up Nona's body and cupped her breasts until the nipples grew even harder. He flicked the solid black bullets with his thumbs and squeezed the firm round orbs.

"I once hacked the FBI's Most Wanted."

His voice became husky, like a man approaching orgasm.

"Could have deleted Bin Laden or Whitey Bulger. Before they caught 'em."

He slapped the left breast. Nona gasped in surprise. He slapped her again and pinched the nipple until she screamed for him to stop.

"Ain't no stopping me. Bitch."

When he slapped her this time it knocked her to her knees. Her face was streaked with tears and she tried to turn away, but Davis hit her across the face.

"I once re-routed a US Airways flight to Alaska."

He squeezed her cheeks and spread the tears into dirty black smudges. The camera shuddered as Davis angled it down toward the bed. He pulled Nona's head forward to the new thing showing in the foreground. It quivered with excitement, as much at his achievements as the fact he was going to make Nona suck it. He got one hand behind her head and pulled it forward.

"Did you know?"

He was really short of breath now.

"On any given day? Right now."

He pulled her face down to his erection.

"There are more flights in the air across America than any other time."

She kept her mouth closed as he nudged his penis at her lips.

"Imagine crashing that party."

He could barely talk now.

"Think about that while you swallow this."

He thrust forward. Nona twisted her head aside and shouted for him to stop. He slapped her again. She screamed. The next slap was a punch and it knocked her head sideways. His erection throbbed. This was fun. Something was knocked over on the bedside cabinet. The motel room door opened and the skinny black pimp came in. Leroy wasn't pimping when he saw the guy with the pimply white backside hit Nona.

"Pack up and fuck off."

Something else was knocked over and voices were raised. Three doors away, the noise woke a Yorkshireman diverted from New York.

Grant sat in silence for a few minutes after the video clicked off. The extent of his misjudgement weighed heavy but not as heavy as the enormity of the threat. He leaned back in his seat and let out a sigh. He couldn't remember what time the disturbance woke him up or when he'd thrown Leroy off the balcony, but the timer in the corner of the video told him exactly when that was.

The disturbance lasted from between just after midnight to half-past twelve. Midnight plus one and zero dark thirty.

"Shit."

Brubaker agreed.

"Yeah."

Grant looked at his watch. Ten-fifteen on the day he'd been due to fly home. The day he'd been advised to avoid flying. Not because of a fire in the flight path. Because of something much bigger. He took a business card out of his pocket and opened his phone. Brubaker noticed the card.

"You need a taxi?"

Grant called the number and waited.

"I need an army."

FIFTY-ONE

Grant didn't call Bruno Morris because he needed a taxi. He called the ex-serviceman because he was black, and as he'd taken great pleasure in telling Grant, the Yorkshireman was never going to pass for black. Bruno didn't take much persuading. A few choice words and a brief explanation were all Grant had to use. The big ugly car was outside the Little Rock Food Mart twenty minutes later.

"Why don't you call the police?"

Bruno watched Grant reload the handgun from a box of shells beneath the cash register. Grant looked at Brubaker, Brubaker looked at Bruno and shrugged.

"He kind of shot himself in the foot with the police."

Bruno indicated the gun.

"Should have called an ambulance then."

Brubaker shook his head.

"Figuratively, not literally. He shot at the police."

Bruno took a sharp intake of breath.

"You shot the cops?"

Grant flicked the cylinder closed and spun the drum.

"I shot the tires."

Bruno held his hands out.

"Oh, good. Because that's so much better."

Grant stripped off the paintball-stained combat jacket and moved to the clothing rail at the back of the store. He glanced at Brubaker.

"Have you got anything bright?"

The old man looked puzzled.

"T-shirts?"

Grant shook his head.

"Jackets. Windcheater's my preference."

Brubaker waved for Grant to look at the far end.

"Think there's something in clearance."

Grant flicked through the coat hangers and found what he was looking for third one in. A horrendous Day-Glo pink lightweight zipper jacket. He shrugged into it but left the zip unfastened then turned to Brubaker.

"You got any bottled water?"

Brubaker indicated the cooler cabinet. Grant smiled.

"And some aftershave?"

Brubaker gave him a "you've got to be kidding" look. Grant shoved the gun in the back of his pants and checked that the windcheater was long enough to cover it even when hanging open. Once he was satisfied, he looked at Bruno.

"They'll be dug in and heavily armed. Who do you bring in when the defenders are dug in?"

Bruno let his breath out slowly.

"The airborne."

Grant nodded.

"The only airborne I know around here is Leroy's. And I kind of shot myself in the foot with them as well."

Bruno tilted his head to one side.

"And of course, I'm black."

Grant stood firm.

"It's not about being black, it's about being local. I couldn't be anything further from local. They'll listen to you."

Bruno straightened.

"You reckon?"

Grant sighed.

"They'd better. Because once he hacks the system, they own American airspace. Do you think the passengers care about black or white?"

He lowered his voice.

"We all bleed red."

Brubaker pointed out the obvious.

"Airborne drop in behind enemy lines. These boys ain't got no chutes no more."

Grant turned to the old man.

"But they've got plenty of firepower. And, I'm guessing, explosives."

He split his attention between the store owner and the cabby.

"Down in the bunker at Notebook Trail."

Then he focused on Bruno.

"I need you to get them mobilized and get them armed. Fast."

A distant rumble turned into an overhead roar of engines as another airliner came in to land. After the debacle at the refineries, any evidence Yates had submitted to the airport was long gone. There'd be no closing airspace anymore. Flights would continue coming and going and they were fast approaching the magic hour, when there were more flights in the air across America than at any other time. The latest plane landed with a screech of tires and the roar of reversed engines. That was one down and hundreds to go.

"Quick as you can. As many as you can."

Grant didn't sugar the pill.

"There's only one road in."

This was as serious as it could get.

"I'll try and slow them down. Keep his finger off the button."

It was Bruno's turn to get serious.

"How you gonna do that? Storm the place on your own?"

Grant smiled and shook his head.

"I'm going to walk up to the door and ask them to let me in."

FIFTY-TWO

Grant drove down the tree-lined country lane and followed the curves in the road. One way in and one way out. Not all the way to Catawba Point because that's where the convoy had set off from but close enough for government work. Walkers Ferry Road curled past the houses near the airport and left the pockets of civilization behind. He kept his headlights on full beam, partly so he wouldn't have an accident at this crucial stage but mainly so the defenders would see him coming from far enough away that they wouldn't get itchy trigger fingers.

The clearing near the junction toward Catawba Point was dusted with moonlight. The dishes on the booster tower glinted in the dark that wasn't really dark at all. Grant remembered doing military exercises at night. Once your eyes adjusted to the dark, a full moon practically turned Salisbury Plain into daylight. Grant wanted them to see him coming. He wanted them to know who he was.

He kept the windows closed despite the late-night heat and the aftershave. The scent was overpowering but preferable to the other smell. He scanned the junction and slowed to a crawl. There was no sign of the convoy, but he knew it was here somewhere. Probably parked round the back in the woods. There was no fallen tree blocking the way this time. There was no group of armed men standing in the road. The armed men were dug in and waiting. Defenders prepared to defend. Grant didn't want them thinking he was going to attack.

He angled the car into the junction and stopped. The headlights cut a swathe across the clearing. The cell phone tower stood out like a futuristic castle, tall and straight and festooned with transmitter arrays. The best signal in Charlotte. So good, even the airport used it.

Grant pulled off the road and edged across the uneven ground of the clearing. The headlights bounced and flickered but didn't reach all the way to the tower. When they did, he stopped again and turned the engine off. The headlights automatically cut out, leaving just the sidelights showing. That wasn't good enough, so he turned the engine back on. The base of the tower was flooded with light. The maintenance door was closed.

Grant took a long, deep breath then let it out slowly. His nerves were steady. His eyes were calm. Despite his mouth being dry, he was ready for this. He picked up the bottled water and got out of the car. The door sounded loud when he closed it. He took three steps toward the tower. The motor faded into the background. Silence enveloped him. He stood in the headlights wearing the bright pink windcheater and held both hands out to his sides like Jesus on the cross.

Then he heard the sound that makes strong men weak.

There was no need to work the bolt action because there was probably a round in the chamber already. The noise was a warning. Seven more warnings rang out across the clearing. The other men were either more disciplined or didn't have bolt-action rifles. Grant could hear scuffling in the bushes but nobody came out. He kept his arms out straight.

"How you boys doing?"

There was no reply.

"Bit late to be out paintballing."

Still no response. They must be working on some kind of radio silence. Or maybe Carter didn't know what to say after being rebuked by Cornelius Stout. Grant was banking on this dirty dozen being Big Dog's puppies. Puppies are always easier to handle. Puppies armed and pointing their guns at you are a different proposition. Grant didn't want to antagonize them.

"It's okay. I come in peace."

The rustling was on the left, and John Carter materialized from the trees. He held his rifle loosely in both hands, pointing down and across his body. The other eleven were doubtless pointing at Grant. He kept his hands out. The bottled water was getting heavy. Carter stepped into the light.

"Maybe. But you might be goin' back in pieces."

Grant lowered his arms slightly to ease the stress on his shoulders.

"Way tonight's shaping up. That could apply to all of us."

He took a step forward.

"I'd like to avoid that."

He waved one hand to indicate the hidden gunmen around him.

"I'm sure you boys do as well."

He took another step.

"But I've got to tell you. The shitstorm that's about to rain down on your heads. That don't seem likely."

He took one more step then stopped. Half a dozen paces from the maintenance door. Two steps from John Carter. Carter raised the rifle and tucked the butt against the pad of his shoulder. Not loose. Not relaxed. The only good sign was that his finger was still outside the trigger guard.

"I ain't never been threatened by a man in a pink tutu."

Grant plucked at the lapels of his jacket and flicked it open to show he wasn't armed, then lowered his hands.

"A tutu's a ballet dress, but I get your point. Reason I'm wearing this is that my yellow one didn't survive the paintballing."

Carter tightened his grip on the rifle.

"I got news for you. The pink one ain't gonna survive neither."

Grant shrugged. He didn't think divide and conquer was going to work tonight, but he still had hopes for the delay and wait for reinforcements tactic. Best delaying tactic is to keep your opponent talking. They rarely shoot you while holding a conversation.

"Well, before you shoot the messenger. I'm the one bringing news."

He twirled one finger to get Carter used to the movement.

"Do you know what a Trojan Horse is?"

Carter snorted a laugh.

"Of course I do. And we don't got that situation here."

Grant nodded and smiled. Something else people tended not to shoot you while you were doing. Smiling.

"Not the wooden horse."

He had another thought.

"Or the condoms. The computer virus."

Grant became aware of crickets chirruping in the undergrowth and birds fluttering in the trees. Sounds of nature that were at odds with the confrontation being enacted in front of them. The noises were peaceful and quiet. Violence felt a long way off. He kept talking and waving his hands and smiling.

"There's this reverse Trojan Wormhole virus that's so nasty it could rip you a new asshole before you get time to hit the escape button."

Carter looked less confident.

"You think I'm worried about getting wormholed?"

Grant shrugged.

"It's not you and me should be worried."

He pointed at the maintenance door.

"It's your boy in there."

He made a typing motion with one hand.

"If he hits the wrong key. Big Dog's world's gonna coming crashing down."

The mention of Big Dog worried Carter.

"And what's that to you?"

Grant took another step toward the cell tower.

"What you think we were talking about on the boat?"

Concentration furrowed Carter's brow.

"I thought he was gonna feed you to the gators."

Grant held his hands out, making sure he didn't drop the bottle.

"Does it look like he fed me to the gators?"

He waved at the maintenance door.

"Who do you think told him to snatch the woman runs the computer store?"

Carter tried to get in front of this.

"Because she knows how to stop the reverse Trojan wormhole?"

Grant nodded.

"She knows how."

He patted his pocket.

"And I've got the code."

He let out a sigh.

"So you'd better say, pass friend. Or get ready for shitstorm dropping time."

FIFTY-THREE

The metal door clanged shut behind Grant and echoed through the iron and concrete structure. Carter stood with his back to the door in case Grant tried to get out. Grant didn't want to get out. The base of the tower was bigger than it looked from outside, but it wasn't big enough for three men and a hostage. The cramped interior was further complicated by jutting metal supports and a spiral staircase to the maintenance hatches for the dishes outside. As the tower grew narrower, the staircase was replaced with a metal ladder fastened to the wall. The only light was a caged bulb on the wall and the glow from the laptop computer. Crash Davis looked up from the desk he was sitting at below the staircase.

"Wow. You really know how to dress for a date."

He wafted a hand in front of his face.

"Think you overdid it with the aftershave though."

He nodded toward a dark corner beyond the desk.

"I'm sure she appreciates the effort though."

Evelyn looked tired and disheveled. She was sitting on the bottom step of the spiral staircase with her arms wrapped tightly around herself. There was no spark or energy when she looked up at Grant. She'd given up. As much as that concerned him, it was the laptop on the desk that he focused on.

"I see you got yourself another charger."

Light from the screen gave Davis' face a Halloween glow. The look in his eye was even scarier. He was looking forward to unleashing Armageddon. Grant couldn't see how far he'd got on the computer screen. He wouldn't have understood it even if he could. That was Evelyn's line of expertise. Grant's was making people do as they were told. The rifle prodding in his back meant he wasn't in a position to do that. Carter nudged Grant forward.

"He's talking about some kind of Trojan wormhole shit."

Davis looked at the man in the Day-Glo pink windcheater and the overpowering aftershave and shook his head.

"No. He's just talking shit."

Grant kept his hands down by his sides because there was no room for the full Resurrection Man pose. The water sloshed in the colored bottle. Color seemed to be a big thing for the white supremacists. Sleeping with a black hooker definitely hadn't put Davis in the Big Dog's good books. If Cornelius Stout knew about the pillow talk he'd be even less impressed.

"I know about the shit you were talking at the Sleepy Nook."

A look of doubt crossed Davis' face. Grant glanced at the laptop and then at Evelyn. Evelyn nodded, a little of the old fire returning to her eyes. She shifted on the step but didn't stand up. Not yet. Grant relaxed his knees and shoulders. Davis put a brave face on it.

"And I know about you throwing Leroy off the balcony."

Grant kept his tone light.

"You saw that, huh?"

Delaying tactics. Keep 'em talking. Wait for reinforcements. Grant tried to gauge the time without glancing at his watch, but he wasn't very good at that. There was no clock on the wall. He guessed it had been maybe half an hour since Bruno set off to recruit the Notebook Trail gang. The Catawba Point Irregulars were deployed around the clearing. This was going to go black versus white ballistic any minute now. The question was how long did Davis need to push a button? And could Grant reach him before that happened?

Delaying tactics. Grant smiled.

"I suppose I should stop denying that."

He relaxed his arms and slowly moved one hand to the back of his trousers.

"But since Leroy's in the morgue and Nona's in a coma…"

He nodded at Davis.

"That makes you the only witness."

Davis stood up straight and banged his head against the spiral staircase. He moved to one side for extra headroom and braced his shoulders.

"Back at ya. Before Leroy came in, only witness in that room was Nona."

Grant's fingers disappeared under the windcheater.

"The pillow talk, you mean?"

He shook his head.

"Not strictly true."

He brought his hand out of his back pocket.

"What you think Big Dog's gonna make of this when he finds out?"

He held the ninety-day chip up and spun it like a coin. He caught it in one hand. The zigzag crack glinted in the light. Evelyn got ready to move. Davis leaned against the wall and let out a lung-emptying sigh.

Carter looked confused but he didn't lower the rifle. He kept it low and firm in the base of Grant's spine. Rifles aren't good close-quarter weapons. They're long and clumsy and not easy to maneuver. The gun in Grant's belt was much better, but the rifle being stuck in his back meant Carter didn't need to maneuver, just pull the trigger. Grant tried to see if his finger was inside the trigger guard without making it obvious. He couldn't tell. He'd also made a tactical error; with the bottled water in one hand and the ninety-day chip in the other, he couldn't draw the gun anyway.

Distraction.

He flicked the chip again to keep everyone's eyes on it.

Davis' sigh became a low chuckle.

"That was just going to be a bit of porn home video."

He didn't sound worried.

"But holding that over me only works if you're in a position to show it to Big Dog. Which you're not."

He pushed off from the wall.

"And it's only a danger if somebody outside this room can see it."

Grant caught the chip and closed his fist.

"Who said nobody else has seen it?"

The doubt crossed Davis' face again but was quickly replaced by a sly look that bordered on madness.

"If the cops had seen it, it'd be in the evidence locker, not your pocket."

Evelyn edged forward from her sitting position. Davis was a full step to the other side of the desk. Grant got ready to flick the coin one more time then nudge the rifle aside and draw the gun. Carter chose just that moment to assert his authority as armed guard. He jabbed the rifle into Grant's back and everybody heard the dull clunk of metal.

"Hold it right there."

Carter sparked to life. Keeping the rifle firmly in Grant's back, he released one hand to lift the bottom of the pink windcheater. He pulled the gun out of Grant's belt and held it up in triumph. Grant let out a sigh. Evelyn sat back, deflated. Crash Davis grinned.

"As I was saying."

The grin disappeared when the first gunshots sounded outside.

FIFTY-FOUR

There was no mistaking the jagged tower sticking up into the night sky despite the trees that surrounded it or the darkness that enveloped it. There was no missing it either, as Bruno Morris discovered when he fired the M16 he'd borrowed from the Notebook Trail armory. Ricochets blasted chunks of concrete from the core. What he was having trouble hitting was the transmitter arrays growing out of the sides like fungus on a dead tree.

There was the added problem of people shooting back at him. That didn't do much for his aim. He might have seen service in warzones across the world, but it had been a long time since anybody had shot at him. It had been a long time since he'd had to run across uneven ground in combat formation too. Three shots ripped turf at his feet and he dived for cover on the edge of the clearing. Grant had been right. The Catawba Point Irregulars were dug in and heavily armed.

"Cover right. Cover right."

Denzel Washburn shouted above the gunfire, then crouched beside Bruno and patted him on the shoulder.

"You okay?"

Bruno turned a begrimed face to the younger man.

"I think I tweaked my back hitting dirt that last time."

Denzel kept low to the ground.

"We don't got no medic."

Bruno smiled through the pain.

"Don't need one. But damn. I missed being part of this."

Gunfire kicked up divots just in front of them. Denzel returned fire to keep the defenders' heads down, then glanced at the taxi driver.

"I never liked the shooting part. It's the camaraderie I miss."

Bruno indicated the other men fighting at their sides.

"Seems like you got the camaraderie covered."

The airborne veterans filtered left to outflank the defenders. Gunfire became erratic as they found cover along the roadside. The distinctive sound of the M16s quested for holes in the defenses. The returning fire was hunting rifles and shotguns, the sounds distinct and different. You could tell who was firing from the sounds of their shots. The M16s were making more noise. The attackers were making inroads too. Helped by the headlights of Evelyn's car, engine still running, as they lit the base of the tower.

Shots from the treeline punched holes in the metal. The defenders had realized the headlights were a problem and were trying to shoot them out. They were missing. Denzel glanced over his shoulder and yelled at the huddle of men in the ditch.

"Flank right. Don't go too wide. Crossfire."

The group moved fast and low to get an angle on the defenders that wouldn't send stray shots into their own men along the roadside. Bruno tugged at Denzel's sleeve.

"The transmitters."

Denzel nodded. All this would be for naught if they allowed the signal to get out. He raised himself up and shouted a reminder over the noise of battle.

"The tower. The tower."

The raised profile was just enough of a target. Turf ripped around him and red mist puffed from his shoulder. The blood splattered Bruno as Denzel went down. He rolled the veteran into the depression they'd been sheltering in and checked the wound.

The hole in front was small but the exit wound could take a fist with room to spare. The only good thing was the blood wasn't pumping. The bullet had missed the artery. Bruno wanted to shout, "Medic," but Denzel had already told him this was a low-manpower assault. He slipped out of his jacket and ripped the sleeve off. Balling the material into a pad, he jammed it into the hole and tied it with his belt. Until the police got reports about the gunfire and sent the cavalry, it was the best he could do. He shuffled to one side and engaged the target again.

He hit the tower. He aimed higher. Three shots blasted the cover off one of the transmitter dishes. A second dish took hits from the right flank. Then another. The attackers were finding their range.

Bullets punched metal in Evelyn's car again.

Sirens sounded in the distance.

Bruno glanced over his shoulder but couldn't tell how far the police were from closing this down. More shots hit the car but nobody extinguished the headlights. The next shot did the second-best thing. Hit the gas tank and blasted the roof and trunk lid into the air. The fireball lit the clearing. The thump of the explosion shook the tower.

FIFTY-FIVE

The four people inside the concrete tomb threw glances of differing levels of panic and control. Evelyn turned to Grant with eyes that showed fear and heartache in equal measure. Carter glanced at Grant then focused on Davis, worry creasing his brow and his eyes pleading for guidance. Davis watched dust and plaster crumble off the walls, then turned his eyes on Grant. His expression was calm and solid and mad as a sack of badgers. Grant tried to comfort Evelyn by ignoring her and staring at Davis. Grant's face was impassive, as if this were nothing out of the ordinary. He knew different though, because he'd told Bruno what to do if the worst came to the worst, and it sounded like he was moving to Plan B.

The explosion subsided, leaving the car a blazing wreck. Bruno watched the flames and remembered Grant's instructions. The Yorkshireman had been proceeding under the hope that the gun cabinet at Notebook Trail might contain explosives as well as firearms. He'd told the taxi driver that unless Grant was outside waving them off that he should assume he'd failed to keep Davis away from the laptop. If that were the case, he should instruct the airborne veterans to do whatever it took to prevent the uplink being made. If they couldn't shoot out enough of the transmitter arrays, they should consider the entire structure a target. The only way to prevent the signal flashing across America and crashing the air traffic control system was to destroy the tower. Raze it to the ground, along with everyone inside.

The gun locker didn't contain any explosives. Bruno had no way of blowing up the cell phone tower. Until now. Evelyn's car gave him the idea. He glanced over his shoulder to where they'd parked their cars. His taxi was a big, solid American car. He'd only just refueled it this afternoon. It was full of petrol. Slam that beast into the tower, and the resulting explosion would reduce it to rubble. Signal aborted. Mission accomplished.

He looked at the maintenance door. Jim Grant hadn't come out to wave them off. It was shit or bust time. He shuffled back out of the firing line and threw one last glance at the jagged finger pointing into the night sky then broke into a jog toward his car. Cold sweat broke out on his brow. Driving into the concrete tower was a one-way ticket. He fished the keys out of his pocket and yanked the door open. Gunfire crackled behind him. Nobody heard the roar as the engine started.

Enter or Escape. Two buttons on the keyboard that held the future of America. Press one, and the world could breathe a sigh of relief. Press the other, and the system would crash. Air traffic control would go into meltdown and the pilots would be flying blind. Some would manage to navigate the airways and perform emergency landings, but many would collide or crash or fall out of the sky. It was an old axiom that the police had to be vigilant the whole time but terrorists only had to be lucky once. Crash Davis was standing three feet from being lucky.

Evelyn moved to the edge of the step she was sitting on and flexed her legs, ready to launch. She was three feet on the other side of the desk. Equidistant. Fifty-fifty chance of who could reach the keyboard first. Except Davis was standing and she was sitting. He had the height advantage, like holding the high ground in a fight or a battle. Pushing up to her feet would waste valuable seconds. All he had to do was take one step and tap a key. She looked at Grant. He blinked. It was all the instruction she needed.

The gunfire continued outside, but there were no further explosions. Yet. Grant knew that was the next step. It was the natural progression. The needs of the many outweighed the needs of the few. Sacrifice was necessary. If he couldn't stop Davis pushing the button. Being an unarmed prisoner guarded by a man with a rifle made that unlikely. Holding a bottle of water and a poker chip wasn't going to cut it. Except he had one last trick up his sleeve.

Bruno put the car in reverse then realized he was the third car in a convoy of four. The attackers had pulled up at the side of the road just before the junction and nobody had left him room to get out. There hadn't seemed to be any need. Either the battle would be won or they'd all be dead. Who needed to move their car in a situation like that? But the situation had changed. He slammed the car into the vehicle behind then rammed the car in front. He did it twice more to make room, then angled out of the parking space and across the road.

He turned the headlights on full beam. The car bounced into the clearing and tore up turf as it skidded on the uneven ground. Bullets pinged off the bodywork. Two shots punched holes in the windshield. He aimed the hood ornament at the metal door at the base of the tower and set up for his attack run.

Grant measured angles and distance. Time was up. Everybody knew it. Evelyn got ready to move. Carter tensed his muscles, becoming rigid and unmoving. Davis looked Grant in the eye. Grant relaxed, took in a long, deep breath through his nose then let it out slowly through his mouth. He softened his eyes, nodded once, then he moved. Fast.

He flicked the ninety-day token at Davis. It spun in the air, drawing the computer geek's eyes. Grant jerked his elbow back and up, catching Carter by surprise. His arm knocked the rifle barrel upwards before Carter could get off a shot. Grant kicked backwards at Carter's knee and it collapsed against the joint the wrong way. Carter screamed in pain.

In one movement, Grant popped the sports lid off the water bottle and pulled a Zippo lighter out of his pocket. He squeezed the bottle and squirted a jet of petrol at Davis. The smell of the fuel overpowered the aftershave now the bottle was open. The spray soaked Davis' head and shoulders as he turned toward the laptop. He managed half a step before Grant rasped the Zippo and tossed it across the room. The man with the pimply arse went up in flames. His hair melted instantly, followed by his eyebrows and nose. The scream was primal and distorted as his lips burned off and his tongue stuck to the roof of his mouth. Despite the pain, he still lunged toward the keyboard.

Enter or Escape.

Two keys. The fate of America. Burning fingers reached for the Enter button. Evelyn pushed off from the bottom step, ignoring the fire that was singeing her hair, and lurched toward the Escape button. Grant dropped the empty bottle.

Enter or Escape.

Evelyn shoulder-charged Davis aside.

Escape.

The screen went blank as the hacker code was revoked. The wail coming out of Davis' mouth was more grief than pain. His extremities looked like dripping wax, but he still had enough strength to go after the man who had thwarted him. The human torch knocked the desk over and charged at Grant.

Bruno picked up speed, crossing the open ground amid a hail of gunfire. The windshield disintegrated and the interior mirror was blasted off its stalk. Pain flared in his shoulder and arm but he kept his foot on the gas. The only thing that slowed him down was the thing that gave him the idea in the first place. Evelyn's car was still burning in front of the tower, forcing Bruno to swerve to get around it before lining up on the maintenance door again. The turf leveled out and the ride became smoother. The gunshots stopped. The clearing fell quiet.

Then the maintenance door opened and a human torch came out.

Grant dodged to one side and tripped over Carter's broken leg. Carter screamed again. Grant tumbled sideways onto the fallen rifle. Davis lost all control, managing to lunge forwards but not change direction. He hit the door like a battering ram and it opened outwards. The agony of his thrashing arms was painful to watch.

Headlights blazed through the door. A car was racing across the clearing. Grant couldn't see who was driving but recognized Bruno's taxi. Davis dropped to his knees, the noise coming out of his mouth more animal than human now. The car veered to one side and hit the concrete tower a glancing blow.

Davis was a screaming tortured monster. The defenders stood open-mouthed. The airborne veterans stopped shooting. Davis thrashed and waved but he was completely engulfed in flames. Grant picked up the rifle and stood in the doorway. He didn't think twice. He shot Davis in the back of the head, and the thrashing corpse stopped thrashing. The silence was all-encompassing. Then distant sirens grew louder and flashing lights flooded the clearing.

RETURN FLIGHT

FIFTY-SIX

"Petrol bomb?"

"More like petrol squeezie bottle."

"What the hell were you thinking?"

Grant winced as the burns ointment was applied. In a curtained cubicle at the emergency department of CMC-Mercy. He'd been lucky and only suffered minor burns, but they still needed treating. Daniel Yates winced alongside him, the detective sharing a trait with many cops in preferring to look at dead people over looking at wounds on the living. Grant looked at the detective to avoid watching the raw patch of skin being smeared with gel.

"Thought it might come in handy. More for the laptop than anything else."

Yates looked away too.

"Well, it sure made a point."

Grant let out a sigh.

"Not sure the collateral damage was worth it."

Yates leaned against the wall.

"You been to see her yet?"

Grant became very still.

"I've seen her."

* * *

The aftermath of the firefight at Walkers Ferry Road took hours to clear up. The long-term effects would last a lot longer. Cell phone coverage around Charlotte dropped by ninety percent. Computer uplink and internet access were down even more. It would be weeks before the tower was fully restored, but at least no planes were crashed and the air traffic control system didn't even suffer a blip. Media clampdown meant outside of the authorities, nobody would ever know. That suited Grant. He'd had a bellyful of Resurrection Man stories in the press.

Casualties were rushed to CMC-Mercy and everybody else was arrested. That was something else that could be sorted out in the fullness of time. Grant vouched for the black veterans and Bruno Morris. Their continued silence would be bought with contributions to the Notebook Trail development and help for the local VA. The Catawba Point Irregulars faced a bleaker future. All apart from Cornelius Stout and his retainers, who managed to deflect any accusations by being ten miles upriver when the attack took place. John Carter bore the brunt of the blame, being the man in charge on the ground. The rest of his crew refused to say anything, standing on their constitutional rights. So long as they had white counsel.

Dawn was feathering the eastern horizon by the time the rush calmed down at the hospital. Different doctors and different nurses but the same professional approach. They didn't need the corporate sign at the entrance to remind them about commitment to care or uncompromising excellence. They had that in spades.

Grant was a long way down the list of casualties awaiting treatment. He didn't wait for permission to go see the one further up the list.

"I'm thinking you should come with a health warning. For any women who get involved with you. Like on cigarette packets."

Grant sat beside Evelyn's bed in the examination room and looked shamefaced. She was right. He couldn't bring himself to employ the usual cop remedy, gallows humor, so he didn't speak. Evelyn showed her strength by employing it herself.

"Not so much the smoking bit as getting set on fire."

Grant held her good hand gently in both of his and looked in her eyes. She smiled at him but couldn't disguise the hint of sadness behind the smile.

"I think I got off lightly."

Grant nodded.

"I think we both did."

Evelyn glanced along the corridor.

"I hear she's awake."

Grant nodded again.

"I called in to see her while you were being triaged."

Evelyn showed her compassion as well.

"How's she doing?"

Grant repeated his earlier assessment.

"She's a tough kid. She'll be fine."

Evelyn looked at him.

"That's not what I asked."

Grant looked in her eyes and saw a wealth of concern and caring. She was a very special woman. He patted her hand and softened his eyes.

"She's going to need plastic surgery and a shitload of makeup. But they say she'll be eighty percent as good as new in a year or so."

Evelyn squeezed his hand in return.

"Did she say why she bought the petrol he used on her?"

"Crash Davis?"

"Yes."

Grant shrugged.

"She just thought she was buying a bottle of petrol. Never thought anything about it."

Evelyn shifted in her seat.

"Yeah. It's funny about bottles of petrol. You never know where they're going to get used."

Grant looked at the singed hair and stripped eyebrows and felt guilty all over again. The redness down one side of her face hadn't quite developed into burns, but the hand she'd used to press the Escape key was blistered. Apart from that, she was right: they'd been lucky.

"I'm sorry."

She fixed him with a steady look.

"Don't be silly. You saved the world."

Grant shrugged.

"It was you who pressed the button. Ten inches to the right, and it would've been a different story."

She raised what was left of her eyebrows.

"As it is. No disruption to air traffic. And you'll be able to fly away home."

That brought the conversation to a full stop. He really liked this woman. He wanted to spend more time with her, but there was no escaping the fact he had to give evidence in the Snake Pass enquiry. Davis had already been in touch with US Airways and booked him on the next available flight. He tried smiling to lessen the blow.

"I think the Charlotte PD will be glad to see the back of me. They've already booked my ticket."

Evelyn nodded her understanding. This was never going to go anywhere. Grant tried the bad news/good news approach.

"Good news is the next flight isn't for three days."

Evelyn smiled.

"So we've got three days then."

Grant leaned forward and kissed her gently on the forehead.

"Unless the knitting circle gets in the way."

ACKNOWLEDGMENTS

I'm going to keep it brief this time. Like the Academy Awards where you've only got 45 seconds to give your acceptance speech. Well, here's my 45 seconds. Thanks to everyone who helped shepherd this book to the shelves. And to Lee Child for letting me steal his name. Happy retirement, James.

Ex-army, retired cop and former scenes of crime officer, **COLIN CAMPBELL** served with the West Yorkshire police for thirty years. He is the author of the UK crime novels *Blue Knight White Cross* and *Northern Ex*, and the US thrillers featuring rogue Yorkshire Cop Jim Grant.

CampbellFiction.com

On the following pages are a few
more great titles from the
Down & Out Books publishing family.

For a complete list of books and to
sign up for our newsletter,
go to DownAndOutBooks.com.

Coldwater
Tom Pitts

Down & Out Books
May 2020
978-1-64396-081-4

A young couple move from San Francisco to the Sacramento sub-urbs to restart their lives. When the vacant house across the street is taken over by who they think are squatters, they're pulled into a battle neither of them bargained for. The gang of unruly drug addicts who've infested their block have a dark and secret history that reaches beyond their neighborhood and all the way to the most powerful and wealthy men in California.

L.A. fixer Calper Dennings is sent by a private party to quell the trouble before it affects his employer. But before he can finish the job, he too is pulled into the violent dark world of a man with endless resources to destroy anyone around him.

Occam's Razor
Joe Clifford

Down & Out Books
June 2020
978-1-64396-106-4

Former NFL prospect Oz Reyes is summoned to Miami by his boss, Delma Dupree, who asks him to investigate what she calls "the wrongful imprisonment" of her stepson.

With the help of an ex-girlfriend her ex-convict brother, Oz uncovers a South Florida rarely seen, one crawling with shifty detectives, rogue assassins, and hard-drinking, sexual deviants—where no one and nothing is what it seems.

Helen Topaz, Henry Dollar
Part Three of the Trevor English Series
Pablo D'Stair

All Due Respect, an imprint of
Down & Out Books
May 2020
978-1-64396-100-2

Manufacturing threats of blackmail against himself, petty crook Trevor English convinces his lover, Helen, to pay off his fictional victimizer.

But when Helen suggests that an investigator be brought in to find out who was behind the extortion, Trevor finds he must either maintain his intricate deception or end his affair—either option capable of spinning his life wildly out of his control.

Shotgun Honey Presents Volume 4: RECOIL
Ron Earl Phillips, editor

Shotgun Honey, an imprint of
Down & Out Books
May 2020
978-1-64396-138-5

With new and established authors from around the world, Shotgun Honey Presents Volume 4: RECOIL delivers stories that explore a darker side of remorse, revenge, circumstance, and humanity.

Contributors: Rusty Barnes, Susan Benson, Sarah M. Chen, Kristy Claxton, Jen Conley, Brandon Daily, Barbara DeMarco-Barrett, Hector Duarte Jr., Danny Gardner, Tia Ja'nae, Carmen Jaramillo, Nick Kolakowski, JJ Landry, Bethany Maines, Tess Makovesky, Alexander Nachaj, David Nemeth, Cindy O'Quinn, Brandon Sears, Johnny Shaw, Kieran Shea, Gigi Vernon, Patrick Whitehurst.

CPSIA information can be obtained
at www.ICGtesting.com
Printed in the USA
BVHW030042110620
581083BV00003BA/336

9 781643 961057